SNAKES IN THE GARDEN

A Novel

L. S. Whiteley

Walker and Company
New York

For Mai

First published in the United States of America in 1990 by
Walker Publishing Company, Inc.

Published simultaneously in Canada by Thomas Allen & Son
Canada, Limited, Markham, Ontario.

Library of Congress Cataloging-in-Publication Data

Whiteley, L. S.
Snakes in the garden : a novel / L. S. Whiteley.
ISBN 0-8027-1113-8
I. Title.
PS3573.H4874S6   1990
813'.54—dc20   89-70762
CIP

Printed in the United States of America

2 4 6 8 10 9 7 5 3 1

Some people claim
There's a woman to blame,
But I know
It's my own damn fault.

Jimmy Buffet
"Margaritaville"

It is invariably saddening to look through new eyes at things upon which you have expended your own powers of adjustment.

F. Scott Fitzgerald
The Great Gatsby

ONE

The night that they found Grandfather, barefoot, checkbook in hand, sprawled out on the ground in one of the back pastures with two bullet holes in the back of his skull, I was in bed with my business partner's wife. Later, when I was informed of his death I admit that I was not exactly grieved. Grandfather and I had never been particularly close. I was, however, surprised. Surprised that he was dead—murdered. And surprised at the manner in which he had been found: face-down in a fresh pile of cow shit. This, I thought, went beyond mere cruelty and humiliation; this, I thought, was obscene, sadistic. A little eighty-five-year-old man, frail as a bird and mean as God. That he, somehow, could have been forced, persuaded, whatever, to lie down in that stinking mess. He was not shoved—this was later confirmed; he went down first on one knee, then on the other, and then leaned over into it, arms outspread. The more I thought about it, the more incredible it seemed. Although perhaps it wasn't incredible at all. Even an eighty-five-year-old misanthrope, whose prime pleasure in life was the destruction of other people, might want desperately to live, to keep sucking down that Big O, and under the right circumstances, the proper inducement, might do almost anything in an attempt to extend the deadline, the cut-off date. Very few of us go gentle into that good night. When the time actually comes, when the Cold Hand is on the shoulder, most of us kick and scream and beg and pray and promise and protest and try to cut deals on the side. But it's all in vain. When the time's up, hell, it's up, and neither love nor money nor your blue-eyed daughter's sweet smile can buy you an extra day. "You can leave that. You won't need it." "But I've worked my whole life for it." "Yes. I know. That's the joke. Don't you get it?" "No. Explain it to me." "You're stalling. Come on." "But wait. Wait! Wait!" What absurd little nervous creatures—running so fast yet going nowhere.

So there I was, mixing it up with the wife of my business partner (an honest man and all-around good fellow) while Grandfather was being removed most rudely from the planet. Jesus, I'm a bastard. I know it; I can't help it. And, in truth, even if I could help it, I wouldn't, because that's just the way I am. Although on occasion, rare and far between, my behavior has been so foul and unwarranted that even I, yes I, have been offended.

Like this entire episode with John's wife. Despicable. Utterly without redemption. The man had never been anything but straightforward with me in all matters, and this was the way in which I chose to repay his trust and friendship: in a bed, in one side of a duplex that I had laid aside expressly for such situations, with his charming young bride of barely two years riding me like a horse. All she needed was a cowboy hat.

But in point of fact it really had nothing to do with John as far as I was concerned. It was entirely his wife—Little Susie. She had been coming on to me for as long as I could remember, winking and blinking. I thought for a long while that she had a spastic eye. Hell, maybe something was wrong between her and John at home. I had no idea. I judge no one and only ask for a fifty yard head start.

Susie started crying after the horse got back to the barn. She said that she could never see me again. Once around the track and a few tears. I was getting off easy, and I knew it.

She slid out of bed, walked naked into the bathroom and turned on the water in the shower. She had managed to work up quite a lather.

She stepped out of the shower wrapped in a towel, shook her wet blond head from side to side like a dog and moved over to the dresser. She was no longer crying. She began putting on her make-up. No words were spoken.

When she had finished with her face, she shook her head again and smiled at herself in the mirror. She picked her clothes up off the floor, wiggled into them, then marched around to my side of the bed, kissed me quickly on the cheek and tousled my hair. I almost slapped her. She had come full circle—child, woman, mother—in less than an hour, and had left me standing in the middle. She shut the door behind her. From the bedroom I could hear the lock click.

I dragged myself out of bed feeling somehow as if I had been used. It was a new experience. I found it to be extremely disagreeable. It angered me no end that this little bitch would have gone to all the time and trouble (not to mention the incredible risks to my financial health and physical well-being) just to roll me once and then cut me loose. Did she imagine that she was doing me a favor? I had better things to do. Maybe it all had something to do with living dangerously, walking on the wild side, or just too much daytime television. I didn't know. I didn't care.

Suddenly I felt rather dirty and went to take a shower myself. The water fell with a force that was almost masochistic. I spun the shower control knobs from hot to cold, from cold to hot, a dozen or more times. I emerged feeling cleansed but not quite purified. In truth, I simply felt stupid. I could only hope that I was not developing a conscience.

I slipped on my jeans and made my way into the kitchen. There the eye was presented with a bright, yet austere, vista of undisturbed disuse—chrome, steel, fluorescent lights, Formica. The refrigerator served as the sole repository for the collective contents of the kitchen: four clean glasses, one silver spoon, a liter bottle of Beefeater gin, several 10-ounce bottles of Schweppes tonic water and a plastic lemon filled with "real" lemon juice; an ice maker and an ice tray brimming with perfectly formed ice cubes rested in the freezer compartment above. I like, whenever possible, to keep things simple.

I fixed myself a gin and tonic and sat down on the sofa in the living room. The only thing of any real value in the entire apartment was a somewhat worn Oriental rug that I'd received in lieu of my share of some money once owed to my cousins and me back during our drug dealing days, back before things got quite so serious and the participants quite so greedy. This poor sap, who had the distinct misfortune of thinking himself a personal friend of one of my cousins, owed us the money— and not an insignificant amount either—for some weed that we had fronted him, which he, in turn, promptly got popped with. A major loser, this guy. I was for letting him off, chalking it up to experience and bad luck—hell, he was about to go to jail anyway; it wasn't as if he had tried to rip us off or anything. But one of my cousins, David, who may have felt some degree of responsibility for the fiasco as he was the reputed "friend" of this moron, insisted that we needed to try to recoup our losses. With David it seemed to be a matter of principle.

So bright and early one Saturday morning, we—my two cousins and I—backed an orange U-Haul truck up to this poor fool's front door and proceeded to cancel his debt. In addition to the rug, I also received a nice bed and dresser. My cousins both sold their cuts for whatever they could get, which, if I remember correctly, was not much. But I, for some odd-ball reason, hung onto my share of the booty. I'll always remember that poor sobbing asshole running frantically from one room to another in his rapidly emptying house, begging us to leave that (something of uncertain value—we knew television sets but not antiques—which was in some way connected with his family's past) and take this (something else, maybe junk) instead. Usually we just took both items in question; it was far simpler and, I believe, infinitely more fair. Finally, when we began to roll up the rug, he cracked totally. He let out a howl that was hardly human and nosedived down on top of it. "No! Please! Please!" he cried, trying to grab up great handfuls of rug. "This was my great-grandmother's! Please! It's been in my family for a hundred years! Anything happens to it, my mother'll kill me!" Calmly, smiling slightly, David went over to him, pried his fingers loose, picked him up and set him down on the bare floor. "That's okay," David assured him. "We won't tell."

TWO

I got up off the sofa and went into the kitchen. As I was rinsing out my glass before returning it to the refrigerator, I thought that I heard something outside. I stepped out onto the porch: rain. I walked around to the back and yanked up the canvas top on my car—a white '57 T-bird, a two-seater, that I bought from a crazy fellow I knew who sold all of his worldly possessions (and even a few things that didn't actually belong to him) and set off for the wilds of Alaska to pan for gold. "I'll come back rich or I won't come back at all!" he announced with marvelous bravado at a going-away party that he threw for himself. So far as I know he was never heard from again. I've always liked to imagine that he struck the mother lode and married an Eskimo. But who knows? Some people just disappear on you.

I clamped the top down into place. The interior was soaked. It was basically a good automobile, but it could have used some work—like maybe a new engine, a new transmission, a new paint job and a new interior. I was not unduly concerned about a little water on the seats. They had gotten wet before. Nevertheless, I thought I'd give the car a chance to dry out a bit before driving it home.

I went back inside and made myself another gin and tonic. I turned on the stereo, dialed up a rock station and sat back down on the sofa. Music filled the rooms of the duplex with an insistent yet simplistic beat that would have thrilled any teenager but only served to make me feel rather old—I'm thirty-six now; at least four years and more than a thousand miles removed from all events recorded here.

I originally bought this duplex about eight years ago, at a

time of great confusion and uncertainty in my life. I was then living in another house with a girl whom I no longer loved and who no longer loved me. If, in fact, either of us had ever actually loved the other is debatable. We were having an excruciatingly difficult time of breaking the thing off. Over a period of more than four years of living together, we had become dependent upon each other to such a degree that we were almost afraid to be alone again. So maybe, after a fashion, there was some love, or at least some need, there somewhere.

Her name was Angie, and she had the finest breasts of any woman I have ever seen, bar none. They were round and firm and rode up high to proud little points that poked out against her shirts even on the hottest of days. These were no overripe day-old melons. These were perfect orbs, so circumferentially perfect as to seem to have required caliper and compass for construction. One look and yes, you knew there was a God. Men stood up when she walked into a room. Women took deep breaths and tried to smile.

She was short, only about five foot three or four, with a tight little butt and a slim waist. She took exceptionally good care of her body; she was into exercise long before it became fashionable.

She had a small button nose and enormous calm brown eyes. Her hair was black and fine and silky; it fell almost to her waist. And when you would sit somewhere and watch her walking away, her hair would swish and sway to a rhythm independent and indifferent.

I first met Angie at college, at the University of Florida at Gainesville. I was in my third year, majoring in having a good time. My family had sent me there to get me out of town. At the time of my departure it had been a matter of some urgency.

Some three years before Angie and her wonderful breasts, I was still selling drugs in partnership with my cousins. Somehow, from one of David's sources (I never entirely understood the whole operation), we were getting one-pound bags of methaqualone powder delivered into our hands upon request. It was rumored that it all came from a Rorer warehouse that had been ripped off somewhere in New England. It could just as likely have been some fruitcake chemist in a garage somewhere turning it out by the quarter-ton lot for all I ever knew. But the

[6]

facts were indisputable: one hour after David made his phone call we—David, his twin brother Daniel and I—would be dividing up one-pound bags of the stuff into sixteen one-ounce baggies for distribution to the hungry population of southwest Florida.

It rapidly became rather ridiculous. People were walking about with a baggie of methaqualone powder in one pocket and empty vitamin E capsules (500 milligrams) in the other; they would stop (often in public, always at parties), load up a cap, pop it into their mouths and go, unsteadily, on their merry way. It was so plentiful that it was almost legal by default. People were smoking it, mixing it with their morning coffee, giving it away as birthday presents, using it as currency to pay off their debts. You could go down to the beach and find no one but tourists in the water. Everyone would be laid out in the sand like corpses after a massacre. A couple of overly energetic people once tried swimming and nearly drowned; many more nearly ended it early for themselves in their automobiles. Cars were winding up in the bay with alarming regularity. Body shops were doing a land-office business. No one that I knew had a car that was wholly in one piece. It became known in local folk lore as The Time of Minimum Driving Skills. And even today, in certain circles, there are undoubtedly those who still reflect back upon this period with a sense of fond, if somewhat cloudy, nostalgia.

But as it is with most good things, it could not go on indefinitely. The local law enforcement officials somehow—I may have inadvertently sold some powder to a narc—zeroed in on me. Ultimately they missed their mark, but not by much. Whoever was doing the informing (we had our suspicions, but could never confirm them) must have been genuinely fond of the powder because when he—I prefer to hope that it was not a she—turned me in to his superiors, he reported the wrong house number. He should not, however, have felt too badly about it; he got the right street and was only off by a couple of digits on the house. It was a mistake anyone could've made.

I'll remember it until the day I die. It was like some kind of an off-balance, slow-motion movie: there I was sitting in the sunshine, on my front porch, totally stoned, generally enjoying the day. There was movement in front of me; my eyes focused.

[7]

A line of unmarked yet obvious police cars came tooling down the street. They pulled to a stop in front of my next door neighbor's house. I was so far gone that it didn't occur to me until much later that they were after me. At the time I remember thinking how peculiar it was that the police should need so many men just to arrest poor old Mr. Peabody. He and his wife were both in their eighties. With shotguns and revolvers glistening in the sun, wearing bullet-proof vests and brand-new baseball caps, the police came charging out of their cars and into my neighbor's yard. I almost applauded it was so dramatic. Men swarmed around the house. They threw themselves into bushes; they crouched under windows. Doors were kicked in; orders were shouted. Radios everywhere crackled unintelligibly. A shotgun went off inside the house (accidentally, I later learned). A window in the front of the house exploded. There were calls of "Officer down!" One misplaced soul began calling for a medic. There was momentary panic. Then it became quiet, very quiet. Inside, old Mr. Peabody and his wife were having simultaneous heart attacks. Soon police officers began filing out of the house. They walked about in Mr. Peabody's yard, smoking cigarettes and looking dejected. Some of the more senior tacticians stood in a circle cursing. Several ambulances arrived. Mr. Peabody and his wife and an officer were loaded up and taken to the hospital. The city was sued.

Several days later word was quietly passed through back-channels to my father, a rather prominent businessman in Sarasota at the time (he was overseeing all of the day-to-day operations of Grandfather's companies—banking, construction, farming, oil, commodity trading, what-have-you), that they, the police, may have missed me once, but they surely would not be so clumsy a second time. That evening out at Grandfather's farm, Devon Woods as it was commonly known—the name referring to the main house, a two-story twenty-room mansion, as well as the twenty-five hundred acres surrounding it—there was much shouting and screaming. Grandfather suggested prison; he thought everyone should go to jail at least once. He claimed that he had been and was no worse off for the experience. Father seemed largely indifferent to the whole affair, but in truth I knew that he was deeply disappointed. Mother and Grandmother both strenuously challenged Grandfather's claims to intimate knowledge of the value of confinement. I sat silently in a chair and listened. There was a lot of finger-pointing; blame was distributed freely. The past tense—"he was," "he had"—was in active use. I began to feel as though I were already dead and gone. It was all remarkably strange. At last, thankfully, reality and reason prevailed: the ladies persuaded the gentlemen that, for the sake of the family name (and this was stressed above all other considerations), I should be sent somewhere a bit more upbeat than the institutions of correction favored so passionately by Grandfather.

Thus was it decided that I should have an education. I was given a generous allowance—partially to dissuade me from independent enterprise—and promptly exported to Gainesville. I was glad to get away. I needed a vacation.

I had seen Angie several times before we actually met. She was working as a waitress in a bar near campus. My friends and I sometimes went there; it was a fairly good bar. We would sit and drink and watch her carrying pitchers of beer from the bar to the tables. There were a lot of other watchers in that place. She could've had any of them. And except for a drunken proposal or two to join us after work for some fun—"Sorry, boys"—there was little communication between her and my friends and me. She treated us like children, which was probably what we deserved.

And so it stood until one day I found myself late for class, hurrying up the stairs in the English department building to reach my classroom before my professor, a real case, locked the door. This particular professor would allow tardiness of five minutes by a stopwatch and no more. You could beat on the door and shout your excuses into the door jamb but it was all for naught. So there I was, vaulting it up the stairs, taking them three at a time, red-faced and breathing like I was closing fast on the four-minute mile, when I whirled around a turn at the top of a flight of stairs and ran right over her. She had been sitting there minding her own business, reading *To Have and Have Not*. I saw her half a second before I hit her. I couldn't stop; my forward momentum carried me, logically, forward. Books, pens, paper and Ernest Hemingway went everywhere. I fell forward; she fell back. I finally came to rest on finger tips and toes suspended some six inches above her. And there, like a true idiot, like the rank amateur that I was (and probably still am), I froze. "Okay, real nice," she said after a few seconds; she was looking me right in the eyes. "Now go back down and let's try it again. And this time, let's see some enthusiasm." I lifted myself up without falling on top of her, helped her up, collected her books for her, apologized quickly and ran on up the stairs. The door to the classroom, as I had suspected, was locked.

When she looked up again and saw me coming back down, she grabbed Ernest and headed for a neutral corner. "Gonna try it from the back too?" she asked. "Locked out," I said. "Professor Fine?" she asked. "The same," I said. We began to talk: Professor Fine, other eccentrics of education, college in general. She was very bright. She was going to school part-time because she wanted to learn—this was a totally alien concept to me. As we talked her eyes seemed to grow softer, her body less rigid. Finally, on impulse, in mid-sentence—something in her laughter may have encouraged me—I stopped her and asked if she would like to go smoke a joint. Much to my surprise she said yes.

That night I took her to dinner and then to a movie and then to bed. God, I really thought that I was something. I actually believed that I was calling the shots. Men, young and old, delude themselves to such degrees that it's downright depressing.

Her story was brief: she was four years older than me but didn't look it; her parents existed somewhere doing something for some reason; she lived in an apartment paid for by a man with a wife and two kids who sold insurance and came to collect the rent on Monday and Wednesday nights; she had been married once before but it didn't take; she worked at the Golden Parrot four nights a week serving beer to college kids for tips; she had a lesbian lover on the side who danced the hootchie-coo in a strip joint; together they shot heroin for fun.

She told me all this in bed the next morning. It was supposed to shock me. I tried to appear as if I knew what was going on, after all I was a college man.

Soon she began skipping her Monday and Wednesday night

sessions to spend more time with me. I was naturally flattered. Her Sugar Daddy dropped her from the role of honor; an eviction notice was served. Her lesbian lover wrote her a long letter in red ink on purple paper, sent along a nickel bag of smack and then faded into the past. "Think of me when the moon is full and remember," her lover wrote. At my insistence she went cold turkey on the junk—I didn't need the competition—and then moved in with me. She immediately began transforming my little rat-hole apartment into a livable home.

At the close of that semester I cashed in my credits and packed my bags. I'd had enough; it was beginning to seem like work. Angie, in a tearful scene, said that she didn't want me to leave. I was overwhelmed; I invited her along. In truth, I couldn't wait to show her off to all of my old friends. I had not been back to Sarasota but once in the last three years, and that was a surreptitious appearance I made at Grandmother's funeral. The subterfuge, however, had been unnecessary. The police were no longer interested in me.

Father told me that Grandmother had died peacefully in her sleep. One morning her maid went in to wake her and found her—she was dead. They marked it down to old age. My other two grandparents on my mother's side died before I was born, and Grandfather had little tolerance for children, so for me, as far as grandparents went, she had always been the sole representative. She had been a great beauty in her youth. There were old photographs of her everywhere. She loved to tell stories about the way things were in Sarasota, and Florida in general, back when she was growing up. I remember her now as a little white-haired lady with delicate hands who wore high ruffled collars and smelled of lilac and sherry.

In her will Grandmother left my cousins—I had five—and me each twenty-five thousand dollars, two hundred and fifty thousand went to each of her three sons, a mass of jewelry was divided up acrimoniously among my girl cousins and the wives of her sons (a real cat fight there; some of the participants still refuse to speak to one another), another small slice was dribbled off to assorted charities, but the bulk of her estate reverted back to Grandfather's control, where it always had been. What my cousins eventually did with their money I have no idea, although several of them were later seen driving around town in expensive new cars. I, again the odd-ball, the pack-rat, put my twenty-five thousand in a money-market fund and just left it there. There was nothing that I really wanted or needed.

Upon my return from my three years in exile, I was awarded, presumably because of my good behavior—I didn't get arrested or disgrace the family name—an entry-level management position with a company which Grandfather had recently purchased at a discount from someone's widow. I have never in my life been more bored. Angie went to work as a waitress again, but this time in a very upscale operation—hanging plants, brass, wood, stained glass, the works. The motif was Olde English, and she truly looked the becoming wench in her barmaid outfit. She made more money—bending over those tables, Jesus, the eyes would pop—working three nights a week than I did for five days.

At the time we were living in a large apartment complex which I despised. I later found out that Grandfather owned it. It was nice and clean and everybody had his or her own parking place and surely no one could have been jealous of anyone else's apartment because they were all exactly alike, but I wanted something different. I wanted something that I could call my own. So I went shopping for a house. Everyone but Grandfather thought that I had lost my mind. Grandfather merely grunted (this was as close to a sign of approval as one was likely to get from him) and asked me if I was still a "dope-head." I found a marvelous old rambling house with three bedrooms that was structurally sound but sorely in need of some work, plopped down a small down payment and set about fixing up the place. When I had finished a neighbor offered to buy it from me—he had a brother who was retiring or something and wanted to live close by—for more than half again what I had paid for it, repairs included. I didn't need to be kicked in the head to know that I was onto something good.

During the summers of my last two years of high school, I had worked as a carpenter—mostly just hauling lumber—for one of Grandfather's construction companies. One of the people that I worked with was John Allen, the man who would later become my business partner. He was only a couple of years older than me and already a lead carpenter. In high school, when he was playing football, his teammates had christened him "Bear", and through the years of our association this remained a fairly accurate description of the man. He was easily six-five and probably weighed close to two-fifty. His hair was long and extended in brown waves from a part at the top of his head down to his shoulders. When you looked at his face what you saw was a handsome face, the color and texture of tanned leather, and a pair of penetrating blue eyes. At a party shortly after I got back from Gainesville, someone happened to mention that John was still in town, working as an independent contractor with a small crew of helpers. Once I discovered that there was money to be made in old buildings, I went looking for him. He was not overly difficult to find; he was listed in the phone book. My plan was simple: we would combine my money (the twenty-five thousand remained virtually untouched) with his experience and contacts; we would buy up some old houses and duplexes with as little cash down as we could get away with, fix them up, move in a better class of tenant at a higher rent rate, keep the properties for a year or so until our investments went long-term on the capital gains, then sell out; we would split up the profits and accept the losses, which fortunately were precious few, on a fifty-fifty basis. We shook on it and went into business. Nowadays, it seems like everybody and his dog is doing the same thing, but back when John and I first got started the field was wide open— at least people weren't writing books about it or trying to peddle their get-rich-quick course on late-night television.

Life in general progressed rather nicely for the next couple of years. John and I were making money; Angie seemed satisfied. She especially enjoyed the house—painting the walls, learning the art of hanging wallpaper, buying furniture, kitchenware, appliances. It kept her busy. She even planted some flowers. Then at some point, one morning like a hundred other mornings, I looked up and noticed that she was decidedly unhappy. I knew what the problem was. In fact, I had been waiting some time for it to break. Angie, I had to keep reminding myself, because she certainly never looked it, was still four years older than me and would always be so. She felt the passing of time more keenly than I did. She felt things slipping away.

There were really only two things in life that Angie

wanted: legitimacy and family. She was a remarkably old-fashioned girl. In spite of all the twists and turns, she had always been angling back to the comforts of comformity and community. First, she wanted to be a wife again. This I refused outright. I was only twenty-seven and did not wish to be tied down any further than I felt I already was. I also disapproved (and still do) of marriage in general—the entire deal seems patently unfair and biased in favor of women. The other thing that Angie wanted, more dearly I have always believed than the first, was to be a mother. In that matter I could be of no help; it was entirely beyond my reach. When Angie was only sixteen she had managed to get herself pregnant. Her parents, naturally distressed, took her to a doctor and had the pregnancy aborted. But while the good doc was in there mucking about, he also tied off her fallopian tubes. A most thorough and thoughtful man. No one, however, bothered to consult with young Angie about the procedure, and it was not until later that she learned of it. By then the damage had been done. There were threats of a biological nature to have her tubes blown open, but nothing ever came of it. With time she grew progressively more depressed, silent and withdrawn. Those two unused bedrooms in that house gnawed at her soul and reminded her daily of what could never be.

Then she remembered drugs. It was like an old friend newly found. Only this time it was cocaine. Up until this point, I would mark it well into our third year together, we had both been relatively drug-free. There was a little pot and hashish, an occasional Quaalude (my favorite), maybe a snort of coke or crystal now and then, but nothing like the snow storm that blew through the door and very nearly took us both with it. I was running just to try to keep up. Things quickly began falling apart: coke by the gram, then by the ounce, then by the pound; dealing again, but this time not for profit, just for stash; needles and hundred dollar bills; more plastic baggies and now little glass vials too; some of the sleaziest people that I have ever had the displeasure of knowing; hollow eyes, eyes without pupils, pupils without eyes; paranoia, mistrust, resentment, anger, insanity; words said that could never be unsaid; fighting, cursing, crying, going to bed, making love; around and around; whirling so fast you couldn't even focus.

It was in this frenzied atmosphere of forward regression that I happened to be out one day (coked-up) looking at a property for John and me. (It's remarkable how well you can function on the surface when really you're so far out of control. It's also amazing to me, in retrospect, how your so-called friends won't try to stop you from killing yourself, won't pull your aside, kick you in the butt and tell you that you're losing it. But then again, often those that one chooses to associate with at times like these are caught up in the same madness too. It's almost like a game to see who'll survive and who won't.) So there I was, riding high, cruising around in my T-bird with the top down and the radio blaring, lost in a town I had lived in almost my entire life, amazed at the rapidly changing landscape. When I saw it, I never looked back. I stopped the car in the middle of the street, left the motor running, walked right up to one of the front doors (it had always been a duplex, not a house that someone had chopped up) and asked if I could see inside. The poor people who were living there at the time were so startled that they let me in. I knew immediately that I needed it, had to have it. The whole concept of the place hit me all at once—a second home, a secret place, a place where I, I alone, could be alone, or with someone else if I chose. A place of peace and parallels, of rest and reflection. It was beautiful. I was overjoyed.

There had been no sign in the yard; it was not even on the market. I had to trace its ownership back through the plat books at the courthouse—the tenants went squirrelly on me when I began to expound upon my vision as to its future use. At first the owner refused to speak with me. He thought that I was crazy, but I persisted. A few days later I came down enough to talk terms with the man. We eventually settled on a fair price.

The duplex was located on a quiet side street near downtown. It was set well back from the street on a deep lot. Along both sides of the property and across the back ran thick flowering hedgerows. A jacaranda tree sat in the front yard, providing color in the spring and some much needed shade during the summer. To ease the inconvenience of eviction, I gave each of the former tenants three hundred dollars. (I know that legally I was under no obligation to do this and probably should not have—it may have set a bad precedent—but I was no good at slumlording; one tear and I would crack.) I then hired a private contractor from out of town, someone that John didn't know, to begin sprucing the place up. The exterior stucco walls were painted an appealing pastel yellow, the barrel-tile roof was painted red—this, I thought, gave the building a certain Spanish flair—one side of the front porch that had been slowly collapsing in upon itself was propped up and stabilized. New appliances and window-unit air conditions were purchased; the bathrooms and kitchens were redone; the floors were sanded and varnished. I moved in a new couple on one side. They were retired and agreed to take responsibility for the care of the yard. They were wonderful people. They kept to themselves, watched a lot of television and asked no questions about my nocturnal comings and goings. Their monthly rent neatly covered my mortgage payments, leaving me with only a small utility bill as the total cost for one side of a duplex to do with as I pleased.

Less than a month after I had gotten everything squared away in my little den of deceit, my little hideaway (I had only had an opportunity to bed a couple of ladies), I discovered a red pair of men's underwear under the bed back at my number-one house. And since I did not wear underwear, red or any other color—too restrictive in my opinion—I suspected that I was not the only one at play. I confronted Angie with the evidence suspended from the end of a broom handle. She lied, then cried, and then confessed. It had been over for a long time. This was simply the last of a series of last straws. The next morning I gave her a check for fifteen hundred dollars, bought her a first-class one-way airplane ticket to Denver (she said that she wanted to go where the air was pure; I thought about Peru but she didn't have a passport) and drove her to the airport. She gave me a kiss and a little wave from her airplane window, and then she was gone.

Even though I now no longer had any practical need for my duplex, I decided nevertheless to keep it. I so enjoyed the thought of it just being there—waiting, secret and ready.

A couple of years after all this happened, I received a postcard in the mail postmarked somewhere (the town's name was blurred) in Colorado. It had been forwarded from my old address—the house which Angie and I had shared—to my new beachhouse. The card, in beautiful flowing script, read:

> *Dear Shithead,*
> *Am marrying a millionaire*
> *in the morning. So fuck you.*
> *Love,*
> *Angie*

And whether she had really bagged herself a big one (she deserved it) or was, in fact, getting punched out by some cowboy on a weekly basis, I never knew. But whatever the case might have been, I still thought that it was extremely considerate of her to send me a card. So few people these days take the time to write.

THREE

The rain was still coming down as I locked up and headed home. My car's headlights—both of them severely out of whack and almost useless for purposes of illumination—sent forlorn beams of light shooting off into space. They were in such bad condition that, if it were not for the police, it probably would have been easier and safer to have driven without them.

I had no idea what time it was getting to be. There were no clocks in either my duplex or my car, and I refused, as a matter of principle, to wear a wristwatch. I do not believe that one should allow time to dictate one's life too closely. I was, however, somewhat surprised when I passed a clock in front of a bank flashing 11:13.

I turned off the Trail and onto Siesta Drive and almost ran over some bozo riding a bicycle in the rain. As I crossed the bridge connecting Siesta Key—the island on which I lived— with the mainland, I got a good whiff of the bay and remembered for the one-millionth time why I love being close to the water, close to life and the smell of its beginnings: there's something fertile and female in that smell, something timeless and reassuring. The lights from the condominiums ringing Sarasota Bay and the expensive homes of Bird Key played out across the water; a lone fisherman in a rain slicker and hat dangled a line into the dark near the end of the bridge; a few boats ran about in the channel, heading out into the Gulf or returning.

The rain beat down upon my car's canvas top with such force that it all but drowned out the radio. Palms and Australian pines silhouetted darkly under streetlights whipped about in the wind. There were few cars on the road, and as I drove I wondered if Kim would be back home yet. She had mentioned something this morning about an art showing that she and several of her fellow art students were having at a gallery downtown. She had asked me to come, but I begged off. I wasn't particularly good at standing around, being polite; I was much better at getting drunk and knocking over barstools. The gallery's owner had been quite excited about Kim's work. He said that it showed great promise. He had spoken of power and purity of form. If the guy wasn't gay, he might have been just trying to get into her pants. Lots of luck, I thought to myself with a satisfied smile. I trusted Kim implicitly.

At every turn in the road my headlights scraped across at least one For Sale sign. It seemed as if every third house were up for sale. I didn't understand exactly why that was, but that was the way it had been on the island lately—a very heavy turnover. I also couldn't help but notice that none of the signs were from Allen-Clay Realty—the name of John's and my company. This did not really disappoint me too much. Real estate sales and property management played a relatively minor role in our overall business strategy; we tended to concentrate our efforts more in the investment arena.

I pulled to a stop in front of my beachhouse—a two-story wooden structure resting atop piles driven into the ground. Kim's little red Volkswagon was already there. I stepped out of my car and immediately sank into several inches of wet sand. Kicking off sand as I went, I climbed the short flight of stairs to the front door.

Kim was something of a fanatic about cleanliness; this may have had something to do with her Oriental heritage. Living with me (a naturally relaxed fellow) in a house surrounded by sand could have made life difficult for anyone. Between the sand and me, it was a losing battle.

I unlocked the door, stepped inside and began removing my shoes—my sole concession to her fanaticism.

"Kim," I shouted from the living room. "Kim, I'm home."

There was no answer.

I thought that she might be upstairs in the bedroom, though it did seem a little early for bed. I walked to the foot of the stairs and shouted again: "Kim, I'm home." I then heard the glass door that led out to the lanai slide open; I went back to the living room.

"Kim, sweetheart, didn't you hear me?" I asked.

She walked up to me without looking at me and threw her arms around my chest. I bent slightly and rested my chin on top of her head. Through my shirt I could feel her wet face, and I knew that she had been crying. I ran my hand down her long black hair and on down her back. Silently we stood in the middle of the room, rocking from side to side.

Kim had come to me by a convoluted route from Vietnam. Twenty-two years old but looking more like fifteen—whenever we would go out together she would have to carry along an ID; her body a perfectly proportioned miniature (only ninety pounds), with a waist so tiny that you could almost fit both hands around it; a happy spirit, full of life and energy, with a freshness, a childlike innocence; a prancing pony and a real little powerhouse in bed.

"What's wrong?" I asked.

Still not looking at me, she took my hand, led me over to the sofa and sat us both down.

"What's wrong?" I asked again. "Come on. Tell me. What's the matter?" I pulled her closer.

She sucked in a great wet sniffle and looked up at me. An oval face, smooth and light brown in color, with sharp planes and exotic angles—eyes, eyebrows, cheekbones, narrow nose and mouth—extending out from the center. Her big brown eyes, rimmed in tears, seemed ready to explode.

I was hoping that it was not her mother again. Her mother became deathly ill about once every six months or so, and all of the children and grandchildren from all over the country and Canada would have to drop whatever they happened to be doing and rush to be by her side. (Fortunately for Kim, her mother only lived over in Fort Lauderdale.) There would be wailing and praying and doom and lament; many confessions of love withheld and respect not shown would be extracted in mournful bedside scenes. With hopes rising and falling like swells in the sea, the vigil would continue for a couple of days—or at least until all of the relatives arrived—then, miraculously, Mom would recover. There would be a big party with lots of whiskey and Vietnamese food to celebrate the miracle of Mom's resurrection. Everyone would sing and dance and drink and eat and laugh and praise the Lord Jesus and Buddha, then they'd all go home again. So far Kim's mother had been brought back from the brink at least five times that I knew of.

"Thomas,—" she began, then stopped. Her bottom lip was quivering; her eyes were blinking fast. This was something serious, I could tell.

"What is it? What's the matter?" I asked, holding both of her small hands in one of mine.

"Thomas, the police called," she said at last.

"The police?" I said. And this truly startled me; I had not been involved in anything illegal since Angie had left. In fact, the day after her departure I took all of my drugs over to David's place and gave them to him to sell for me on a consignment basis.

"They said that they found your grandfather out at his farm," Kim said. "Somebody shot him. Killed him. They wanted to speak with you. I told them you weren't here."

"Grandfather?" I asked.

"Here's the number you suppose to call." She pressed a piece of paper into my hand. "They asked where you were. Where were you, Thomas?"

"Dead?" I asked.

"Why would anybody kill your grandfather?" asked Kim. "Little old man. Never hurt nobody."

"Grandfather's dead?"

"Call them, Thomas." She closed my hand around the piece of paper. "Call them now." She got up and walked toward the kitchen. "You hungry?" she asked.

"Jesus, I can't believe it," I said. "Grandfather dead. Why I was just—"

"I stopped on the way home and got you something for dinner," she called from the kitchen. "You eaten yet?"

"Yeah," I said. "I mean, no. I mean, fix me something, okay?"

Kim stuck her head out around the door and gave me a curious look.

Feeling none too stable, I slid over to the end of the sofa. "Jesus," I said, looking down at my hands. My palms were sweating. On the piece of paper that Kim had given me was a telephone number and a name. I wiped my hands off on my jeans, picked up the phone and dialed the number.

After the third ring a bored female voice came on the line: "Sarasota County Sheriff's Department."

This stunned me for a second until I realized that naturally the Sheriff's Department and not the police would have jurisdiction in the case since Devon Woods was located in the county.

"Uh, yes, hello," I managed to say. "May I speak to Officer, I mean, uh, Deputy Dawson, please?"

"One moment." The line clicked off and I could feel myself being electronically switched and rerouted through the Sheriff's Department building.

"Johnson, Homicide," said another bored voice; this one male.

"Uh, yes. Is Deputy Dawson there, please?" I asked.

"Detective Dawson just stepped out," yawned Johnson, Homicide. "Perhaps I can help you?"

"Well, I don't know," I said. "My name is Thomas Clay and Detective—"

"Ah, Mr. Clay,"—the voice picking up noticeably—"so glad you called. Did you just get in?"

Mentally I could see Johnson, Homicide reaching across his cluttered desk, sliding over a memo pad and writing down the time, then underlining it. 11:35 P.M.

"No," I said. "I've been here for awhile."

"Right," laughed Johnson, Homicide, obviously unconvinced. "Well, Detective Dawson should be back within the half hour. Does he have your number?"

"Yes," I said. "I believe so. He's already called here once."

"Good," said Johnson, Homicide. "We'll be in touch."

And he hung up.

"Okay," I said into the buzzing phone and then hung up too.

Kim brought in a plate and set it down on the coffee table in front of me.

"What they say?" she asked. Out of her back pocket, she pulled a red cloth napkin wrapped around a knife and fork and handed it to me.

"They'll call back," I said.

[23]

In front of me was a steaming platefull of ravioli in meat sauce.

"Ravioli?" I asked stupidly.

"Stuffed with cheese and spinach," said Kim. "I got it at that new little Italian restaurant on 41. Nice clean place. You like Parmesan cheese?"

"Yes, please," I said, cutting a noodle in half and running it around in the meat sauce. "And do we have any wine?"

"Yes," she said, disappearing into the kitchen.

The ravioli was scalding hot; I had to chew quickly to keep from burning myself.

"What kind?" I asked.

"Cheap kind," she said, reappearing with two glasses of white wine and a green shaker of Kraft Parmesan cheese. She set the glasses down on the table and began shaking the cheese out over the ravioli.

"Thank you," I said, looking up at her.

She kissed me on the forehead, set the cheese down and picked up the wine. "Here," she said, handing one of the glasses to me.

We clinked glasses and drank.

She sat beside me and watched as I ate. I speared half a ravioli and offered it to her. Her mouth closed around the fork. "Mmm," she said, giving me the thumbs-up sign. "Good."

"Have you eaten?" I asked.

"Yes," she said. "Before you got home."

And as I continued to eat—it may have been the ravioli that triggered it—into my brain, full-blown, complete with color and sound, sprang a repeat of my first set of concrete and verifiable recollections concerning Grandfather and Devon Woods: I must have been about four years old at the time; there was a party, a celebration of some sort, out at Devon Woods; cars lined both sides of the entrance road leading up to the main house for almost a quarter of a mile; Grandfather had ordered one of his prime steers butchered and barbecued for the occasion. Above an open pit dug in the ground an enormous slab of meat turned slowly, filling the air with a wonderful smell; the grease and the fat and the sauce sliding off the slab fell back with a sharp hissing sound onto the red-hot coals below; the man who turned the spit and ladled on the sauce—

one of Grandfather's hands, a dark-faced toothless migrant worker—was so drunk that from time to time he would reach out and take a swig from the bottle of the specially mixed barbecue sauce instead of his whiskey bottle; eventually he had to be given a chair to sit in so that he would not fall into the fire. In the garden, near the spit, there were long rough-wood trestle tables set up and heaped high with food; at another table were dozens of bottles of liquor and hundreds of clean and dirty glasses mixed together; several large garbage cans lined with some type of sanitized plastic were filled with ice and beer and soft drinks; people in coats and ties and fine dresses and large hats strolled the grounds with plates in their hands, eating and drinking and laughing; we children—Grand-father's lot as well as those children and grandchildren of his business associates and guests—ran about, screamed and hol-lered, ate and drank and ran about some more. At some point during the festivities one of my young girl cousins, Laura, must have become over-excited; she began throwing up. I can still see her in that pretty white frill dress, with her long blond hair swirling in the breeze, backing through the crowd, the crowd parting quickly, allowing her to pass, her big blue eyes filled with terror and confusion, throwing up in great heaves; her head extended, neck and arms out so as not to soil her little dress, backing up blindly, throwing up loudly. Grand-father spotted her coming his way and immediately called over his dogs who were lolling about under the tables and trees; and a red-eyed rangy pack of beasts, they were. The animals leaped to their feet at Grandfather's command and came running; Grandfather pointed at the trail that Laura was leaving and shouted, "Get it!"; the beasts fell to and began licking it up. Laura retreated; the dogs advanced; Grandfather cheered his animals on; "Don't let any of that good gravy go to waste!" he shouted. Women shrieked and screamed and turned away in disgust; men, trying to be men—many of them in some way or other dependent upon Grandfather for their livelihoods— laughed and applauded and cheered. Finally one brave woman shot out of the crowd, snatched little Laura up in her arms and rushed her, still spewing, into the house. Grandfather laughed and shouted and patted his dogs on their thick twitching heads. Then suddenly turning, Grandfather saw me standing there next to him, very much enjoying the whole thing, and Grandfather stopped laughing; his eyes narrowed to little pinpoints, red dots like his dogs' eyes; with one long and bony finger he began jabbing me in the stomach, backing me up with each jab; "Well, boy," he demanded, punctuating each word with a poke in the stomach, "who's gonna feed my dogs now? Huh? Who's gonna fed 'em now?" I was stunned, horrified; Grandfather was jabbing; people were watching and laughing; the dogs were milling about, sniffing the ground, sniffing my feet; I tried to speak but couldn't. Grandfather kept jabbing me, backing me up, demanding to know who was going to feed his dogs. Finally he backed me into a rosebush; thorns shot through my backside; I let out a loud yelp, leaped forward, then scrambled past him; knocking over chairs and bumping into people, I made a beeline for the safety of the house. The men cheered; Grandfather laughed; an associate handed Grandfather a drink and led him over to a group of red-faced hysterical men. Little Laura never entirely got over the experience; to this day she will have nothing to do with dogs of any size or breed. As for myself, I learned to be on alert against all adults, and Grandfather in particular.

I felt a hand resting lightly on my arm. I turned and looked at Kim—beautiful, with those big sad almond eyes, eyes that at twenty-two had already seen more sorrow and suffering than most Americans would see in a lifetime.

"I'm sorry about your grandfather," she said. "He was a nice man."

" 'Nice' might not be exactly the right word," I said.

"He was nice to me," she insisted. "That time you took me with you out to his farm, he showed me some of his horses."

"He also asked you why your people lost your country," I reminded her.

"Well," she said after a moment, "at least he was interested."

In its purest form, this was vintage Malcolm Clay: make them feel comfortable, smile a bit, then blam, hit them with a question, an insult, something—something that would embarrass, something that they could not explain. In every situation Grandfather had to try to win, to come out on top. Even against someone like Kim—from whom he could have hoped no possible gain. Maybe he had not been certificably or clinically insane, but he had certainly been dancing close to the outer edge.

"Thomas," said Kim, her voice low, almost a whisper, "the police asked me where you were. Where were you, Thomas?"

"Well, I knew that you wouldn't be home," I said, trying to appear confident in my story, "what with your art show and all, so after work I stopped by Mr. Wong's and had a bit to eat, shrimp in curry sauce." I lifted a fork of ravioli to my mouth, checked myself and lowered the fork back down to the plate. "Then I went over to the Beach Club, had a few drinks, talked to some people, listened to some lies and then came on home."

"All right," she said, her eyes calm, knowing. "But if you want to, you can say you were with me."

"Thanks," I said. "But I imagine quite a few people saw you at the gallery without me."

"Yes," she said. "They probably did."

I wanted to reach out to her, to hold her, to confess and promise that I would never again do anything that might hurt her. But I couldn't. There's something inside of me, something cold, something that calculates and double-thinks every situation, plays it out in my head in advance, something dark that I may have inherited from old, now gone, Malcolm Clay that will not allow me to open up to others, to respond in a normal fashion to offerings of friendship and affection.

Kim finished off the rest of her wine and stood up.

"I'm going upstairs to take a shower," she announced. "Come up when you ready."

"Okay, sure," I said. "I'll just wait here for that detective's call."

"All right," she said. Then she kissed me and drifted on up the stairs.

I waited. The telephone, however, never rang. Instead there was a loud knock at the front door. I moved over to the door and opened it.

A man about my height—six foot—or maybe a few inches taller, wearing a gray three-piece suit, stood in the rain, smiling. His hair was wet and brown and cut in a slightly longish style; a trimmed mustache curved across his upper lip; his teeth were white, his skin well-tanned.

"Thomas Clay?" the man asked after a moment.

"Yes," I said.

The man's smile grew wider.

In his right hand I noticed that he carried a brown leather briefcase. "Are you with the Sheriff's Department?" I asked.

"Not technically," the man responded. "May I come in?" He cupped his left hand, held it out and let it fill with rainwater. "I'll explain."

I stood to one side and motioned him in.

He stepped into the room and glanced around. "Nice place," he remarked; his eyes were already working—searching, checking, remembering.

There was something vaguely familiar about that face, those eyes.

"Mind if I sit down?" he asked. He was still smiling.

"Please," I said.

The man eased himself down onto the sofa. I flopped into a recliner next to him.

The man looked at me and continued to smile.

And then I recognized him. I knew who he was. He and I had been in the same grade together throughout elementary and high school. I had not seen him since our senior year. By that time we were both running with entirely different groups—I with the dopers and the drop-outs and the girls who would spread for you on the first date; he with the clean crowd, or maybe he had been alone. To me he had always been the quintessential punk—straight arrow and straight A's. Even as a child I had disliked him. He was just too damn good and neat and polite and smart. At some point, during the fourth or fifth grade I think it was, I became so annoyed with his general goodness that I tried to flush his head down a toilet in the boys' bathroom. He had made one too many A + + for me. This, in turn, led to my first run-in with organized authority, school or otherwise. I was spanked, suspended from school for a week and made to apologize. It was a harbinger of a future to be filled with censure and reprimand. And now here he was: sitting on my sofa, smiling like a man whose entire existence had just been justified. Truly, a most unwelcome development.

"Mason Brooks," I said. "Jesus Christ, it's been a long time."

"A long time," he repeated.

We sat and looked at each other. Neither of us made an attempt to reach out and shake the other's hand.

"So what is it? You've grown up to be a policeman? A detective?" I asked.

"As I said, not technically."

"Then tell me. Technically."

"Well, you see, on occasion I perform certain services for the Governor," he allowed.

"Certain services, huh?" I was somewhat skeptical.

"Yes," he said. "Anyway, I was over in Miami on some state business when the Governor called. He had heard about your grandfather and asked me to hop over and see if there was anything I could do, here, on the ground, in an advisory capacity, so to speak."

"And when the Governor says hop, you hop."

Brooks smiled and popped open his briefcase. He took out a yellow legal pad, plucked a gold Cross pen out of his inner coat pocket and twirled up a point. With the pad and pen poised on his knee, he looked back at me.

"Before we get started," he said, "the Governor has asked me to convey his condolences. The Governor was very fond of your grandfather."

"The Governor must be a fool or a masochist or both," I said, leaning back in my chair.

"I take it then that you didn't like your grandfather?" he asked. He was writing now.

"I may not have liked him," I said, "but I didn't dislike him enough to kill him."

"Not personally?" he asked.

"Not personally or by proxy," I said.

Brooks smiled and continued writing.

"According to Detective Dawson—now he's with the Sheriff's Department—"

"I know," I said.

Brooks stopped writing and looked up. "You know?"

"He called here. He left a message."

"Oh yes, of course. He spoke to your wife."

"Girlfriend," I corrected.

"Girlfriend." Brooks made a note on his legal pad. "So according to Detective Dawson—is that her?" He pointed at the ceiling, toward the sound of someone taking a shower. "Your girlfriend?"

"Yes."

"Nice."

"Right," I said.

"Anyway, according to Detective Dawson, who was at the murder scene, your grandfather, Mr. Malcolm Clay, was shot twice in the back of the head at close range with a small caliber weapon in a field behind his house sometime this evening. The exact time of death has not yet been established." He paused. "Any questions?"

"Just one," I said. "What the fuck are you doing here?"

"I thought that I had already explained that," said Brooks patiently.

"You said you worked for the Governor. But what does that have to do with you being here, in my house, asking me a bunch of questions?"

"The Governor and your grandfather were friends, allies in many important causes, causes important to the state."

"I'll bet."

"The Governor," Brooks continued, "asked me to look into his death, to assist the local authorities in whatever ways might be possible, to insure that your grandfather's murderer is brought to justice."

"Oh, justice. So that's what we're talking about?"

"Yes," said Brooks. "Murder and justice."

For several seconds, in a silence surrounded by the sound of falling water—the rain outside, the shower inside—we stared at each other.

Then Brooks began again: "Now when Detective Dawson called here, he reports that you weren't home. Is that correct?"

"Correct," I said.

"So the obvious question is, where were you?"

"Well, I stopped by Beck's Place after work and had a few beers," I said. "And no, I didn't talk to anyone I knew, and there's probably no way to confirm that I was there. You'll just have to trust me."

"We'll do better than that. We'll check it."

"Check, check," I said. "Knock yourself out."

Brooks pointed at the plate of half-eaten ravioli on the coffee table. "It looks as if you're just getting around to dinner. Almost midnight. Rather late, isn't it? Perhaps you've had a busy night."

"I like to eat late," I said. "I always eat late."

"Sure," said Brooks; he was still writing. "Okay, now when was the last time you saw your grandfather alive?"

"Well, let me think." I picked up my glass of wine and took a sip. I was trying to decide whether or not to tell the truth. Eventually I opted for the course with which I was most familiar. "I don't recall precisely, but I would guess about a month ago."

"About a month ago," echoed Brooks.

Something in his voice told me that he knew more than he was letting on.

Brooks scribbled off a few more lines, then returned the pen to his pocket and slid the legal pad into his briefcase.

He stood up and looked around the room. "Guess that's about it for now."

Brooks turned, got almost to the door, then stopped and turned back. "You know, whoever whacked your grandfather must've really hated the old boy," he observed.

"Why do you say that?" I asked.

"Because," explained Brooks, "when the body was discovered it was found lying face-down in six inches of cow shit."

"Why that's, that's—"

"You got that right," agreed Brooks. "Brains, mud, cow shit and blood. One hell of an unpretty sight. Detective Dawson reports that the ambulance boys were out there raising hell about it."

"Jesus," I said. "I don't believe it."

"What you believe or don't believe really doesn't make a good goddamn to me," said Brooks, opening the door. "A nasty way to die, though. Well, good night."

"Yeah," I said, not bothering to get up. "Good night."

And as Brooks closed the door I wondered if he already knew that I had been out at Devon Woods earlier that evening. I also wondered if maybe I should call a lawyer.

FOUR

I could hear Kim moving about upstairs. I knew that she would not sleep tonight; she might get in bed but she would not close her eyes. Death in any form was traumatic for her. One of her brothers, who had been a captain in the South Vietnamese Army, was gunned down by his own troops and his body left by the side of the road when he tried to stop his men from retreating before the fall of Da Nang in early 1975. According to Kim, his spirit would wander the Vietnamese countryside for eternity. After the North Vietnamese took over the country her father, who had been a lawyer with certain political ties to the old regime, and one of her sisters, who had worked at the American embassy in some vague capacity, were both sent away to a re-education camp, where, at some point during their scholastic ascent, they were taken out into the fields together and shot as slow learners. I once asked Kim why her family had not fled earlier, when they had a chance, and she had given me a look mixed with pity and pain—pity for me, the hopeless American, and pain for herself, for her family—and had said because they (her family) had always believed the U.S. government's promise that they would be taken care of, as they were considered to be high-risk. And besides, her father had insisted right up to the time the tanks were rolling through the streets of Saigon that the B-52's would return, that it was all a master stroke of American strategy to lure the North Vietnamese out into the open. But the big bombers never came back, and the U.S. government, in the final dying spasms of its great idealistic adventure, decided that enough was too much and promises were only words and one less country in the world was only one less country. Even now, Kim still could not bear to watch the news on television—she walked out of the room when it came on—because it was all too real for her. "If I wanted to see that stuff," she once told me, "I'd just go to bed and dream." Yes, soldiers, she had nightmares too.

Above my head I could trace her movements from the bedroom to the bathroom, back to the bedroom, into the hall, into the other bedroom which was used as a sort of study, then back to the bedroom again. Eventually I heard the bed creak, and I knew that she had finally landed.

I took my plate and knife and fork and wine glass into the kitchen and set them down in the sink. I turned on the water and watched the remains of the ravioli in meat sauce wash off the plate and on down the drain. Gone as if it had never existed.

I reached up into a cabinet, brought down a tall glass and made myself a liberal gin and tonic. Beefeater and Schweppes again. Except here at home, instead of a plastic lemon filled with lemon juice, I had fresh wedges of lime preserved for my use in a small Tuperware bowl. Kim really knew how to spoil a fool.

With the ice in my drink clinking against the sides of the glass, I stepped out onto the lanai. Fortunately the wind was blowing from out of the east so no rain was coming in through the screens. The rain and the night had siphoned off some of the heat and had left a pleasant crispness in the air. In front of me, in clay pots and hanging out of baskets suspended from the ceiling, a jungle of plants pushed and swayed against one another. To my surprise I saw my two cats sleeping in separate chairs at opposite corners of the lanai. Kim usually had these animals banished to the great outdoors. It was not that she particularly disliked cats, it was just that she held the opinion that animals should be of some practical, rather than ornamental, value. She was especially repulsed by the people one often sees fawning over small aggressive dogs.

My cats—Tom, a solid white long-haired male, and Blackie, a solid black long-haired female—had come into my hands as a result of chance and coincidence. There was no attempt at calculated cuteness here. Two different girls who lived with me at two different times brought these animals with them along with their other assorted possessions when they came to stay. And later, when they left—I was as happy with their departures as with their arrivals, if I remember correctly—they left their cats behind. They (the cats) had both been rendered sexually neutral, so they were relatively docile. Both of them lived under the illusion that the beach was their private domain. They were spoiled and insufferably arrogant. Perhaps it was their arrogance that appealed to me. I could identify with their indifference.

As I lowered myself down into a wicker chair, my black cat lifted her head, gave me a none-too-kind look, then tucked her head back under a paw. The other one, the white one, could have slept through a hurricane. He was primarily a day cat anyway—he believed that he was invisible when on the beach.

Of all the places in my house, of all the rooms and amenities, the place of which I was most fond was my lanai: white wicker furniture, a curtain of green plants, the white sand beyond, and beyond that the blue of the Gulf of Mexico; the constant breeze and the smell of the sea; the sound of the surf; and at night the moon and the stars—a vista of openness and space, life and movement. Essentially it was a porch screened-in on three sides that butted up against the back of the house; a sliding glass door connected it with the rest. Off to the right was a small sun deck of weathered wood. Three steps down led to the beach; a hundred more, the Gulf of Mexico.

Coming back through the sliding glass door from the lanai, one first entered the dining area. An oval-shaped table, four caneback chairs, one china cabinet—all made of teak wood. To the left of the dining area was the kitchen. Stove, refrigerator, dishwasher, microwave—all the conveniences of a modern American kitchen. Next to the kitchen was a little half bath. Though necessary this room was singularly unremarkable.

The rest of the downstairs was given over to the living room. Against one wall was a fireplace. Admittedly a fireplace in south Florida may have seemed somewhat superfluous, but on those occasions when the temperature dropped, it had proven a wonderful extravagance. Most of the year an embroidered silk screen blocked the fireplace opening; two small rubber trees in clay pots stood alongside the screen. A brown leather sofa (almost identical to the one in my duplex) was centered against one wall. In front of the sofa was a large oak campaign chest, about fifteen inches high; this served as a coffee table. Two small end tables were positioned at each end of the sofa. A white fabric recliner, a mahogany secretary bookcase (an antique given to me by my parents) and a television set rounded out the living room.

Running along the wall opposite the fireplace, a stairway led upstairs.

At the top of the stairs was another bathroom. A skylight was fitted into the roof above the bathtub. This was one feature of the house about which I always remained uncertain; I could never get used to taking a shower or a bath and looking up and seeing clouds and birds drifting by.

Down the hallway, off to one side, was my study. An old roll-top desk and swivel arm chair were placed against one wall. Three bookcases which Kim had painted a strange dark blue contained my books. I probably had close to a thousand volumes in my little library. (It's rather strange, I've always felt, that I didn't acquire a taste for reading until after I was finished with school; but then again, being force-fed large quantities of unrequested material is hardly conducive to stimulating an appetite of any type.)

Across the hall was the master bedroom. A double bed, a dresser, a chest of drawers and two night stands—all matching mahogany and all antique—were scattered about the room. These various pieces, like the secretary downstairs, were given to me by my parents when they moved to Spain. Several years before they had surreptitiously purchased a little seaside villa on the island of Majorca. Their move came as a major surprise to me; it was a surprise to everyone. After having worked for Grandfather in one capacity or another for more than thirty years—and getting paid very well for it too—one day Father decided that he'd had enough fun and quit. This sparked a near riot within the family and among the personnel of Grandfather's various companies. Father's brothers screamed; underlings scrambled for positions. In a scene that took place out at Devon Woods which I happened to witness—I was out there on another matter—Grandfather accused Father of disloyalty and selfishness. This brought a slight smile to Father's face. He dropped the keys to his office into Grandfather's lap and left without saying a word. My parents sold their home, sold or gave away most of the things, memorabilia, whatever, that they had acquired over the years and bade farewell to America. They left taking only four suitcases with them. They have not been back since, and from what I can discern from their letters and telephone calls, they seem not to miss the good ole US of A in the least.

As it was with my antique rug at my duplex so was it here at my beachhouse that I had one item which I valued above all others. That item was a painting—again a gift from my parents. It hung in the bedroom on the wall opposite my bed. Since earliest childhood this painting has been a source of continual fascination for me. The painting itself shows in the foreground a pair of black patent leather boots propped up on a low table and crossed at the instep; from the size of the boots and the angle of the bootlegs' incline we know that they are being worn by a man sitting outside of our immediate range of view. Behind the boots, coming toward us, is a young naked girl; she has long black hair falling over small shoulders; the boots effectively block out most of the lower half of her body. In her hands she is carrying a small metal bejeweled box; the box is held up in front of her breasts; she is about to pass through an archway covered with a thin gauze-like curtain; a long bony white hand is extended out from behind the archway, poised to sweep the curtain aside. Behind the girl, off to one side, is an opening cut into a thick outer wall; through the opening one can see the watchtowers and the minarets and the glistening domes of an old Middle Eastern city and the stark blue desert skies above.

I can recall being very young and asking Father what the painting was supposed to mean, and Father had explained that it could mean whatever the artist and I wished for it to mean. This struck me as a splendid concept. I was deeply moved when Father brought the painting over to my house just before they left for Spain. "It might be worth some money," he said, handing it to me. This supposition was positively confirmed one afternoon several years later when Kim spotted a painting by the same artist (now long since dead) in a gallery downtown. I called the owner and asked him to drop by and give me an estimate on what he thought my painting could be sold for. One look and he told me that he knew a man out on Longboat Key who would pay twenty-five thousand for it today, but he suggested that we place it in his gallery at thirty-five thousand and see what happened. I thanked him and promptly had the painting added to my homeowner's insurance policy. I was not interested in the money. I liked the painting; though not so much that I myself would have paid the twenty-five, thirty or thirty-five thousand for it, but enough to keep it and forego whatever immediate gains could have been realized from its sale.

It might appear to some that my sense of priorities was somewhat skewed—others might say, screwed. But I have always loved art, and paintings in particular. I learned early in life, mostly by means of observation, that the pursuit of money solely for money's sake, simply to add a few more zeros after one's name, is a vain and unworthy goal. There needs to be something more, or else it's all just clocking time and hoping for a soft landing.

FIVE

The alarm went off and she slapped it dead. An annoying brightness was edging in around the curtains; somewhere nearby a seagull shrieked insistently. I rolled over and immediately went back to sleep. Soon I could feel a sharp little bony knee probing my back, pumping for my kidneys. This was our usual wake-up routine: the alarm, a five minute respite, then the knee.

I flopped out of bed and made my way on uncertain feet for the bathroom. With a sudden violence Kim ripped open the curtains, flooding the bedroom with a hard white light. She looked at me and smiled. She seemed quite pleased with herself.

I staggered on toward the bathroom and shut the door behind me. I felt foul; I looked foul. I decided not to shave. I ran my fingers through my hair and sneered at myself in the mirror. My eyes were puffy and rimmed in red. I shot a couple of drops of Visine into each eye, brushed my teeth and stepped into the shower. The water from the pulsating shower head threw itself down upon me with a wonderfully erratic rhythm. I could almost feel the brain cells coming to life again.

After my shower I wrapped a towel around my waist and, still dripping water, padded back into the bedroom. Kim had raised all of the windows and opened the glass door that led out to a little balcony positioned over the lanai. (This was usually where I began my day; even during the height of summer it remained relatively cool out here until well past mid-morning.) A Gulf breeze was swirling through the room, kicking up the curtains and sending loose pieces of paper scattering about. Outside, on the porch, on a little table, was a cup of coffee and a newspaper. Kim walked by me, gave me a quick kiss, slipped her silk bathrobe off her shoulders and stepped, brown and firm, into the bathroom.

I proceeded to get dressed. I pulled on a pair of blue jeans and selected a clean shirt. One of the many obvious advantages of working for one's self is that you do not need to dress to try to impress other people. In the case of John and myself there were, however, certain occasions, such as meetings with bankers and investors, that did mandate more formal attire. But as a rule, for the office and ourselves, we opted for a relaxed dress code. This was most fortunate for John. For I have never in my life seen anyone who looked more uncomfortable, more ill at ease, than my business partner in a suit and tie. It just didn't work for him. He always reminded me of someone in court accused of some heinous crime trying to convince a jury that, contrary to the evidence and the eyewitnesses, he was not the man they sought. Sadly the whole effect collapsed under its own preposterous weight; he looked guilty as hell. Eventually I was able to wean him away from the three-pice suits and substitute some lightweight linen jackets and colorful silk shirts. He still looked guilty but at least there was no pretense—which was really what made the money boys itch.

Out on the balcony my newspaper was flapping and my coffee was getting cold. I went out to join them. I sat down in a wrought iron arm chair and propped my feet up on the railing. From this height I had an unobstructed view of the beach for almost 180°: joggers and fast walkers; children splashing in the surf; tourists searching for shells; an elderly gentleman wearing a golf hat, walking in circles, flapping his arms; sailboats and speedboats; surfers skipping school; the beach ballerina (a regular), her hair wild like seaweed, spinning and leaping to the music in her head; some arrogant asshole out running with his dog (I once nailed this animal for befouling my beachfront; a well-aimed rock caught him in mid-crap); someone playing a radio too loud; two other people throwing a frisbee; Europeans with enormous stomachs protruding over obscene bathing suits, guzzling their morning beers; young trim, already well-versed in the art of manipulation, walking and smiling and looking, always looking—an arm in a bikini, a beaconing wave.

I waved back.

"Friends?" asked Kim, standing behind me.

I had not heard her come out of the bathroom.

"Birds," I said, without turning around. "Migratory birds, looking for a place to land."

She went back inside and began to dress.

I took a sip of my coffee and opened the paper.

Thursday. September 21. There was no mention of Grandfather on the front page; I was mildly disappointed. That date—the twenty-first—or one very near it, was for some reason special, of some sort of significance. I couldn't quite put it together. Farther down the page was the explanation—a picture of a forlorn-looking farmer in a feed cap standing in the middle of a North Dakota cornfield in six inches of snow. The caption read: LAST DAY OF SUMMER. This was typical Florida newspaper humor; they loved to stick it to the Yankees whenever possible.

"You going to work today?" called out Kim in front of the mirror.

"Sure," I said. "Why not?"

"Well, I just didn't know," she said. There was a note of uncertainty, discomfort in her voice; again, death and wandering souls throwing her off. "Should we send flowers?"

"To whom?" I asked. "He's dead. He never liked flowers anyway. Those gardens out at Devon Woods were one of my grandmother's projects. He just allowed the gardeners to keep them up."

"I wish I could've met her," said Kim. "Your grandmother, I mean."

"You would've liked her," I assured her. "She would've liked you."

She came out onto the porch. She was dressed now. She looked at me, then out at the Gulf. She sighed slightly and nodded her head at nothing.

"Okay," she said, still a little off beat. "See you tonight." She bent and kissed me on the mouth, letting it linger there for a second longer than usual, then she turned away. I heard her going down the stairs, then on out the door.

Yes, she and Grandmother would have gotten along splendidly. In many respects they were a lot alike—both of them

[41]

physically small yet strong-willed and intense, with a low tolerance for fools but still with a surprising capacity for caring. They knew what they wanted and had the patience to wait for it. It was easy to imagine them together having lunch, talking art, going to galleries. Kim could have shown Grandmother what she was working on and Grandmother would have admired it, for in her time she had been something of an artist herself.

In fact it was art, or more precisely the pursuit of art—Grandmother's demand for a studio from which to do her seascapes—that had originally forced Grandfather to build the little beach house in which I was now so pleasantly established. It may not have looked it, but it was one of the sturdiest structures on the beach. In one form or another it had been standing for more than sixty years. At the time that it was built—1925, according to title search documents; one of the first buildings on the beach, according to an early aerial photograph—Grandfather and Grandmother (already quite prosperous) were living in a large house overlooking Sarasota Bay. Grandfather set foot in the place only one time, and that was primarily to inspect the workmanship of a sub-contractor he was considering for another project. He disliked the beach and the Gulf in particular. He claimed that swimming in salt water caused sterility, and he loved to expound upon his theory in mixed company.

Shortly after Grandmother had taken up her palette and brushes and settled down at her easel, a singularly intrusive individual began construction of another house next door. The hammering and sawing and shouting and cursing broke her concentration, Grandmother complained; so Grandfather bought out the neighbor and then at her insistence went on to buy up an additional half of a mile of sand on either side of her little studio to prevent any future fools from similarly disrupting her creative solitude. It was always a source of some amusement for those of us within the family who knew the true history of Grandfather's rise to wealth and fame that this particular purchase of one mile of virgin beachfront property in 1925, which would later net him millions (he parcelled it out a little bit at a time like bread crumbs to starving sparrows), was often cited in newspaper and magazine articles about him as an example of his vision and foresight. Better, I suppose, to make the right move for the wrong reason than the wrong move for the right reason.

After more than twenty-five years of putting color to canvas, suddenly and without explanation, Grandmother abandoned her art and turned the beach house over to her sons and their families to use as they wished. By the time I was born a pattern of alternating weekends of usage among families had already developed. (It seemed that Father and his two brothers got along together rather poorly in social settings.) And on our weekends: I can remember being probably four or five years old and standing at the water's edge, utterly amazed at the seemingly endless expanse of blue stretching away before me, standing and staring, and the heat and light, and then from behind Father would scoop me up and swing me into his shoulders where I would sit hugging his head for support as he marched us out into the surf, and Father would jump and I would shriek with laughter and the waves would break around us and then roll on toward shore, and then later, dried off and in a change of clothes, with the sun dropping red over the horizon, the cook-out—the steaks rare and char-broiled; this before we found out that good food was bad for you—and the cherries and orange slices, still tasting faintly of gin, from the Tom Collins that my parents would drink, and the women guests lounging about in their two piece bathing suits (I was observant even then), though not quite bikinis yet, and a couple of years on and the swimming parties and the birthday parties with my little friends from school. And one birthday party in particular (call it my eighth): all of my little guests—all boys—and myself dressed up in soldier suits with oversized helmets and plastic rifles, and the screaming and shouting as we assaulted the beach, making little popping noises with our mouths, heaving shells for grenades, then spinning and clutching our chests and falling into the surf, and there, face-down, arms outspread, holding our breath as long as possible, we would lie limp and let the waves wash our mortally wounded bodies up onto the beach, and then after a few minutes (long enough to become bored with being dead), we'd jump up again, springing magically back to life, and continue our bloodless battle against all things evil and un-American. Looking back on it now it all seems extremely remote and somewhat sad—a time of innocence and can-do confidence, a time when all good little soldiers went to bed early and dreamed of days of greater glory just ahead.

Then at some point during my first year of high school, in an unusual example of concord and agreement within the family, my parents and the parents of my cousins passed possession of the property on to the next generation. Their reason for this magnanimous gesture was never clear to me, but whatever it was, I approved wholeheartedly. My cousins and I were each given a key and a lecture on the responsibilities of wealth and position in a grown-up world. Quite soon, however, the lectures were forgotten, and with my older cousins— all out of the same litter—leading the way, the beach house was quickly transformed into a combination bordello, flop house and opium den. It was wonderful. There were black lights and day-glo posters and candles and ashtrays overflowing with cigarettes and half-smoked joints (this was 1967 and things were just beginning to break) and beer bottles and tequila bottles and garbage everywhere. Upstairs, it was mattresses wall to wall, sperm- and blood-stained, as many as half a dozen to a room; with a couple of singles tossed into the hall for good measure. Occasionally some anonymous female person on speed or hoping to make herself indispensable or perhaps doing penitence for her sins would attempt to repair some of the damage, but on the whole the place was a marvelous disaster and a general threat to health, both physical and mental.

And so it was here, amid the trash and the bottles and the unconscious bodies, in a room that would later become my study, that I first made love to a girl—no, love is entirely the wrong word here; in fact, it mocks the word and its meaning because this was sex, in and out, pure and simple. She was a small girl with brown hair, not unattractive. Unpardonably I have forgotten her name, though I must have known it once; it was well-advertised in every toilet stall, on every wall in every boys' bathroom in school. She was easy, a little high school whore, a phone number and a fuck. Early on she had discovered, or had been told (and had believed) that she had only one thing to offer, and that realization made her quiet and sad. It was rumored that she had stopped wearing underwear on dates because the boys always kept her panties as souvenirs. Somehow I was able to buy a half pint of rum, and somehow again, I don't recall the details, we arrived at the beach house. There were undoubtedly other people there and many things happening, but all of that is a mere blur to me now. I can only remember thinking that she drank her rum and coke too slowly. I was drinking too, trying to hurry things along. Eventually we found ourselves at the bottom of the bottle. I put my arm around her, for support as much as for affection, and led her upstairs—or maybe she led me. We entered the first room we came to. We tripped and fell together onto an unoccupied mattress. We probably laughed. The room was so dark that I couldn't tell if anyone else was in the room, and frankly I was so eager that I couldn't have cared. We kissed and hugged and groped about. First, a breast—she undid her bra—a bare breast. I was ecstatic. Then a hand on a knee. Then slowly, carefully, trying to maneuver between skin and fabric, I slipped my hand up under her dress. I didn't know what to expect. I knew that everyone had said that she would do it, would buck like a horse and moan like someone in pain, but still I couldn't believe it, couldn't believe that any girl would actually do the deed. So, blind and dumb, petrified, I continued my crawl, hoping, praying that she wouldn't scream. Then suddenly my hand brushed against a little tuft of hair and she let out a moan and I almost wasted my effort right there in my jeans. Anatomically I was still very much an amateur; she had to guide me in, and then a couple of good strokes and another moan—it was the moaning that did me—and that was it, it was over. Not very romantic I know, but at least I was over the hurdle, in the club.

And then from out of the dark, from across the room, there came the slow, methodical, almost weary clapping of a single pair of hands. "Not bad," said a voice (male). "Wanta swap?" And this really shook me. It confused me; it brought me most rudely back to the real world. Before I had not cared; now I was concerned. "No," I managed to blurt out before I entirely realized what I was saying. I was only fourteen and somewhat horrified at the debauched nature of the suggestion and the casual manner in which it had been delivered. "Okay," laughed the voice. And I recognized the laugh, and then put the voice together with it—my cousin James, four years older than me, a former high school star athlete and exemplary student who recently, after having experienced some sort of brainbursting revelation (a three day acid trip on an uninhabited mangrove island in the middle of the Gulf), had dropped all pretense of caring and was now coasting on a reserve of goodwill through the remainder of his senior year. He had allowed his straight, Indian-like black hair to drop to his shoulders. His old beer buddies didn't know what to think; his parents were scandalized.

The snap of a match cut the dark. He lit a candle. His handsome face smiled at me. He was sitting on a mattress, naked from the waist up; his lean body roped with muscles; his back propped against a wall. "A joint?" he asked, holding one out in front of me, twirling it between his fingers. "Sure," I said in an unsteady voice as my bulging, disbelieving eyes fixed themselves on the naked girl slumped against his shoulder. Patricia Sue Patterson, the blond, blue-eyed, big-breasted Miss Everything back at my high school. Sitting there calmly: her enormous nipples pointed skyward, an idiot's grin spreading wide and white across her lovely lips, her famous baby blues unfocused. Soft and smiling, beautiful beyond beauty, in the prime of her prime, the queen of dreams. It was a sobering sight. James lit the joint and flipped it across the room. He smiled again. He looked over at Patricia Sue and then at me, then he laughed and blew out the candle.

And there, again in the dark, with the image of Patricia Sue Patterson's goddess-like body burned into my brain, creating fever and sweat, I realized that almost simultaneously I had lost my virginity, experienced sex in its most primitive form, and had turned down one of the greatest pieces of ass I might ever be offered in my life. And I knew further, without needing to be told, without bringing the matter to a vote, that no amount of begging or pleading or crawling across the floor could now change the irrevocable and ill-considered refusal I had just uttered mere seconds before. I was crushed by the rapidity of it all and the scarcity of second chances.

Then some four to five years on, as my cousins and I each went our various and separate ways, each acquiring as we went a home—apartment, whatever—of sorts, and soon with no

[46]

longer any definable need for a place in which to do anything we could not do in our own modest abodes, the keys, one by one, without ceremony, perhaps without even thanks (one afternoon a key simply left on a table), began returning, making their way back up the chain—child to parent, then child to parent again—until finally, collectively, all of them came to rest in Grandfather's palm. Grandfather wasted little time; he had little time to waste. He promptly had the building boarded up and padlocked.

And thus the matter stood for close to ten years—nailed shut, locked tight. Then at some point, a year or so after Angie had departed for the hinterlands, a powerful hurricane packing winds in excess of one hundred miles per hour swept out of the Gulf of Mexico and punched its way up along the southwest coast of Florida. Buildings were destroyed; people were killed. The beach house fared far better than most of the buildings on the beach, but did not escape entirely unscathed—one side of the house, whole and intact, was ripped away and deposited in a canal several hundred yards away. After the storm had passed the other property owners naturally began to rebuild. But Grandfather refused. He seemed to enjoy the idea of leaving the beachhouse the way it was—exposed to the elements, slowly being reclaimed by the sand and the sea and the wind and the rain. For him, in its present state of impending collapse it was a monument to something (Grandmother had been dead now for more than five years), revenge for some injury, real or imagined. The city was entirely unsympathetic and threatened to condemn the building if he didn't fix it up or tear it down. He sent their letters back unopened; he told their emissaries to their faces that he was out. Proceedings were initiated; the newspaper picked up the story. And I saw a wonderful opportunity. By this time I had been in the real estate game for about four years, and I thought that I was on top of the situation. This was old hat for me—buying from widows, from the financially strapped, auction sells, foreclosure sells. John and I had done it all and had come out shining.

So, fearing nothing, totally confident, I proposed to Grandfather that he sell to me rather than risk losing the property altogether. At first Grandfather pretended to be uninterested, swore that he would burn it down himself before he'd let the city or anyone else have it, then several weeks later, inexplicably, he called to say that we should talk. It wasn't going to be cheap I soon learned—Grandfather was no weeping widow—and the terms were hard to the point of being almost unreasonable. He demanded half of the purchase price in cash as a downpayment; he made the grand gesture, after much haggling and some excellent acting, of agreeing to hold paper on the balance for fifteen years at 10%. Ordinarily I would have balked at a deal structure liked this, walked away and laughed, but there was just something about buying that building, dealing with Grandfather and coming out on top, out-foxing the old fox himself.

I now realize that it was entirely misdirected ego on my part. To raise the downpayment I had to sell the house that I was then living in, put a short-term second mortgage on my duplex, borrow additional funds from the bank and finally from my parents too. But it was all going to be worth it I kept telling myself, though as the mountain of debt continued steadily to rise I was not nearly so cocky. Eventually I was able to put together the money that was needed and the deal was done; the papers were signed (no handshakes) and I took possession.

Inside of the house a foot of sand had accumulated; everything was soaked and the wood was beginning to rot; weeds and mushrooms were shooting up out of unlikely places; birds were nesting in corners; disintegrating mattresses, broken pieces of furniture, rusty appliances, old garbage and things unrecognizable were scattered about; and there amid the rubble, signs of recent human habitation—used condoms. "Some people'll fuck anywhere," muttered John, shaking his head in disgust. (I had observed recently that he was becoming something of a moralist, and this disturbed me.) With John still voicing dismay and disapproval, he and I began repairs on the exterior, rebuilding the outer wall, while two other men whom I had hired cleaned up the interior—removed everything, hauled it away; washed, scrubbed and disinfected the place from floor to ceiling. Finally the beachhouse was once again livable and I moved in. Although for the first couple of weeks, until I had gotten water and electrical hook-ups, it was a bit like camping out. But regardless it was mine, a house on the beach, mine, mine, mine.

Then came the telephone call (the first incoming call that I received) and the other shoe dropped. "Where's my money?" demanded a shrill voice at the other end of the line. I was stunned. All right, so I was a few days late with my first mortgage payment—I knew it; but I didn't think that the world would come to an abrupt end. "Well," I began slowly, calmly, as though I were speaking with a child. "I want my money!" shouted the voice "Now!" Again I tried to explain that I had been forced to do this, to do that, unexpected costs, unseen damage and so on. "Read the contract," interrupted the voice. "Section 12. Paragraph (c)." And Grandfather, his voice high and excited, began to read. The small print. I had not read the contract myself word for word; Grandfather's lawyer had drawn it up and I had assumed, stupidly, that it was a standard contract. In essence what Grandfather's special clause said was that if I fell behind in my mortgage payments so much as only thirty days he could (and now I knew, would) immediately, and with little legal recourse left to me, foreclose on the property, and I (worldly, clever, totally together me) would lose the huge downpayment I had already paid out, as well as the house and all of the improvements thereon. Now I could see the trap; now I could see Grandfather leering at me from the other end of the long table as I signed those fateful papers. It was beautiful. I almost felt like congratulating him, or strangling him. I started to say something, but Grandfather quickly cut me off. "Pay up! Grow up!" he shouted into the receiver and then slammed it down. I got out my contract and read it. Every word. Grandfather had me by the proverbial short hairs.

There was, however, one thing which Grandfather had not counted on, nor for that matter had I—my business partner, my friend, John Allen. The next day he made the mortgage payment for me. I didn't even ask him to; he volunteered. (I desperately did not want to go back to my parents for more money—a fact that Grandfather knew well. They had already lent me a substantial sum. Father had been advising against the entire enterprise from the beginning, from becoming involved with Grandfather at all. "He's different," Father had insisted.) John further suggested that we sell off another building that he and I owned jointly to help ease my cash flow problem. John's motives for doing all of this were somewhat mixed—friendship, yes, truly, in its purest and most noble form; but also, I have always believed, the satisfaction of having himself proven right, of having recognized a snake when he saw one.

Eventually I was able to work things out, but for awhile there it was touch and go. Reflecting back upon the whole affair several days later, I couldn't understand why Grandfather had called me in the first place, why he would have instructed his lawyer to insert a trip clause into a contract and then have called me to warn me about it, threatened me with it, brag about it, whatever. But then Grandfather was a man of enormous contradictions, and some of the things that he did seemed not to make sense, seemed illogical to others, but below the surface, far below the surface, there was a definite method to his madness.

After that first month I made every additional payment in person—drove out to Devon Woods with a cashier's check, hand-delivered it and requested a receipt. "Almost got you, didn't I, boy?" laughed Grandfather the following month as he handed over the receipt. His laughter had nothing to do with humor. "Next time I'll take you and your big hairy friend too," he threatened, his little rat-eyes sparkling. "Maybe there won't be a next time," I said. "Not if you're smart," he snorted, slamming his receipt book shut and stalking out of the room.

Needless to say I never again entered into a contract with Grandfather. In some situations escaping with one's own skin is almost as gratifying as winning.

SIX

Morning was marching on and I knew that I had a telephone call to make. I gathered up my coffee cup and my newspaper and went downstairs. In the kitchen I decided to fix myself a second cup of coffee. As the water was boiling, I searched through Kim's cabinet of exotic spices and Oriental herbs and found, in the back, a small unopened bottle of brandy—B & B. I rarely had a drink before five in the afternoon, but today was special. I felt that I needed to fortify myself against the coming events of the day.

With my coffee and brandy in one hand and my newspaper under my arm, I moved into the living room. It was slightly after ten o'clock; I knew that John would already be at the office. He was an early riser, probably a holdover from his construction days. I took a sip of my coffee and dialed his home.

The first ring.

The second ring.

Then: "Hello."

"Susie?"

No answer.

"Susie, this is Thomas."

"I thought I told you I couldn't see you again."

"You did," I said. "And you were absolutely right."

Silence again.

"Susie, the reason I'm calling is, is that, well, last night someone killed my grandfather. Murdered him. Shot him in the head."

"Oh," she said, betraying no emotions whatsoever. "I'm sorry."

"Right," I said. "But you see the deal is that the cops are going to probably want to know where I was last night."

Again, more silence.

"And I might have to tell the truth," I added, hoping to shake her loose.

"You must do what you must do," she said.

"Right," I agreed. "But you see that might mean that I might have to say that I was with you last night at my duplex."

"But you weren't," she said calmly. "Not last night or any other night. And I've certainly never been to any duplex of yours. And I'll swear to that on a stack of Bibles in any courtroom anywhere."

"What?" I asked. "What did you say?"

"You heard me," she said. "Last night never happened. And unless you want to join your grandfather, you'd better remember that."

"I see," I said, and I knew what she meant. John loved her, loved her so much that a murder—one, two or a double with a suicide—would not be beyond the realm of possibilities.

"Good," she said. "Just forget about me, Thomas. Forget about me and anything that didn't happen last night. And don't call here again unless you want to talk to John."

And she hung up.

And again, for the second time in less than twelve hours, I was left holding a buzzing telephone.

I put the phone down, feeling as if I had been screwed and deserved it. I was not really mad at Susie, or even disappointed. She had her problems and I had mine. I took another sip of my coffee and brandy and decided to let things develop as they would. There was little to be gained by plotting and planning.

I shook open the newspaper and spread it out on the campaign chest in front of me. I wanted to find Grandfather. I flipped through the pages quickly; I was expecting bold print, black borders. There was nothing. This genuinely surprised me. Surely someone from the newspaper would have had adequate time and opportunity to find out about Grandfather's death before they went to press. Undoubtedly they had certain necessary connections, monitored police bands, emergency frequencies and such. I went back through the paper again. Slowly this time. Still nothing.

There was, however, something about a couple of other members of the family. Michele Clay (my oldest cousin, the older sister of James and Laura) and Vanessa Clay (David's and Daniel's step-mother)—both of them pictured there on the society page, glittering in evening gowns, adorned with diamond necklaces and long hanging earrings; their hair, blond and shoulder-length, cut in a similar style, turning inward just so at the ends; their faces, tanned and smooth; their eyes, hard and arrogant. They had that well-preserved look that women with enough money can buy. They were both about the same age, both bumping up against the underside of the big four-O. With drinks in their hands and wonderfully false smiles on their faces, they projected an image, even on the printed page, of smug contempt and manicured conceit. The caption at their feet explained their purpose, their reason for their superior smiles and upturned noses: they were there (there being the Van Wezel Performing Arts Hall, one of Sarasota's more striking structures) to attend the last performance of the last play of the summer theatrical season—a traditional charity gig. The play, which I thought was extremely appropriate for these two, was *Macbeth*.

Michele and Vanessa had known each other for close to twenty years. They had been roommates together during their first year at Radcliffe, and friends ever since—more than friends. But before either of them were to reach those ivy halls, a year before, there occurred an incredibly unseemly episode— unseemly even by our family's standards—involving Michele, which would later effect both of their lives in ways that neither of them could have foreseen or even imagined.

It began at some vague point during Michele's last year of high school. She had already been accepted at Radcliffe and found herself requiring a medical examination as part of that school's policy for admission. So quite naturally she, as everyone else in the family did when in need of medical attention, turned to David's and Daniel's father—a doctor, known locally as Doctor Jack. And how and where exactly, precisely, flesh first found flesh, I don't know; I don't even really care—though there were some rather snide comments circulating at the time about it beginning and ending in the stirrups. Somehow, regardless, she became involved romantically, or more to the point, sexually with Doctor Jack—her uncle, my uncle. I have always theorized that this was her first sexual encounter. In short, Doctor Jack got Michele pregnant, and to correct his error he was obliged to abort his own handiwork. Eventually Michele was sent off to college with a clean bill of health—or at least with a clean uterus—but the experience and the ensuing scandal scarred her deeply. After that I never again saw her in the company of a man; in fact, she would often go out of her way to avoid them.

Word of the whole sorry affair soon began to leak out. Michele's father, Philip Clay, a big man with a short fuse and an oversized sense of his own worth, then serving his first and last term in Washington as the representative of the good people of Florida's 13th congressional district—he was persuaded not to seek re-election after the appearance of press reports detailing the leasing of a building which he owned to the federal government at an outrageously inflated price; he would later go on to become a highly respected Washington-based lobbyist for the citrus industry—threatened to come back to Sarasota and kill his brother. Prudently Doctor Jack discovered a hitherto unknown urge to visit the ruins of Rome and left on the next plane out. His wife stayed home and began to drink.

After several months things quieted down and Doctor Jack returned saying that he was sick of spaghetti. For awhile life again seemed to progress more or less normally. Then one bright night, close to Christmas, Doctor Jack's wife took out her little red MG and ran it flat-out, full-speed into a reinforced concrete barrier at the end of one of the bridges linking Siesta Key to the mainland. She had been drinking; there was an empty fifth of vodka in the car. They called it an accident (probably for David's and Daniel's sake), but it always looked like something else to me. The drawbridge attendant was even quoted as saying that, from where he was sitting (he had been reading a magazine and looked up when he heard an engine rev), it appeared as if she had been aiming at the end of the bridge all along.

Michele didn't come home for her aunt's funeral. In fact

she didn't come home again until later that summer, and when she finally did return she brought Vanessa with her. And in the fall, when she headed back to school, she was flying solo—for Vanessa had already become Mrs. Doctor Jack Number Two.

I slammed the newspaper shut and flipped it on the floor. My hands and face were covered with newsprint. I went into the bathroom and washed them off. Passing through the kitchen again, I stopped and poured another healthy shot of brandy into my coffee cup. I walked out onto the lanai and downed my drink in one gulp. If I'd had a dog I would have kicked it. I was late for work, generally disgusted and a little drunk. And my day was just getting started.

SEVEN

The offices of Allen-Clay Realty were located east of town in a campus-like complex of three- and four-story buildings surrounded by blooming tropical bushes and towering oak trees. The buildings, with their fronts facing outward, were set in a circle around a small greenish-colored pond (probably once a cow pond) which was called a lake. In Florida any body of water with at least three fish and a frog in it, that is used in commercial or residential construction, is referred to majestically as a lake. We occupied a back-corner suite of rooms on the third floor of a four-story building. The exterior was mirrored glass; the interior was polished chrome, pastels, potted plants and elevators.

I slipped my car into my designated parking spot and made my way, blinking, through the sunshine, past the mirrored walls and up the elevator to the third floor. I pushed open the door marked Allen-Clay Realty and entered an air-conditioned buzz of efficiency and progress. A large barrel-chested gentleman with thinning close-cropped hair was seated on a leather sofa earnestly studying his shoe. To me he looked suspiciously like some type of police person.

Behind a waist-high curved counter, standing there amid her computers and printers and copiers and telephones, was our receptionist, Julie Lawrence, a stunning redhead with bright green eyes who used to sleep with both John and me (though not in the same bed at the same time) until she realized that neither of us was ever going to marry her. Her goals in life were clear—to get married, quit work, have two biologically perfect children and retire to a backyard swimming pool. She was still looking. Her face, usually a model of composure and control, wore a strained look.

She motioned me over to the counter. Nodding her head in the direction of the large gentleman who was now shifting through a pile of magazines on the table next to him, she whispered: "Some men from the Sheriff's Department are here, and one of them is back in your office right now." Her voice was urgent, conspiratorial.

"My office?" I asked, surprised and somewhat angered.

"I tried to stop him," explained Julie apologetically. "But he said you wouldn't mind."

"Okay," I said. "Don't worry about it. Let's just carry on as normal."

"All right," she said. She shifted gears and addressed the gentleman who had gone back to examining his shoe—he was obviously unimpressed with our periodical selection: "Can I get you a cup of coffee, sir?"

"Yeah, sweetie," croaked the big man. "That would be right nice of you."

Julie cast a spider's smile at him and headed off toward the coffee machine. Julie was not a woman to be trifled with. In addition to being a splendid receptionist and secretary, she was also in charge of complaints and the collection of rents. She did all of the real work in the place. She pursued her duties with a singular, if slightly unorthodox, vigor. She enjoyed telling new tenants that if they didn't pay their rents when due she would have their mail stopped. The amazing thing to me was that so many people believed her and lived in fear of her postal powers. Sometimes she exhibited a little too much zeal and originality, and had to be reined in a bit. One memorable afternoon shortly after we had established ourselves here in our new offices, I was in the back in my little cell contemplating life and the cosmos (one of my favorite pastimes) when I heard loud voices coming from the reception area. I went up front to investigate. On one side of the counter was a tall thin man in soiled working clothes, a short fat woman, two sunbaked children and a dog. Julie was on the other side of the counter trying to be polite. The gist of the argument, I soon discerned, was overdue rents (six months worth) followed by an eviction notice—fairly standard procedure. I could see that there was nothing to be gained by arguing (what was done was done), but people do love to talk, shout, demand justice, even when they're in the wrong. The conversation rapidly became more heated and somewhat personal. At some point the fat woman gave a secret hand signal to the children and they began to cry and the dog to bark. This was apparently more than Julie could stand—it was a Monday, I believe. In one swift fluid motion she reached into her purse (she always carried a large formless embroidered bag), whipped out a black western-style revolver with a six inch barrel and shoved three inches of the barrel into the man's flapping mouth. Everyone froze; the dog ceased barking. It became marvelously quiet. With the pistol still firmly planted in the man's mouth, Julie slipped quickly over the top of the counter and slid down to the floor. She then backed the wide-eyed family—they all had their hands in the air, even the children, which I thought was cute—out of the door and halfway down the hall. She was speaking to them in a low purposeful tone. In a couple of minutes Julie returned. She was alone and as calm as if she had just been out for a breath of air. "The Johnsons," she said to me by way of explanation, as if this were supposed to mean something. "Oh," I said, not knowing what else to say. She walked past me and around behind the counter again. "Is that thing loaded?" I asked. She smiled at me. "Naturally," she said, slipping the revolver back into her bag. "If it weren't, what would be the point?" "Quite right," I agreed, and with this new perspective on the meaning of life I took the rest of the day off.

I left the large gentleman still fiddling with his foot and went to find out who was intruding upon my privacy. As I passed the conference room I glanced inside. A long walnut table and twelve padded armchairs were squeezed into this room. Against one wall, almost covering the entire wall, was a large and rather curious painting which Kim had done for us (and for which she made us pay her; "Otherwise I couldn't consider myself an artist," she had patiently explained)—a jungle scene with pairs of red and yellow eyes peeking out through jagged parts in the spreading foliage. No one was in the room.

Down the corridor in front of me were four offices, two to a side. The outer offices, the rooms with the windows, were

John's and mine. My office was at the end of the corridor; it was a corner office. John and I had flipped for it and I had won. Perks as such did not mean much to me. But since I did spend a considerable portion of my working day looking out the window, watching the ducks bobbing across the pond and mating on the banks, I thought that to a certain extent I deserved two windows. The other two offices belonged to our small yet highly effective sales staff—a couple of naturally aggressive women who did all of our sales work. (I was not very good at sales; people sensed my genuine indifference.) The doors were all open, and I could see that the offices were empty. Up ahead I could also see that my door was open too.

I stopped just outside my doorway and looked in. The papers on my desk and credenza appeard to have been shuffled and carelessly restacked. Arching up from behind my desk was a broad back in blue pinstripes; the head and hands were out of sight, going through one of my bottom drawers.

"Hey, don't you need a search warrant or something to do that?" I demanded, stepping into the room.

"Probably," responded a voice—a voice with an unpleasantly familiar ring to it. "Probably I do."

A drawer slid into place and Brooks' head popped up. He was smiling. "Good morning," he said.

Brooks moved around from behind the desk and took a seat in a chair on the other side. "Well, come on in," he said, waving toward my desk. "It's your office, isn't it?"

"It certainly is," I said crisply. I marched past him and sat down in my chair.

Brooks already had his pad and pen out; he seemed eager to get started.

"Did you find anything?" I asked. "Anything incriminating?"

"Unfortunately not," said Brooks cheerfully.

His breezy manner, to say nothing of the obvious liberties he had taken with my property, annoyed me considerably.

"Are you always so goddamn happy in the morning?" I inquired.

"I can't help it," Brooks confessed. "I just love my work. You get to meet so many interesting people—like, for example, that bartender over at Beck's Place. A wonderful sense of humor. And you know what's strange, interesting?"

"What?" I asked, not wanting to hear the answer.

"He, amazingly, cannot recall you having been there last night."

"There's no real reason he should. I didn't start any fights or dance naked on any of the pool tables."

"And for that I'm quite sure he—and everyone else—is grateful," said Brooks, writing again. "But, in point of fact, you didn't actually go there last night, did you?"

"Well, perhaps it was the night before last," I conceded.

"Yes, perhaps it was," agreed Brooks. "But you see now, right now, all that we're concerned with is last night. The coroner's office has tentatively established the time to death at somewhere between 8:00 and 9:00. Now last night, no other night, only last night, between 8:00 and 9:00, where were you, Tommy?"

"Thomas," I said. "Not Tommy. Not Tom. Thomas."

"Okay, sure, Tom," he said. "Now last night between 8:00 and 9:00, where were you?"

"Don't I get to have a lawyer?" I asked half in jest.

Brooks stopped writing; he looked up.

"If you feel that you require legal counsel in order to answer my questions, please feel free to call one," he said in a tone of business-like correctness. "But as yet you have not been formally charged with any crimes. I am merely trying to fill in some background."

I could see that it was going to be a long and tedious day.

"I was with a lady," I said.

"What's her name?" He was writing again.

"A married lady."

"Yes," he said, not seeming to grasp my meaning. "What's her name?"

"Married," I said. "Get it. A husband."

"Oh," he said. He stopped writing. "A husband, huh?"

"Seems like they've all got 'em," I said.

"And you have no compunction about having affairs with married women?" he asked.

His attitude of moral superiority surprised me somewhat.

"Well, they're the ones who are married," I said, "not me."

"A fine distinction," he observed, scratching away at his pad again, "All right, now what's her name?"

"It won't do you any good," I said. "Don't you understand? She's married. She's got a husband. A big husband."

"And she won't corroborate your story?"

"She'll deny it."

"She would lie?"

"People do," I said.

"How do you know that?"

I bent forward across my desk.

"Well, don't tell anybody," I whispered, "but I once told a lie myself."

"No, I mean, how do you know that she won't corroborate your story?"

"Because I've already called her and asked her," I explained.

"So then you felt the need to establish an alibi for yourself," he said. "Curious. Very curious."

He filled up the page and flipped it over.

Down the corridor I could hear the heavy approach of footsteps. The sound drew nearer and then materalized in the person of John Allen.

"Thomas, there's some cop out front that just told me somebody knocked off your grandfather," he blurted out. His face was intense, disturbed. "What a bitch, man!"

"A bitch," I agreed, standing up. "John, this is Mason Brooks. Brooks, John Allen, my business partner."

"John," said Brooks warmly. He stood up, lifted one of John's hands and shook it vigorously.

John turned to look at me. His mouth was slightly open. He had not noticed Brooks when he had first entered the room.

"Brooks here is looking into my grandfather's death for the Governor's office," I explained. "My grandfather and the Governor were apparently political pals."

"Oh," said John, not quite understanding the whole setup.

"Mr. Malcolm Clay made some great contributions to this state," Brooks assured us.

"To the Governor's re-election campaign is more like it," I countered.

Brooks looked at me as if he wished to say something

further. Instead he turned toward John who was still standing in the center of the room. "Sit down, sit down," said Brooks, indicating an empty chair.

"Well, I don't wanta bust up nothing," said John.

"Oh, we're just having a little chat," said Brooks, smiling. "Old times, you know."

John sat down somewhat reluctantly.

"Speaking of old times I can remember watching you play football back in high school."

"You can?" asked John.

"Sure," said Brooks. "I was a couple of grades behind you in school. Tom and I were both in the same grade."

"You were?"

"Absolutely," said Brooks. "In fact there was one game in particular which I'll never forget. The state regional championship between Sarasota and Fort Myers."

"That was a long time ago," sighed John.

"Only a lifetime or two," laughed Brooks.

"You're right there," agreed John.

"I remember it was fourth down and . . ."

And, and, and, ad infinitum. Nothing bored me more than sports talk, with the possible exception of car talk. But John— Jesus Christ, he was eating it up. Sitting there on the edge of his seat, reliving through the eyes of another his moment in the sun. The cheering crowd, the flying colors, the energy, the excitement. John had peaked out at eighteen on a football field on a Saturday afternoon now long gone. Nothing that he could ever achieve in his life would again equal or even approach that brief shining spasm of magic and glory. He might become rich and successful, admired by friend, feared by foe, but he would never again come close to the high that he knew that day when the earth stood still and he ran. Watching him now, his eyes fixed, a smile on his lips, the words of his triumph ringing in his ears, I could almost feel sorry for him. Almost. Because at least, and in spite of it all, he did have his one golden moment, his time that was his time alone, which no one could deny him or take away; and this was more, a hell of a lot more, than most people take to the grave with them. And so on he ran, on into the the past, with the crowd cheering and the flags waving and the goal post like a crucifix looming up ahead.

". . . and then you scooped it up and ran 80 yards for the TD. God, that was great! Really great!" concluded Brooks.

"And I'll tell you something weird," added John. "I didn't even know what I'd done until after I'd done it. Until somebody came up to me and told me we'd won."

"Amazing, John," said Brooks. "May I call you John?"

"Sure. What else you gonna call me?"

"Great, John."

"And what was your name again?" asked John, extending his hand.

"Mason."

"Right. Mason."

They shook hands again and smiled.

Brooks was good, very good. With a little easy flattery he had succeeded in quelling any feeling of suspicion or discomfort which John might have initially harbored.

"Have you been living here in town since school?" asked Brooks casually.

"Yeah," said John. "Never been north of Atlanta. Can't see the need."

"I couldn't agree with you more," smiled Brooks. "Looks like you guys are doing pretty well right here."

"It pays the bills and keeps us out of jail," said John.

They both laughed.

"You married, John?" asked Brooks. He had not written a word since John had come into the room. In fact, at some point he had even returned his pen to his pocket.

"Oh, sure," said John. He reached around behind his back and pulled out his wallet.

"Is your wife originally from Sarasota too?"

"Nah," said John. "She's from Ohio." John opened his wallet and showed Brooks a photograph.

"Pretty," said Brooks, looking quickly at me. "Very pretty. What's her name?"

"Susie. Little Susie, I call her," said John proudly. "You know like the song." And John favored us with a sample: " 'Wake up, Little Susie, wake up.' "

"The Everly Brothers," declared Brooks.

"Right," said John, smiling. He turned toward me and pointed at Brooks. "Here's a man that knows his music."

I nodded my head and sank a little lower in my chair.

"Check this," said John. He flipped over the photograph in his wallet and flashed his famous Polaroid of Susie lying naked on a bed, looking somehow simultaneously embarrassed and defiant.

"Extraordinary," said Brooks.

"No shit," agreed John, snapping the wallet shut and returning it to his pocket. He was smiling wider than ever.

"Do you and your wife have any kids?" asked Brooks.

"Not yet, but we're working on it."

"Good luck to you."

"Luck, hell," laughed John. "It's damn hard work. We've tried every fucking position but standing on our heads."

"A labor of love," observed Brooks.

"I guess."

The conversation drifted into fifteen long seconds of silence.

"Well," said John, rising, "nice talking with you, Mason."

"Same here, John," said Brooks. "A real pleasure."

They shook hands once again.

John turned toward the door, then stopped and turned back to me. "I've already been out this morning to look at that place on Tenth Street. Let's just forget about it. It's gonna need too much work."

"All right," I said.

"Well, be seeing you guys," said John with a wave of his hand as he stepped out of the door.

"Later," I said.

"Good-bye," said Brooks.

And John's footsteps faded on down the hall.

"Little Susie, eh?" asked Brooks gleefully.

"I haven't got the slightest idea what you're referring to," I said.

Brooks slipped his legal pad into his briefcase.

"Your partner's a big man."

"Big," I agreed.

"You know, Tom, this case just may prove to be more rewarding then I had first imagined," smiled Brooks, standing up.

I said nothing; I looked at him. He looked back at me.

[65]

And if at any time during the last twenty or more years I had had any regrets, doubts or second thoughts about having shoved Mason Brooks' overlarge head into the toilet in the boys' bathroom they were now utterly and finally for all time erased: he was a first-rate top-flight asshole.

"Hey, Brooks, tell me something," I said finally. "How'd you people keep my grandfather's death out of the newspaper?"

"You looked for it then?" asked Brooks.

"Naturally."

"A couple of years ago a rather famous psychologist did an interesting study on criminals and publicity," said Brooks, switching his briefcase from one hand to the other. "He found that many murderers were quite proud of their crimes and loved to read about them."

"Sounds fascinating," I said. "Send me a copy."

"That might not be necessary. You might already know more about that than I do."

"You're a funny man, Brooks," I said. "Now tell me, how'd you keep it out of the paper and why?"

"Well, we needed a little extra time," explained Brooks, now standing in the doorway, "so I called up Bill Hobson. You know Bill, don't you? He's the managing editor over at the *Herald-Tribune*. I asked him to sit on the story for twenty-four hours. We wanted to see what would float to the surface."

"And what did?" I asked.

"Slime," said Brooks, already turning. "Slime and fish shit. As always."

EIGHT

Yes, I knew Bill Hobson, all right. In fact, I had seen him just a week or so before in one of the downtown bars that had recently been designated this season's upscale outpost for the terminally trendy. He was squiring around some leggy young thing who moved about the bar with her lovely unsmiling face tilted upward at an exaggerated angle. She looked like she was waiting for someone to come along and take her picture—or her pulse. It was a royal treat to watch her drink. I kept expecting (hoping) that she would dribble her daiquiri down the front of her dress. But she never did; she had obviously been practicing.

Hobson had arrived in town about three years ago from Tallahassee where he had been the *Herald-Tribune's* bureau chief. He was an interesting fellow: handsome, intelligent, witty, quick with the jokes, good with the ladies. Whenever our paths would cross we would always buy each other drinks and he would detail the latest dirt on the locals for me. I liked him. In truth I was somewhat envious of him. We were both the same age and he was already the managing editor of a major chain newspaper with a daily circulation of more than a hundred thousand. He was on a fast track going somewhere. For Hobson, Sarasota was merely a pleasant place to pause before his next move up the ladder.

Tucked away in the back of one of my desk drawers, I found a telephone book, weeded out the newspaper's phone number and put through a call. After a little zigzagging among secretaries and assorted newspaper personnel, Hobson came on the line: "Hello."

"Bill, this is Thomas Clay. How's everything in the newspaper game?"

"Well, they haven't shut us down yet."

"So I've seen," I said.

"I bet I can guess why you're calling," said Hobson. "I bet you're wondering about a little item missing from this morning's edition."

"No," I said. "I've already had an interview with the Grand Inquisitor and he explained the conspiracy to me."

"Ah, so Mr. Brooks is already out beating the bush?"

"He's trying," I said. "No, the reason that I called was that I was wondering what you could tell me about Brooks."

"I thought Mason mentioned something to me about you guys going to the same school together."

"We did," I conceded. "But we were never exactly close."

"Yes," said Hobson. "I can see how you and Mason might not have had a lot in common."

"Well, we both disliked each other," I said. "And still do."

"That's a beginning," laughed Hobson. "A definite beginning."

"Come on, Bill," I said. "Fill me in. What's the deal on Brooks? You know him, don't you?"

"Yeah, I know all about Mason Brooks. He told me his life story one night in Tallahassee over a bottle of Chivas."

"Well, what's it going to take to hear it? Another bottle of Chivas?"

"No," said Hobson. "For you, Thomas, my friend, it's gratis. This time."

"I owe you."

"I'll collect."

"Okay," I said.

"All right. Let's see. Mason Brooks was born in a log cabin and had to walk four miles—"

"Wait," I said. "Skip his adolescence in the wilderness and begin after high school."

"Then you're going to miss the part about how he kilt a bar when he were three."

"I can live with the loss," I assured him. "After high school, okay?"

"It's your debt."

"Terrific."

"All right," began Hobson again, "after high school Mason joined the Marines and—"

"The Marines?" I asked.

"Yes, sir."

"Jesus Christ," I said.

"He joined the Marines, went through Basic Training and then on to Officer's Training School. As a second lieutenant he was shipped off to Vietnam to make the world safe for democracy."

"Mason Brooks?" I asked.

"The same," confirmed Hobson. "He was assigned a rifle platoon, served thirteen months, then extended his tour. He just couldn't seem to get enough of it. He told me that for the first time in his life it made him feel like he was really doing something worthwhile. He was wounded twice, won himself a shitload of medals and came out a captain."

"What? He was some kind of a hero?"

"Not to hear him tell it. But then they don't give those things out for sitting in the shade and doing nothing. I saw them myself. They were for real."

"Weird," I said. "Really weird."

"He came back home, drifted around a bit, then settled down in Tallahassee. He joined the Tallahassee police force and went to FSU at night. He graduated and went on to law school, all the while supporting himself by being a cop. Eventually he took the tests or whatever and became a detective. Then he graduated from law school. And this was where he faced his big dilemma. Because you see he enjoyed being a cop, especially a detective. He said it was like a human chess game for him, trying to figure out the other guy's moves before he made them. But his wife—"

"His wife?" I asked.

"Oh yeah. Somewhere down the line, in college or somewhere, he met a girl and married her. But his wife wanted to be a lawyer's wife rather than a policeman's wife. So he tried lawyering for awhile. But you see he was missing the juice, the excitement of running down dark alleys and firing at fleeing felons. So after a couple of years he quit the law and went back

[69]

to police work, and his wife quit him. And I think that really stung him, it left him hanging out on a limb."

"Did he ever drop?" I asked.

"Nope, I think he's still out there," said Hobson. "Anyway, by this time Mason had established some pretty solid contacts in both the law business and in politics too. And so when our beloved Governor came into office he was looking around for some capable young men to help him. Mason was recommended and he signed on. And ever since he's been the Governor's shining boy. He's done everything from driving whores home at four in the morning to setting up multi-million dollar trade deals for the state overseas. He's like the Governor's right hand."

"Now I know which hand the Governor wipes his ass with," I said.

"Whatever. And according to the grapevine when the Governor makes his bid for the Senate next year Mason'll be there right alongside him. Maybe it's his Marine training, but he's loyal to the Governor almost to a point that's beyond reason. He's one guy I'd hate to have on my ass. He just doesn't give up."

"Well, thanks, Bill," I said. "Next time I need a little cheering up I'll be sure not to call you."

"I'm always here," said Hobson.

"Yeah, well, okay."

"Listen, Thomas," said Hobson, "since I've already got you on the phone let me ask you something. We're working up a story for tomorrow's edition on your grandfather's murder, and I'd like to get a relative's reaction."

"You can say that I'm devastated. Simply devastated."

"Devastated," laughed Hobson. "Wonderful. Devastated. That's one of my favorite words and we haven't used it in a week."

"Right," I said.

"Devastated," repeated Hobson. "That's great." And still laughing he hung up.

NINE

My office was beginning to seem too small, the walls too close. I needed to get out, out where there was air and space. I told Julie that if anyone called looking for me to say that I was in mourning, and I left. I got in my car and began to drive. I knew where I was going.

Overhead the sun boiled bright. The day's colors, predominantly green and blue, were heightened to an almost hallucinogenic degree. I turned on the radio and let the road wind away. And so on I drove: out past where the suburbs and the shopping centers thinned; past the last lame used car dealer with the sunlight blinking back off the windshields of the wrecks; past the burger barn that had changed owners ten times in the last ten years; past the tax-dodge industrial parks and the vacant warehouses; past the drive-in converted into an open-air flea market; past the vegetable and fruit stands; past the mobile home parks, the development tracts, the half-filled graveyards and the gravel pits; past the interstate overpass and on, on into the country. The country: green and flat, stretching out in all directions, unbroken, open; the scrub pines and the cabbage palms; the satellite disks and the pick-up trucks; the sumac and the moss-draped cedars; the horses and cattle; the roadside wildflowers blooming red and blue and gold; the road itself bleached white by the sun. And then, up ahead, like a warning or a threat, I saw the sign—Devon Woods—and I turned down the drive.

According to local legend the main house had been built shortly after the Civil War by a northern colonel for his southern bride to replace the one that he had been ordered to burn (belonging to the woman's father) on Sherman's march to the sea. A couple of years after the house was completed, the colonel took a shotgun blast in the back and the woman returned to her people in Georgia. Over the next sixty or so years, for better or worse, expanding and contracting, the house and the land changed hands many times. Finally in the 1930's Grandfather bought the place, intact and functioning, from a man who went broke, and then crazy, looking for oil in southwest Florida. Grandfather always took special satisfaction from the fact that the farm had once belonged to a man (the man from whom he'd bought it) who had snubbed him and Grandmother socially. At first he had planned to call his acres Sweet Revenge but was eventually persuaded by Grandmother to settle on Devon Woods instead.

Geographically located some ten miles due east of downtown Sarasota, it was a strange and unsettling place, a place where things seemed out of balance, a place of surprise and often unpleasant discovery—white fences circling a sea of violently churning green; white barns and stables and other assorted buildings standing out like islands in that long-stalked sea of specially imported grass; horses (Arabian and quarter) with their necks stuck out over the fencing, watching with calm unconcern whatever transpired; cattle (Black Angus and unusual-looking generic crossbreeds) grazing in distant pastures; orange groves and fields of lettuce and tomatoes and strawberries; an airstrip and an empty hangar (coming back from Tampa one foggy night some thirty years before, Grandfather overshot the runway and landed in a swamp, and Grandmother made him surrender his Cessna); and the main house, white, massive, two stories, twenty rooms, with eight huge columns and a veranda across the front; flowering walks and sculpture-filled gardens (many of the statues headless and armless); an oak-lined drive of white pebbles winding for more than a quarter of a mile up to the main home itself; and the whole twenty-five hundred acres dotted with ponds and streams and woods, dark and wild.

After Grandmother died Grandfather rarely left Devon Woods. All business of any real importance was conducted by phone or else on the premises. A steady stream of bankers, brokers, and lawyers could be seen roaring down the white pebbled road in their BMWs, Mercedes and Porsches. The road was narrow and a game of chicken rapidly developed between competing factions. Cars would go flying off the road, into oak trees, into fences, into pastures. It became quite commonplace to see grown men in three-piece business suits screaming and shouting and cursing and wrestling in the grass and dirt beside the wreckage of their autos. Only one fatal accident was ever recorded. One moon-bright night two lawyers carrying trust deeds to be signed refused to blink. They hit head-on, went through their respective windshields and came to rest (final) on the hoods of their colleague's automobile. The ultimate merger, Grandfather was heard to observe. It was one of the most hazardous quarter mile stretches of road in Sarasota County, and that was the way that Grandfather liked it.

As I pulled to a stop in front of the main house I noticed a shiny new black Corvette parked over by the stables. This puzzled me slightly as no one in the family or, for that matter, anyone that I knew, drove such a car.

I left my own set of wheels in the middle of the drive, walked up the steps to the front door and rang the doorbell. Inside I could hear the chimes going off in a rush of rhythmic explosions. I turned around to wait. A wide green swath of manicured lawn threw itself out before me. All of the trees within a hundred yards of the house had been chopped down by the old colonel to deny his enemies cover in case they should have tried attacking his home. In the end, however, it did him little good. Now the cleared land offered one a wonderful open vista of level and undisturbed tranquility to meditate upon.

Behind me the door squeaked open. I turned to see a pair of intense red-rimmed eyes peeking out through a three inch crack.

"Simon?" I asked.

The door swung open quickly. A hand darted out and snatched me inside.

"Oh, Mr. Thomas, Mr. Thomas, Mr. Thomas," wailed a fractured voice, getting progressively higher and more distraught.

The house was completely dark. The lights were all off,

the curtains drawn against the sun. I took off my sunglasses and tried to see.

"Oh, Mr. Thomas, Mr. Thomas," began the voice again.

"Settle down now, Simon," I said, reaching out blindly and grabbing a frail and bony arm. "Jesus, I can't see a damn thing." I felt along the length of one wall, found a switch and flicked it on. The entranceway flooded with light. "Now come on over here and sit down," I said. Gently I guided my charge over to a caneback chair positioned against a wall and eased him down.

For more than half a century, Simon had been Grandfather's personal servant, his man Friday. He had coordinated Grandfather's wardrobe and seen to his grooming needs. From a custom-built barber's chair bolted to the floor in the master bathroom, Simon would shave Grandfather every morning and cut his hair twice a month. He took pride in his work and was answerable to no one but Grandfather—a fact which he would flaunt before the rest of the household staff. Physically he was a small man, but he carried himself with great dignity. He walked with his head up, his shoulders back, as if he were balancing something atop his head. He was almost phobic about his own appearance and grooming. Every day for the last fifty years, he had worn a freshly washed, board-stiff, starched white shirt. Somewhere down the line his ancestral blood had been corrupted—another fact about which he was exceedingly proud. His nose was high and slender, his skin more of a light cocoa color than black, his hair straight and just beginning to turn white. He had already run through four wives and was presently breaking in a fifth, less than a third his age. To me he had always seemed almost magical, so much younger than his years. But now, hunched over in the chair, with the light from overhead beaming down on him, he looked like just another little old man slapped down by fate unkind.

"The police, they was here," said Simon, looking up. "They talked to all us inside, then went out to talk with the others."

"Well, Simon, that's their job."

"Yes sir, Mr. Thomas, I knowed that," continued Simon. "But they was asking 'bout you."

"Oh yeah?"

"Yes sir. Asked when you was last out here. So I told 'em.

I'm sorry, Mr. Thomas, but I had to, I had to tell 'em. The man said I could go to jail for helping with murder after the fact. Said I'd never get out of prison alive. Don't wanta go to no prison, Mr. Thomas."

"That's all right, Simon," I said, placing my hand lightly on his shoulder. "You did the right thing. This man, what did he look like?"

"Big. Big man. Tall as you. More. Mustache. Lots of hair. Said he was a special something or 'nother. Made the man show me his badge though 'fore I'd talk to him. And he showed me, all right. Quick enough."

"You did just fine, Simon. Don't worry about a thing."

"Yes sir, Mr. Thomas. But I still didn't wanta tell."

"Tell?" I asked.

" 'Bout last night. 'Bout the fighting and the yelling," explained Simon. "But they made me. Said I'd die in prison. I'm too old for no jail."

"Aren't we all," I said. "Well, don't worry about it. You did what you had to do."

"Yes sir, Mr. Thomas. But what's gonna happen to us now?"

"What do you mean?" I asked.

"I mean now that Mr. Malcolm's gone, what's gonna happen to us?"

"Well, I don't really know," I said. "I guess you should just keep coming in to work until somebody tells you not to."

"Yes sir, Mr. Thomas, yes sir. That sound like a fine idea." Simon stood up and looked around at the darkened rooms. "You hungry, Mr. Thomas? You look like you could use some lunch."

"Yes, Simon," I said. "I think I could. See what you can scrape up for me. A sandwich or something. And maybe a drink. A gin and tonic. I'll be outside, okay?"

"Yes sir, Mr. Thomas," said Simon, the tone of his voice picking up somewhat. "Right away."

And now with his anxieties as to his immediate future at least temporarily assuaged, Simon hurried off toward the kitchen, snapping on lights as he went.

And soon the house began coming to life: light, sound, air, movement.

I stepped into the reception hall—a narrow room running half the width of the house, almost totally devoid of furniture. The floor was laid out in one foot squares of alternating black and white Italian marble; overhead was a crystal chandelier. The room presented a barren and hostile introduction to the rest of the house.

Behind me one of the housemaids was now busily opening curtains, shutters and windows. The outer walls were two feet thick and the ceilings twelve feet high. Once the air was circulating through the house, it became quite livable within. A central heating and cooling system had been installed some twenty years back, but it was rarely used, even on the most uncomfortable of days.

Over to my left, in the main dining room, another house-maid was arranging a centerpiece of cut flowers. The highly polished surface of the dining table reflected the flowers back in a multi-hued blur. The table, which could provide seating for sixteen, was centered over an enormous yellow and gray antique rug. Under the rug were floors of Indian teak. The walls were covered with panels of satin damask. Against one wall stood a long sideboard and more flowers. A fireplace with elaborate molding around it was set into another wall. On either side of the fireplace was a door.

Through one door was the bar and lounge—an eighteenth century London pub. Not a replica; the real thing. A couple of years after Grandmother and Grandfather had bought the house, they embarked on a little shopping trip to Europe to buy furniture and pieces of art and the like. In England, while Grandmother was cruising for Chippendale and Gainsbor-oughs, Grandfather would cool his heels in a certain pub near their hotel. And the more time that he spent there, the more he liked it. So before their departure for the Continent, Grand-father bought it: the interior—walls, ceilings, floors, fixtures. He had it dismantled piece by piece, crated up and shipped (along with the workmen) to Devon Woods, where it was later reassembled. Personally it was my favorite room in the house. A fireplace almost large enough to stand in. Deep leather chairs. Dark wood paneling. Venetian-stained, lead-glass windows. An L-shaped mahogany bar with a brass footrail. It was a man's sort of room, a room for brandies and Tampa cigars, bawdy jokes and business conspiracies.

The other door led back to the kitchen, the pantries and servants' area, where the staff could relax and watch television and eat their lunches in private. And then farther on down the corridor—the breakfast room, with its high wide windows to catch the morning sun opening out onto a garden terrace.

Off to my right another housemaid (one whom I could not recall having seen before; I would certainly have remembered— young, Latin, big black eyes, a secret smile) was in the library turning on lights and dusting shelves. And again: more wood paneling, another large fireplace, leather wingback chairs, scattered tables and desks, books to the ceiling, the ceiling carved and crisscrossed with exposed beams, marble busts on pedestals, and along one wall, clustered together, a dozen or more paintings in gilded frames.

The girl stopped dusting for a moment and looked over at me. Her black hair spread smoothly across her shoulders in dramatic contrast to the white of her uniform. I nodded my head and smiled. The girl nodded back and then disappeared into the adjoining room, the game room—a wonderful place for those who enjoyed losing. In the middle of the room was a magnificent pool table set atop an arched stainless steel base. Two slightly defective slot machines which almost everyone played but which never paid off occupied one corner. In another corner was a poker table circled with captain's chairs. I was tempted to follow after the young senorita and try out a little of my Spanish on her and maybe stir up some games of our own, but decided to delay the encounter until a more appropriate time. After all, officially, I was still in a state of shock and bereavement.

Directly in front of me was the great hall, the largest room in the house—fifty feet by forty feet. The floor was a continuation of the same black and white Italian marble from the reception hall. Six spaced columns of Mexican onyx separated these two rooms. Fifteenth- and sixteenth-century Flemish tapestries depicting scenes of boar hunts and battles hung against the walls. Into one of these walls another elaborate fireplace was set; around it was gathered a small grouping of sofas and tables and chairs. The far wall was made up of a series of French windows giving access to Grandmother's garden located behind the house. More cut flowers were set out on the tables, and overhead was another crystal chandelier.

The young maid circled out of the game room and into the great hall. Trailing a feather duster along the backs of sofas and chairs, she swished across the floor. She stopped in front of a small chest positioned at the bottom of the stairs and, with some degree of earnestness, began to dust. Behind her a winding mahogany staircase led the way up to an interlocking maze of rooms above—five guest rooms; Grandmother's bedroom, cream-colored and delicate; her sitting room off to one side (one of the stranger rooms in the house; overlooking the fields and pastures; black walls, black curtains, black carpeting, one old rocking chair and a loud ticking clock); then Grandfather's bedroom (huge yet also rather spartan; a couple of chairs, a dresser and a four-poster bed set in the center of the room with white mosquito netting rolled up on top); and then on through a connecting door, his office (desks, tables, chairs; books, papers, magazines, folded, crumpled, discarded).

I stepped forward a few feet and leaned up against one of the columns at the entranceway to the great hall. From here I had an unobstructed view of the young maid at work. She noticed me looking at her and stopped her dusting. She turned and headed up the stairs, then stopped again. Straddling a step, one foot above, one foot below, her uniform pulled tight across her hips, she slipped a hand up under her dress and began stroking the inside of her thigh. I stood there for a moment watching her—her big black eyes looking back at me—and then I called out to her. *"Mañana,"* I said. It was just bad timing for me. The girl nodded her head, straightened herself up and smiled. *"Mañana, for sure,"* she called back and then took the whole package on upstairs.

Outside the sun bore down unceasingly. I sneaked into my sunglasses and made my way across a wide patio of Spanish tile and into Grandmother's garden. It was really two gardens, one overlapping the other at the edges. First, a rose garden: circular, orderly, a gazebo in the middle, statues, stone benches, shady nooks, a fountain bubbling loudly. And then off to the left, running along a path leading over to the bath-house and pool area—hibiscus, bougainvillaea, poinsettias, oleanders and day lilies leaping out in random and jungle-like chaos.

But it was not flowers which interested me. It was cars. Or more precisely, one car. That black Corvette parked next to the main stable. I went over to have a closer look.

It was new and clean. It had recently been polished. There wasn't a scratch on it. The top was down. There were no loose papers in sight to give the slightest hint of ownership. I popped open the glove compartment. The glove compartment was empty. I touched one of the seats. The seat was hot.

I was getting hot too. I could feel wet patches forming on my shirt. At the other end of the stable, I spotted a chair propped up in the open doorway. I left the car baking itself for someone's pleasant return and entered the pungent cool of horses and hay.

It was here, here in this stable, in a cleared space, from the age of about four on up until we were ten or so and could no longer be told, coerced or commanded, that we—David and Daniel and I—would box, perform for Grandfather and the field hands. Fitted with enormous gloves (which I, for one, could barely hold up) and little satin trunks, we would be led out of empty stalls and into a sweating circle of men—most of them shouting and laughing and betting in rapid-fire Spanish. Grand-father would put all three of us within the circle, hold a crisp new dollar bill over our heads and then let the dollar go. When the dollar hit the ground we were all supposed to start swing-ing, and the last one left standing won the dollar. That was the theory. In practice, though, whoever was positioned to the left of David was usually hit with a right cross the second the dollar began its descent. I can remember on more than one occasion sitting in the dirt, watching the dollar drifting slowly down. Most of the time David won. Grandfather would pat him on the head and tell him that he, undoubtedly, would go far in this world. And David, with the dollar clutched between his gloves, would smile.

I sat down in the chair and waited for my lunch. It must have been close to three o'clock, and I was hungry. Soon, from around the corner, bearing a large silver serving tray, walking almost comically erect, Simon appeared.

"You ain't planning on eating here, is you, Mr. Thomas?" asked Simon in a voice of obvious disapproval.

"Sure," I said. "Why not?"

"Well, it's a little, uh, you know, aromic," ventured Simon, peering into the stable.

"Aromic?" I asked.

"Yes sir."

"It's no worse than a lot of places I've eaten," I assured him.

"Whatever you say, Mr. Thomas." Simon placed the tray down on a workbench just inside the doorway. "If you need anything else just pick up that phone there"—he pointed to a telephone on the wall—"and call the kitchen."

"Thank you, Simon," I said. "But this looks like more than enough."

"Yes sir," said Simon with a half bow, and then shaking his head and walking not quite so erect now, he disappeared back around the corner.

Simon had brought me a thick ham sandwich and a healthy gin and tonic. The ham was smoked and just a bit on the salty side. It made the drink taste all that much the better. And as I ate I recalled another episode that had taken place in this same stable some years before.

Again, it was David and Daniel and me; by this time we were probably twelve or so. It was some type of school holiday, and we were spending a few days out at Devon Woods, riding horses, going fishing, walking through the fields, generally looking for trouble. One night, late, David tip-toed into my room and told me to get dressed; he had something to show me. With Daniel following and complaining, we sneaked downstairs and out of the house. On light feet we crossed through the yard and crawled up into the hay loft in the stable. And there—eyes bulging, mouths open—we watched a willing young brown-skinned beauty lying naked on a horse blanket spread out on the dirt floor in the center of the stable, drinking cheap whiskey straight out of a bottle and taking on a line of migrant workers forming up in front of her open legs. It was an amazing scene. It totally destroyed whatever images of female innocence I might have previously possessed. Afterward, I could not again look at or think about girls in the same way. For now I had seen with my own startled and disbelieving eyes what woman flesh was capable of. In the back of my mind there would always be that wild-eyed young girl, with her long black hair fanned out around her shining face, laid out on her back, working her hips a mile a minute, howling for more whiskey and calling out to each of the men in turn, calling out in a voice of high strained urgency, calling out: *"José! José! Mi amor! José!"*

TEN

I was about to call up to the house and order myself another drink—the last one having gone down quite satisfactorily—when off in the distance I sighted a piece of yellow tape clinging to a barbed wire fence, fluttering in the breeze. I walked over to investigate. It was police tape, crime scene tape; the words DO NOT CROSS were imprinted on it. Here, I thought, right here. I looked back toward the house and, in my mind's eye, followed a path which Grandfather might have taken to arrive unhappily at this spot. There was nothing on the ground now, and not much nearby—a clump of bushes; farther along, the beginnings of a tree line; cattle grazing obliviously; a white egret perched on a fence post, watching; green grass and blue sky. The very picture of rural repose. It seemed unlike a place for death and dying.

"Well, look what the cat drug in," called out a cheerful voice from behind me.

I turned around, and emerging from the undergrowth were Brooks and the large gentleman from the office.

"They say they always return to the scene of the crime," continued Brooks in the same tone of fraternal goodwill, "but I just didn't believe it. A world of wonder."

"I wouldn't know anything about that," I said.

"Well, you're here, aren't you?" asked Brooks, stopping next to me.

"You're a riot, Brooks," I said. "Why don't you get yourself a clown suit and join the circus."

Smiling, one to a side, they stood there looking down at me. Brooks was starting to get on my nerves in the worst sort of way. I turned my attention over to his large companion. In the bright sunlight the man's thinning close-cropped hair seemed to evaporate altogether, leaving only a square-shaped skull hanging in space.

"Oh, I don't think you know Detective Dawson," said Brooks. "He's my liaison. He's coordinating things for me locally with the Sheriff's Department."

"Detective," I said, nodding my head.

The detective nodded back coolly.

"So this is where it happened," I said, turning toward Brooks again.

"What leads you to that conclusion?" he asked.

I pointed to the tape.

"Observant," said Brooks. He stepped over to the barbed wire fence, untied the tape and slipped it into his coat pocket. He placed a foot on the bottom strand of wire and leaned up against one of the posts. "The way we see it so far is that your grandfather and whoever did him came out of the back of the house, through the garden, and then through that gate over there. Your grandfather was barefooted. He had a checkbook with him. Maybe he thought he could buy his way out. They stopped here. Your grandfather went down on his knees—voluntarily or not, we don't know—then over into a fresh pile of cow shit, face-first, his arms out from his side. And there, after a few seconds—his mouth and nasal passages were clean—a gun was placed against the back of his head and he was shot twice."

"Jesus," I said. "What type of person would shove a little old man down in a pile of cow shit before shooting him? I mean that's really extreme."

"Maybe the same type of person that would shove a nine-year-old kid into a urinal," suggested Brooks.

"I was wondering when we'd get around to that," I said.

"We're there now," said Brooks.

"So you're still mad at me 'cause I tried to flush your head down the toilet back in the fifth grade," I said.

"It was the fourth grade," asserted Brooks. "And it was a urinal, and you shoved from behind."

"Whatever," I said.

[84]

"And as far as being mad goes," continued Brooks, "I don't get mad, I get even."

"Ah, the Joseph Kennedy School of Reciprocal Response," I observed. "You see what good it did his sons. Bad karma. Someone always wants to get just a little bit more even."

"As you so aptly put it," said Brooks, "whatever."

Detective Dawson looked as though he could live without all of this verbal sparring. He jacked a cigarette out of a pack and into his mouth and lit it. A weary stream of blue smoke floated up from one corner of his mouth and then drifted away.

"Who found his body?" I asked after a moment.

"A foreman named Abbott," said Brooks. "You know him?"

"Of course," I said. "He's been here for years."

"According to Mr. Abbott every day after work he and the rest of the men go have a few cold ones at a little beer-joint down the road. We're checking on that. This Abbott claims that when he arrived back at the farm at around 9:30, he noticed several head of cattle wandering around in front of the main house. Upon further investigation he discovered that the back gate was open. As he went to close it he says that he happened to look over this way and saw the body. He then phoned the Sheriff's Department. The Sheriff's Department recorded the call to its 911 number at 9:43."

"Well, you must have found some fingerprints," I said. "Like on the gate maybe, or footprints out here."

"The gate was clean," said Brooks. "And it began raining last night around 9:00, so any footprints worth preserving were already mud puddles by the time the detectives got here. There were, however, some fairly good prints inside. We haven't matched them yet, but would you care to take a guess as to whom they might belong?"

Silently I cursed myself. It had been a foolish thing to lie about. I should have known that Brooks would have had little difficulty in finding out that I had been here last night.

Brooks smiled and pushed himself away from the fence post. "You see, there were no signs of forcible entry. So we can reasonably assume that whoever shot your grandfather must have been known to him, must have been let in by him. Or perhaps by the butler. What was his name, Detective?"

Detective Dawson fumbled out a notepad and scanned a page. "Simon Williams," reported the detective.

"All right," I said. "Jesus. I don't know why I didn't mention it before."

"Mention it? Hell," laughed Brooks. "I asked you and you flat out lied. I asked you when you had last seen your grandfather alive and you said about a month ago. That wasn't even close."

"All right, all right," I said, feeling stupid and a little bit confused. "So I was out here last night. Big deal. Hang me."

"We'll try," Brooks assured me.

"Look, I had some business with him, and I knew that if I said that I was out here it would look bad. It was just an honest mistake."

"Honest?" laughed Brooks. "Did you hear that, Detective?"

"I heard," said Detective Dawson.

"This Mr. Williams," continued Brooks in a more serious vein, "says that you arrived at 7:30, and by the time he got ready to go home, around 8:00, he could hear you and your grandfather in the library fighting like cats and dogs."

"It was just part of the game," I explained.

"Did the game include two slugs in the back of the head?" demanded Brooks.

"Jesus Christ," I said. "I came out here to make a mortgage payment on a note that he held on my house. The payment is due on the first of each month, but I always wait until the last of the month just to piss him off, just to get him excited, so that he'll think I'm going to be late and he can foreclose on me. It's a game. I do it every month. He gets mad, yells at me, tells me I'm worthless. I laugh at him and give him the check. Sometimes he even gets so excited he tears up the check. He yells at me some more, bitches about the whole family, the whole world. Then he calms down, gives me a drink and I go home. It's like therapy or something."

"But not last night?" asked Brooks.

"Yes. Last night too," I said. "Exactly like every other time. When I left here last night he was alive and happy. He had insulted me, found fault with everything from the President to the weather and generally declared the world unworthy of his presence. He was in excellent spirits."

"Strange game," said Brooks, looking over at Detective Dawson.

"Strange," agreed the detective, scribbling away at his little notepad.

Brooks stepped forward, took a hold of my arm and twirled me around. "Come on," he said. "I want to show you something."

With Detective Dawson trailing behind us, Brooks ushered me across the pasture and into the undergrowth. After a few feet he stopped. There was a foul smell in the air. He directed my attention over to the right. On the ground, in the shadows, there lay a large black dog. The animal was obviously dead. His eyes were open; his mouth frozen in a snarl of white gleaming attack.

"That's Kraft!" I exclaimed.

"Kraft?" asked Brooks.

"Yes," I said, bending down. "Kraft. He's my cousin's dog."

"Which cousin?" asked Brooks.

"James," I said. "James Clay."

"That would explain these." Brooks dropped two thin pieces of metal attached to a chain into my hand. "We found them around the dog's neck."

I read the name stamped into the metal. "Yes," I said. "These are James' old dog tags. He was in the Army, in Vietnam. I guess he put them on Kraft for a joke." I stood up and handed the tags back to Brooks.

"What do you suppose he was doing out here?" asked Brooks.

"He lives here," I said.

"Not the dog. Your cousin."

"That's who I'm talking about," I explained.

"Your cousin lives out here?"

"Yes," I said.

"Where?" asked Brooks.

"Here," I said. "Out there." I swept my hand out in front of me in a wide all-encompassing arc.

"Your cousin lives out here on the farm, is that it?"

"Well, yes and no," I said. "He doesn't live here. On the

farm. Like in a building or a room or a house. But *on* the farm. Out there. In the fields, in the pastures, in the woods. He camps out. He's got a tent and all kinds of camping shit."

"Your cousin, James Clay, lives out here, camps out here, on the farm, in a tent?" asked Brooks.

"Yes," I said.

Brooks and Detective Dawson exchanged quick covert glances.

"How long's he been out here?" asked Brooks.

"I don't know," I said. "I guess it's been more than five years now."

"That's a long time for a camping trip," observed Brooks. "What makes you think he's still out here?"

"Well, there's his dog," I said. "He wouldn't leave him out here alone."

"And when did you last see him, your cousin, talk to him?"

"Like I said, it's been about five years. He came out here with his dog to live. He couldn't handle it anymore, so he came out here."

"Couldn't handle what?" asked Brooks.

"Life. People. Whatever drives people away."

"But how do you know he's still here, except for the dog, if you haven't seen him in five years?"

"Well, sometimes the field hands run across him," I said, "or where he's been, and I hear about it."

"So he just lives out here, huh? What does he do for food?"

"He fishes. He sets traps for small game. He eats a lot of nuts and berries, I guess."

"Oh, great," said Brooks. "He's some kind of wild man-Robinson Crusoe-Ewell Gibbens character. That's just wonderful."

"He's no wild man," I said.

"Sure," said Brooks, looking out across the fields, thinking. "You said that he sets traps for small game, right?"

"Yes," I said.

"What about hunting? He does a little hunting too, doesn't he?"

"No," I said. "No hunting. No guns."

"No guns?" asked Brooks. "Why not?"

"It's got something to do with Vietnam," I explained. "His experiences, what he saw. He once told me that he had been around enough guns for one lifetime. He said that he wouldn't have one in his house—well, he didn't really have a house, he had a boat. He said that he wouldn't even use one to protect himself."

"Sounds like he got scorched," said Brooks. "What happened to him?"

"I don't know. He never told me, never seemed to want to talk about it. I only know that he hates guns. After he got back from Vietnam, he bought himself this leaky-ass old sailboat and headed for the islands. After several years of that he turned up again back in Sarasota, living on that sorry wreck down at the marina. He had a job, some type of construction work I think it was. Later I heard that he was going to get married. Except that when it came his time to say 'I do' he said 'I don't'. Then he sold his boat and moved out here with Kraft."

"Hmm," said Brooks. He shoved his hands into his back pockets and started pacing quietly back and forth. Suddenly he stopped and spun on his heels. "Who's his contact out here?" he demanded. "He must have someone. I don't give a damn how much of a lone wolf you are, you can't just live out here totally cut off and not need a few basic supplies from time to time. It's not possible."

"I don't know," I said. "I suppose it could be one of the field hands. They'd probably front for him for a few bucks. Ask around. You might find out."

"We will," said Brooks sharply. "And we'll find out."

There was no breeze in the bushes. Flies buzzed and mosquitoes bit.

"Any significance in the dog's name, Kraft?" asked Brooks.

"No," I said. "Not really. I think it had something to do with the fact that when he was a puppy he wouldn't eat dog food, so James had to feed him slices of cheese to keep him alive."

"Cute," said Brooks. "One thing I love is cuteness."

Somewhere off behind us, I could hear the roar of farm machinery and men shouting to each other.

Brooks looked down at the dog, then over at Detective Dawson. "What do you think, Detective?" he asked.

Detective Dawson flipped his notepad shut and slipped it into his shirt pocket. "Well," began the detective, running his hand over the top of his head, "I guess the cousin could've whacked the old guy, done the dog, then maybe himself. Generally have gone nuts. In which case we might never find his body. There's plenty of room out here to lose a body if you didn't want it found."

"But that doesn't make any sense," I objected. "First of all, he's not nuts. And second, like I told you before, he doesn't like guns. And third, he wouldn't shoot his dog. He loved him."

"You don't have to like guns to use one," said Detective Dawson. "And you'd be surprised what people can do to those that they claim to love. I've seen it. When these guys go they like to take a friend or sometimes the whole family with 'em. It can be a fucking massacre."

"No way," I said. "Not James."

"Well, time'll tell," said Brooks, turning and leading the way out of the undergrowth. We walked out of the bushes, through the pasture and on through the gate.

"Is that your 'Vette over there?" I asked.

"A loan," said Brooks. "You like it?"

"It's all right for a cop car," I said.

"The DEA confiscated it from some shrimper up in Bradenton who was bringing in more coke than catch."

"Great," I said. I stopped and let Brooks and Detective Dawson walk on. "See you boys later," I called out.

Brooks looked back quickly. "You can bet on it," he said. He was smiling.

ELEVEN

I stood there, waiting, until Brooks and Detective Dawson were out of sight—the black Corvette disappearing with a roar behind a churning cloud of white dust—and then walked over to the bunkhouse to look up Mr. Fulton Theodore Abbott. The bunkhouse, a long low rough wood building, was located next to the main stable. The building itself was divided into two sections—the larger section was given over to the ten or so members of the permanent work force who chose, for reasons financial or personal, to reside there on the premises. The remaining one-third of the building was, and had been for a good number of years, home to Fulton, as Mr. Abbott was commonly known. (Migrant workers made up the rest of the work crews, and they, for the most part, lived in a small run-down trailer park nearby.)

I stopped outside of Fulton's unit and looked through the screen door into the room—one large room like a studio apartment. Across the room, with his back to me, wearing a blue work shirt and jeans, I could see Fulton seated at a cluttered desk, writing. He was a small trim man, barely topping five feet. His hair was white and parted high, his eyes clear and gray, his skin brown and leathery. He was well into his eighties, a year younger than Grandfather, yet still remarkably spry and agile. Every day, in every sort of weather, he would mount a coal-black stallion and ride off into the fields. And there, atop his magnificent animal, like some lost cavalryman, out of time and place, he would shout, cajole and curse at the men below. And the work would get done.

Fulton and Grandfather had grown up together as boys. In

fact, at some point, Grandfather's father, my great-grandfather, took Fulton into his house and raised him as his own. As Fulton and Grandfather grew to manhood they gradually drifted apart, and then at some later date came together again. After Grandfather bought Devon Woods, Fulton moved out there to manage the farming operations and had been there ever since. The similarities in appearance between the two were often noted by others but not discussed within the family. When the subject arose, the subject was quickly dropped, as was any subject concerning any member of the family. Family matters were simply not considered suitable for conversation. There was a certain secretiveness about affairs of the family, and one learned early that questions only brought rebuffs.

I tapped lightly on the doorframe. The entire front of the building shook.

Fulton's hand went up at his desk. "Come on in," he said, without turning to see who it was. "Be with you in a moment."

I stepped into the room; Fulton continued to write.

A ceiling fan in imminent danger of becoming airborne whirled overhead. All of the windows were open; there was no air conditioner. The walls, corner to corner, floor to ceiling, were lined with shelves constructed of concrete blocks and long stained planks of sturdy lumber. Books at odd angles and objects of no discernible value were packed into the shelves. In the middle of one wall, in the only opening available—books above, below and to the sides—was a painting of a young naked woman. I had seen this painting on many occasions. There was something about the woman's face that was strangely familiar. What it was exactly I couldn't quite say.

Shifting his weight to one side, Fulton lifted himself up slightly from his chair and let loose with a loud reverberating fart. For such a physically small man, he was capable of powerful eruptions. When I was younger this had seemed an extraordinary gift. He could end discussions with no chance for rebuttal—grown men coughing, cursing, fleeing in all directions; horses, dogs snorting, sniffing, pawing at the ground. Now, however, the situation seemed somewhat less wondrous. In recent years Fulton had lost almost complete anal control; he was on call twenty-four hours. To a large extent I attributed his condition to a lifetime of bachelor cooking, cheap whiskey (though he could afford better) and sulfur-tainted water.

I moved over to a window and tried breathing through my mouth.

Fulton wrote poems and short stories (and had done so since his youth). He sent his efforts to small literary publications and, in turn, received their magazines as payment. Around his desk, two feet high and rising, these magazines were stacked—unread.

Fulton slammed a notebook shut. "Done," he declared. He turned in his seat; his eyes swept over me. "Well, Thomas," he said, rising, "a sad day it is, my boy." He crossed over to a small table on which a bottle and several glasses set. "Care to join me in a drink to the dead?" he asked.

"No thanks," I said. "I just came by to warn you about one of those cops—Brooks."

"Warn *me?*" he asked, pouring himself out an inch of Heaven Hill. "I have done nothing about which to be warned. My conduct in all matters is irreproachable."

"Right," I said. "But you see this Brooks character is looking for James' contact, through which presumably he hopes to find James."

"I am not anyone's contact," asserted Fulton. "I am James' friend and he is mine."

"Right. Okay, I understand all that," I said. "But you see what this Brooks guy wants to do is to somehow tie James in with Grandfather's murder. They found Kraft out there in the back pasture. He was dead—shot."

"A good animal. A noble heart. I am sorry to hear that," said Fulton. "But from what I gathered from my own limited conversation with Mr. Brooks and Detective Dawson is that it is you and not James or myself who should be concerned. You are number one on a very short list of prime suspects."

"You don't actually think I did it, do you?" I asked, somewhat insulted.

"I have not given it much thought one way or the other," he said, knocking back his whiskey. "What is done, is done."

"Jesus," I said, "that's a helluva sorry attitude."

"Murder," Fulton assured me, "is a sorry business."

A hot gust of air suddenly blew into the room, sending

several loose pieces of paper from Fulton's desk into the air and then onto the floor. Fulton bent down and began collecting them. A silent one eased out. "Phew," snarled Fulton, fanning his hand behind the offending orifice. "I've got to get that thing fixed."

"Good luck," I said and walked back outside.

It was a real stinker.

TWELVE

I arrived back at my beachhouse just as the sun was going down. Kim was in the kitchen preparing something for dinner that smelled delicious. I came up behind her and kissed her on the top of her head. She arched her back and wiggled her little butt up against me. I ran my hand up under her shirt and grabbed a firm and eager breast. There was a sudden clanking of metal against metal. She spun around, threw her arms about my neck, lifted herself up on her toes and gave me a hard kiss in return.

"Hold that thought," I said, disengaging myself.

Kim went back to her pans and sauces. I made myself a gin and tonic and went out onto the lanai. I sat down in one of the wicker chairs and settled in for the show.

This was my favorite part of the day (it almost made some of the things that I did seem worthwhile): the sun, a blazing orange ball, edging down through strips of sky shot pink and purple; an expanse of shimmering blue waiting to receive; birds flying northward in scattered flocks, seeking shelter for the night; a few boats dotting the horizon; a dolphin momentarily breaking the surface, then the water smoothing over; tourists, whole families, clicking cameras, pointing, squealing ("Okay, now one of you and Uncle Arthur"); a heron on spindly legs cautiously investigating something at the water's edge; little ladies in large hats tip-toeing toward the water with cocktails in hand; sea oats swaying in the breeze; and now the birds, by the hundreds, by the thousands—in places the beach black with birds—swooping, rising, falling, gliding on the air currents; pelicans skimming the surface, inches above the water, then an abrupt rising half turn and a slam-dunk dinner snatched from the sea; lovers holding hands; joggers forever jogging; drunks and deep-thinkers walking alone, concentrating on their feet; then quickly, the sun halved, then quartered; the people stopping, almost as if magically frozen in place, watching, waiting, like primitives paralyzed with fear, for that second when the sun is no more; then gone, the sun sinking below the horizon; and the people freed now, released, moving on again, hurrying along the sand, back to safety and comfort, back to rooms, lights, television sets and conversations of no importance; and it all happening too fast—fading to black.

"Dinner be ready in fifteen minutes," said Kim, coming out onto the lanai. She handed me a fresh drink and took my empty glass. Outside, lying on the sun deck, she spotted my two cats. She stepped over to the screen door and began talking to them in Vietnamese. They stood up, sloped over to the door and began meowing back at Kim. Kim laughed and opened the door a crack. They slipped in quickly, looked around uncertainly for a moment, then leaped into separate chairs.

"Cats," said Kim, shaking her head. "They beginning to learn Vietnamese."

"Yeah," I said. "Bilingual cats, that's all we need."

Kim kissed me again and went back inside.

The first time I saw Kim was in an Italian restaurant. Angie had been gone about two years, and I was currently living alone. Kim was working as a waitress in the restaurant. I was sitting at one of her tables. I might have been a bit drunk. As I was placing my order I tried out a little of my witty banter on her. She was decidedly unimpressed. This annoyed me. After a delay which seemed overly long, she brought my dinner to the table. Perhaps a little too pointedly I said, "Why don't you get a job in a Chinese restaurant? I bet you'd get bigger tits—tips, I mean." Holding my linguine and clam sauce in her right hand, she stood there for a good thirty seconds looking at me, trying to decide where to put the plate. Eventually she set it down on the table and said, "I not Chinese." Then she walked away.

The next night again found me back at the same restaurant, again at one of her tables. This time aside from placing my order I said nothing to her. When she brought my check to the table—eight dollars or less, I believe it was—I handed her a twenty and told her to keep the change. She looked at the twenty, then back at me. "So now you think you can buy me," she said. "No," I responded, somewhat flustered, "I just wanted to—" "Yes," she said. "Good night." And then she walked away again.

I eventually had to go back to that restaurant every night for a week before she would smile at me and talk to me as if I were human. It took another week of every night dinners and big tips before she would go out with me. But once she did— go out with me—it only took one date (a couple of drinks after work) before we were in bed. She had obviously already decided.

I have always felt that initially she began living with me (after our fourth date and my third invitation) because she liked my house, liked living on the beach. Later, other things developed between us.

Kim's reason for living in Sarasota in the first place was to attend the Ringling School of Art and Design, which she did during the day on a part-time basis. After she moved in with me, I suggested that she quit her job and go to school full-time. At first she refused. "Who pay for my tuition, for my paints? Who pay to put gas in my car?" "I will," I said. "You pay. Okay," she said. And that was that.

Kim's English was mostly self-taught and by no means perfect. She made heavy use of contractions and often dropped the contracted verb completely or else accented it so softly that it was indiscernible to the human ear. She also had a tendency to experiment with words whose meanings she did not entirely understand, and their misuse, on occasion, could produce some highly comic results. But on the whole, for a second language, I thought that she did marvelously well. Much better than I could ever have done.

Her full and legal name was Kim Tai Ky, though I had seen it arranged three different ways on three different documents. I once asked her about that and she gave me a rather vague answer, so I pursued it no further. It really didn't matter to me what her name was as long as it was pronounceable and did not contain any obscene connotations.

After Kim's father and sister had been recycled for having attitudes incompatible with the new realities of a unified

Vietnam, the remaining elements of her family—mother, brothers, sisters, aunts and uncles—decided that the glories of socialism were overstated. They pooled their funds, bought a boat and the services of a captain for a small fortune in gold and set a departure date for the next moonless night. When they showed up at the rendezvous site at the appointed hour they were greeted, unexpectedly, by the captain, his entire family and a dozen or so other eager escapees. There were undoubtedly some harsh words and threats, but the bridges were already burned and there was little else to do except to curse and pray. So clinging to their possessions, close to thirty people climbed into the fisherman's flimsy craft and cast themselves off into the night.

The next day in the rain on the open sea, Kim celebrated her thirteenth birthday and watched an old woman die.

Then another ten days on—five of them without food or water—and a little more than half of the original few were plucked, puking and crying, out of the Gulf of Thailand by an inbound freighter and deposited unceremoniously (a cargo net slung from ship to shore) into the hands of the Thai authorities. Their photographs, fingerprints and statements were taken, then they were passed along to a group of song-singing Christians who laid claim to their souls. They eventually wound up in a refugee camp in northeast Thailand where, for two years, they endured the preaching and the singing and the stares of visiting do-gooders and congressmen—some (the congressmen), still stinking of Mekong whiskey and a rough night on Patpong Road. (Their quick tickets out, it was explained to them—namely the dead father and sister—had already been cancelled so they would have to wait like everyone else.) At last some sponsors were found and the proper officials bribed the proper amounts and they—the surviving family members—were loaded onto a plane and shipped to the United States. Upon arrival they were each given a small American flag to wave at the cameras and a bible printed in Vietnamse and told that they were in the land of liberty. "Be grateful. See you on Sunday."

When Kim was telling me this tale (on our first date) she happened to mention in a rather offhanded manner that those who had died in their boat—and in the thousands of other little boats—were said to have died fighting for freedom. The enormity of that statement and the force of its literal interpretation did not fully impact upon me until several days later. But finally when it did I found myself sitting, open-mouthed, in my car at a green light, staring straight ahead, with the cars behind me honking their horns and goose bumps running up and down my arms.

"Five minutes," warned Kim from the kitchen.

"All right," I said. I pulled myself up out of my chair and re-entered the house. "I guess I ought to call my parents," I said. "I don't know whether they know yet or not."

"Okay," agreed Kim. "It might be more private upstairs if you want."

"That doesn't matter," I said. "There won't be any crying. I'll just call from in here."

I sat down on the sofa in the living room and dug the scrap of paper with their telephone number on it out of my wallet. As I dialed the number I tried to figure out what time it was in Spain. It was probably close to midnight, I decided. I hoped that they wouldn't be asleep.

After the fourth ring a familiar voice came to my ear. "Hello."

"Hello," I said.

"Ah, Thomas," called out Father happily. "I told your mother that I thought we might hear from you tonight."

"So you know then," I said.

"Yes. Fulton phoned us earlier."

"And so when are you folks coming back?" I asked. "No one has set a date for the funeral yet."

"Well, son, I don't think we'll be coming back."

"What?" I asked, unsure if I was hearing correctly.

"No, I don't think so," said Father. "I know that you may not understand that, and I hope you won't ask me to explain it, but that's the way things are. And I'd be very much surprised if any of my brothers showed up either."

"Well, okay," I managed to say. "I mean, sure. Like it's entirely up to you."

"Good," said Father.

"Do you need me to do anything for you at this end?" I asked.

[99]

"No," said Father. "Things will pretty much play out on their own."

"All right," I said. "Well, how's the weather over there? How's Mother?"

"She's fine," said Father. "She's upstairs asleep now. She'll be sorry she missed you. We had some friends over this evening for a little dinner party."

"Oh, that's nice," I said, not knowing what else to say. "Well, okay then. I guess that's that. Hope I didn't disturb you."

"Not at all," Father assured me. "Take care of yourself, son."

"Sure," I said. "You too."

And the line went dead.

I sat there for a moment as if I had been slapped in the face, and then I set the telephone down.

Kim stepped into the dining area and began laying out place mats. She looked over at me. "When they coming back?" she asked.

"They're not," I said.

"Not coming back for his own father's funeral?" asked Kim, a handful of silverware arrested in midair.

"No," I said. "They're going to stay in Spain."

"Weird," she said, turning her attention back to the table. "Real weird."

And that, I thought, was putting it mildly.

After dinner (shrimp Alfredo and a large green salad) Kim and I moved back into the living room and settled down on the sofa. As I sipped another gin and tonic Kim began telling me about her day, about a young male model who had posed nude for her drawing class, and how, much to the delight of all of the sketchers, he had been unable to keep a certain extension peculiar to the male anatomy in a relaxed and stationary mode. But before Kim could bring her story to a conclusion there arose the sudden, loud and insistent pounding of a fist against the front door. I got up, went to the door and opened it. And standing there in the harsh glare of the headlights from the passing cars, smiling at me with teeth large and white, was Brooks, still dressed in his pinstripe suit, carrying his briefcase.

"Don't you have a home, or a hotel room, or a hole or something to crawl into?" I asked.

"I knew you'd be pleased to see me," said Brooks, brushing past me, stepping into the room.

"Well, come on in since you're in," I said, closing the door behind him.

Brooks looked around the room quickly. His eyes lit on Kim. "Hello there," he said. "You must be Kim."

Kim looked up at him but said nothing.

"I hope I'm not interrupting anything," said Brooks, turning back toward me.

"How'd you know her name?" I asked.

"We have our methods," smiled Brooks.

"I'll bet," I said.

Brooks sat down on the sofa next to Kim. "Just a quiet evening at home, huh?" he observed.

"Until now," I said. "I believe we have a little arsenic left. Care for a drink?"

"Whatever you're having," said Brooks, pointing to my glass.

"Arsenic and tonic," I said.

"Sounds good."

"Great."

I went into the kitchen and began fixing a drink for Brooks. I dropped four ice cubes into a tall glass, added an ounce of gin and filled it up the rest of the way with tonic. I was in the refrigerator selecting a wedge of lime when I heard them—Kim and Brooks in the living room talking together in Vietnamese. This really bothered me; I had no idea what was being discussed. I stood there silently with the lime in my hand and listened to them. They sounded like a couple of irate birds. All that ding-dong crap. I picked up Brooks' drink and quickly drank it myself. Into the same glass this time I poured almost eight ounces of gin, splashed in a bit of tonic water and tossed the lime wedge into the garbage. Maybe he'll have a nice little wreck on his way back to wherever he's staying, I thought to myself happily as I stirred the drink. Or at least get picked up for a DUI.

I walked back into the living room. Brooks had his yellow legal pad out and his pen in his hand. He looked at me and said something to Kim, still in Vietnamese. Kim smiled slightly; Brooks laughed.

"It sounds like you speak that shit pretty well," I said.

"*Titi.*" said Brooks, slipping his legal pad back into his briefcase. "A little bit."

"Wonderful," I said, handing Brooks his drink.

Brooks took the glass and set it down on the table beside him. I picked up my own drink and moved over to the recliner.

"What were you fellows talking about?" I asked.

"You don't speak the language?" asked Brooks.

"Only English," I said. "Barely."

"A shame," said Brooks. He snapped his briefcase shut.

"How's your case coming?" I asked.

"It's coming."

"But no arrests?"

"In time," said Brooks.

I raised my glass for a toast. "To your case then."

"To justice," countered Brooks.

"Here, here," I said.

Brooks took a small sip of his gin and gin. His eyes brightened. He looked over at me quickly. I nodded my head. Brooks' face eased into a smile, then he turned the drink up and drained its contents. He set the glass down carefully on the table. He was still smiling.

"Well, I guess that'll do it for me," he said, standing, looking quite steady.

"You wouldn't like another, would you?" I asked.

"No thanks," he said. "Half a pint's enough."

Brooks said something further to Kim, again in Vietnamese. She smiled and said thank you in English.

Brooks then looked back at me. "Well, I'm sure we'll be seeing each other again," he said. "Soon."

"I'll be counting the hours," I said.

Brooks made his way to the door, opened it, then stopped and turned. "Oh, I almost forgot," he said, not forgetting a damn thing. "The ballistics report came in just before I left. It confirmed my suspicions. Your grandfather and that dog were both killed with the same weapon. A .22. You don't by chance own one, do you? A .22."

"No," I said.

"I didn't think so," said Brooks, and then he turned and walked out the door.

I sat there and listened: footsteps, a car door, an engine, a car pulling away, then gone.

"Well?" I said, looking at Kim.

"Well, what?" she responded.

"What was all that bird talk about?"

"Bird talk?" she asked, her little nose lifting itself higher.

"You and Brooks, what were you talking about?"

"He was asking me questions. About you," she said.

"Such as?"

"When did you get home last night? What time? Did you seem upset? Were your shoes muddy? Your clothes dirty? Like that."

"And what did you tell him?"

"I told him the truth. We have nothing to hide, do we?"

"No," I said. "Of course not. You should always tell the truth."

"Then why didn't you?" she asked. She stood up and crossed the room to the foot of the stairs.

"Why didn't I what?"

"Tell the truth."

"About what?"

"About that gun," she said.

"The .22? Well, technically, I did tell the truth. In a limited sort of way."

"Okay," she said. She began climbing the stairs. "I just hope you don't get too smart for your shoes."

"That's, 'Too big for your britches.' "

"Yes," she said, disappearing on up the stairs. "That too."

THIRTEEN

I was lying in bed, watching Kim getting dressed. Through the window above my head, the sunlight of another hot day shone in brightly.

"I don't have to go, you know," Kim said, wiggling into a pair of red slacks. "I could stay here with you if you wanted me to."

"No," I said. "Go on. You've been planning on this thing for weeks. Your mother's birthday is very important to her. As people get older they attach a greater significance to birthdays. It's like spitting in the eye of God."

"I don't think you should say things like that," said Kim. She placed her overnight bag on the bed and began putting a neat little pile of things into it.

"It's true," I said. "It's ritual, almost pagan. A flaunting of the fact that in spite of everything, all of the roadblocks and wrong turns, you've made it, survived one more year."

"Well, that may be," said Kim, zipping up her bag. "But you still shouldn't say things like that. It bring you bad luck."

"All right," I said. "I'll try to be better."

Kim picked a blue T-shirt out of the dresser, flapped it once in the air, then slipped it over her head. She shook her hair free.

I got up out of bed and looked out the window. Cutting along the horizon I could see a few scattered sails; on the beach itself there were surprisingly few people about.

"Ready," she announced, turning.

"All right," I said. I pulled on a pair of jeans and followed Kim down the hallway. At the head of the stairs, she stopped and I caught up with her. I took the bag out of her hand and put an arm around her waist. Together, arm in arm, we walked down the stairs, through the living room and outside.

The sunlight, reflecting off the sand, came rushing up with a force that was almost physical. Blinking fast, we made our way over to Kim's car. I opened the door and flipped her bag into the back seat. "Write if you get work," I said.

"What?" she asked.

"Drive carefully and wear your seat belt."

She kissed me. "I be back Sunday night."

"Say hello to your mother for me."

"Sure," she said. She kissed me again and climbed into the car. She sat there for a moment looking up at me as if she wished to say something more—or as if she wished that I would. But nothing was said. Finally her hand reached for the ignition switch. The engine coughed, wheezed, protested, then caught. The car vibrated violently for a second and then settled into a rhythmic beat. She turned and smiled at me with those sad and uncertain eyes, and then backed the car out onto the road. A gear jammed into place, a hand shot out of the window, and the little car sputtered away.

I walked back inside and fixed myself a cup of coffee. Standing in the kitchen, I drank the coffee—this time omitting the brandy kicker. Through the sliding glass door, I noticed that the cats had been left in last night. I stepped out onto the lanai and let them outside. They seemed quite anxious to escape the confines of their screened-in cage.

With a second cup of coffee in hand, I moved on upstairs and took a shower. Again, uncharacteristically, I elected not to shave. My beard was becoming somewhat more defined; my appearance now greatly matched my mood. I sat down on the edge of the bed and tried to decide whether or not I should go to work. After a few minutes of depressed indecision, I got up and slipped on a shirt. Anything was better than sitting around and thinking.

As I pulled into the parking lot I spotted a black Corvette half hidden behind a large flowering bush. Somehow this didn't surprise me.

In the reception area sat Detective Dawson, still examining his famous shoes, still looking as bored as ever. From in front of her glowing computer screen, Julie looked up quickly, thrust a stack of papers into my hands, and said, "In your office." Immediately she went back to her keyboard. The novelty of murder and detectives had obviously worn off for her. No more exciting now than bill collectors—which, in a sense, they were. Society's bill collectors. This thought pleased me immensely.

Down the corridor I could hear the high chatter of little voices. John was out of his office, but our sales staff—Linda Hall (a fluffy blond with bountiful breasts) and Clara Jamieson (a trim brunette whose steely eyes and tight smile had always fascinated me)—was in, and on the phones. Linda waved and blew me a kiss. Clara ignored me.

Up ahead, through the open doorway to my office, I could see Brooks sitting in a chair, flipping pages in a real estate magazine. He was wearing another three-peice suit—this one, off-white and expensive-looking.

"Good morning," he said cheerfully, sliding the magazine onto a table.

I dropped the papers that Julie had given me on my desk and sat down. I picked up my telephone and pressed Julie's button. "Miss Lawrence, would you please bring me that can of bug spray. We have an enormous cockroach in here." I leaned back in my chair and waited.

Smiling, Brooks slipped a hand into his coat pocket and produced a pack of cigarettes. He tapped one out and lit it.

On my desk, facing whoever was seated across from me, was a small sign which read NO SMOKING PLEASE. I picked up this sign and waved it at Brooks.

Brooks reached out, took the sign in his hands and snapped off the NO. He tossed the abbreviated sign back onto my desk and flipped the NO into the air. It landed in my lap.

The sign was made of a hard thick plastic. Breaking it in half would have been difficult enough, but popping off a corner as easily as Brooks had done, was quite a feat. I tried not to show that I was impressed.

I was about to counter his performance by saying something insulting when Julie burst into the room, the spray can ready. "Where?" she demanded. Julie disliked all insects, and cockroaches in particular.

"There," I said, pointing at Brooks.

Julie looked at Brooks, then back at me. "Oh, for God's sake," she said, setting the spray can down on the desk. "Like I don't have enough to do." She turned and walked out the door. "Like I really need this cheap shit. On the money I make. Hell, I'm going . . ." And her voice trailed off into a mumbled string of expletives.

"You're going to lose a good girl there if you keep playing around," said Brooks.

"Which girl?" I asked.

"Good question," observed Brooks. "You could lose more than one."

"Look, it's always a joy to see you," I said, "but I'm busy. What do you want?"

"The truth."

"Just the facts, ma'am."

"Cute," said Brooks, flicking the ash from his cigarette onto the carpet. "Did I tell you how fond I am of cuteness?"

"You told me."

"And you told me that you never owned a .22."

"No, I didn't," I said. "You asked me did I *own* one. Own—as in now, today, the present."

"Word games, huh?"

"You have to ask exact questions if you want exact answers," I explained.

"Okay. Try this: you once owned a .22 caliber, ten-shot, semiautomatic, blue-steel Ruger, right?"

"You must know that," I said, "or you wouldn't be here wasting my time. And you must also know that it was stolen from my house more than six months ago."

"Yes," agreed Brooks. "I have the burglary report right here." He picked up his briefcase and patted it. "But, curiously, nothing else in the house was stolen."

"As you say, curious. Did you find my pistol?"

"No," said Brooks. "If we had you might already be in jail."

"Well, keep me posted." I leaned forward in my chair and began shuffling through the papers on my desk.

"I'm going to do more than that," said Brooks, standing.

"I'm going to nail your ass to the wall if you're even the least bit dirty."

"You take your work entirely too seriously," I said.

"Before this is over with I'm going to teach you about serious," threatened Brooks. "That's a promise." He ground out his cigarette in an empty coffee cup on my desk.

"Splendid," I said. "Come again. Any time."

Brooks stood there for a second looking at me, his eyes hard, his fists clenched. Then he blew out a laugh that was more of a sneer and walked out of the room.

I was not overly distressed that they had learned about the pistol. I was expecting it. Though perhaps not quite so soon. They didn't seem too far behind, or maybe they were already ahead.

As I sat there debating my situation Linda appreared in the doorway.

"May I come in?" she asked.

"Sure," I said.

Linda had worked for us for more than five years. She was good at her job and threw herself into it wholeheartedly, body first. She had closed more than a few deals on her back. I was not one to moralize, for I too had shared her favors. She was always there and always willing. (I admire that in a woman.) One afternoon, shortly after she had joined us, she and I arranged for a little midday tryst in a house that she had listed. For reasons known only to her, she liked, whenever possible and practical, to meet at one of the properties that she was selling. Maybe it gave her a more intimate feeling toward the places. I don't know. When I arrived at the house I found her sitting in her car, gazing up at the structure lovingly. We entered the house together. It had been locked up for several months and was empty. As I walked through the house she slid onto the carpet and began removing her clothes. "Hurry up," she called out. "I have to show it in an hour." I checked all the doors, pulled the drapes, then joined her on the floor. And soon, like a couple of rabid teenagers, we were going at it. Then she began to sing. Her song was always the same and sometimes a bit monotonous, though it was better than some I'd heard. At least the lyrics were agreeable—"Yes, yes, yes, yes," she would gasp encouragingly. And so there we were, in some stranger's house doing the double-backed beast with her singing her joyous song. Then suddenly she stopped, yelped something unintelligible and started pushing and squirming. And now she had a different tune—"No, no, no, no," she complained breathlessly. Well, all right, I thought, a little variation. Then I felt them too. I stopped and looked down the length of our connected bodies and saw that we were covered with fleas. Hundreds of them. I jumped up, she jumped up, and we began slapping and scratching and dancing about. I ran into the shower and turned the handle. No water; obviously it had already been cut off outside somewhere. The fleas bit, we jumped, and the fleas bit some more. The situation was hopeless; there was nowhere to hide. So half-dressed—to hell with the neighbors—still dancing and scratching and slapping, we slammed out of the house, ran to our cars and sped away. The drive back to my house seemed to take forever. It was pure torture. I believe I hit every red light possible. Eventually I got home, ripped off my clothes just inside the doorway and leaped into the shower. Had I not been made of sterner stuff it could have put me off sex for good. As it was it merely discouraged me from making love in vacant houses.

Linda swirled into my office, circled lightly around behind my chair and laid her large freeflowing breasts on top of my head. "I heard about your grandfather," she purred, her arms coming up around me. "I just can't tell you how terribly sorry I am."

"Thanks," I said.

She rubbed her breasts generously across my head. "If there's anything I can do for you, let me know."

"You'll be the first," I said.

She bent herself down over the back of my chair and set her mouth upside down over mine. Hair and breasts and arms and face—I felt as if I were being swallowed alive. In fact, I was already passing into a slow state of perfumed asphyxiation when a sharp tapping sound—fingernails—at my door brought Linda up straight.

In the doorway, looking in disapprovingly, stood Clara with a piece of paper in her hand.

"Well," said Linda, patting my shoulder and smoothing her hair, "my sympathies." She walked around in front of my desk, stopped between Clara and me, and turned. Silently she mouthed the words, "Call me." Then she pressed her lips together, turned again and exited the room.

In passing neither woman spoke; neither of them even looked at the other.

"I thought you might want to check this," said Clara, stepping forward, the piece of paper extended. She stopped on the other side of my desk and dropped the paper. "It's the Bowman contract."

This was a mere formality, a courtesy really. Clara was the consummate professional. Rarely, if ever, did she make mistakes. Soldier straight, she stood there in front of me as my eyes passed over words and numbers that obviously had meaning but which, to my mind, didn't register anything.

Clara was strictly business, trim and efficient, a well-oiled machine. It was her dispassionate disposition which so attracted me. I had always fantasized that anyone as cold and correct as she was at the office would be dynamite in bed. No one could maintain that composure twenty-four hours a day. She had to let it out sometime, and I wanted to be there when it happened. I wanted to hear her shout and scream and howl and moan—or a least pant a bit.

I lingered over the document for a half minute longer than necessary.

"Anything wrong?" she asked.

"No," I said, looking up sorrowfully. Maybe this was my chance, I thought. Maybe she'd respond to a death in the family.

"Good," she said, and she plucked the paper out of my hand, and then, without a further word, without a hint of condolence, she walked out of the room, leaving me and my fantasies forever unfulfilled.

FOURTEEN

It soon became apparent that I would accomplish little in the office today. I needed answers; for if I didn't supply them Brooks clearly would. And his answers, I feared, would prove to be less than satisfactory. So I went to visit my cousin Daniel.

Daniel owned a large two-story house on the mainland overlooking Sarasota Bay. Its location was strategically perfect for his occupation—the importation and distribution of cocaine. Somehow Daniel had happily avoided growing up. (Not that I had reached any lofty heights of adulthood, but I was marginally more mature than he was.) He still enjoyed playing games, and he took it all very seriously. He was the worst kind of sportsman. To him the money, the drugs, the houses, the cars, the boats, the women were merely the most visible means of keeping score. Daniel—10,010. The rest of the poor suckers—zip. His outlook on life was somewhat unrealistic, I thought. His twin brother David and I had both long since given up these games—well, selling dope at least—for more mundane pursuits. But Daniel had persisted. Alone, walking the tightrope, looking down, laughing at the crowds below. Constantly and in every way possible, he kept trying to prove that he was better, smarter, more daring than those he knew, associated with. And making an illicit living (major money) was a large part of that proof, to himself and to others.

I pulled to a stop in front of Daniel's house and got out of my car. All that one could see from where I was standing was a high spiked wooden fence running around the property. On the other side of the fence I could hear dogs barking. I knew that he was home.

Whenever Daniel left his house, even for the shortest periods of time, say a brief excursion to the 7-Eleven for beer and cigarettes, he would invariably lock his dogs inside. If they were outside that meant Daniel was inside. Once when Daniel had been away on a little business trip to the Bahamas some lightweight had broken into his house, and his dogs—two large black and tan female Dobermans—had kept the man company for more than twenty-four hours. They had a pretty good time with him too. Upon his return home Daniel found the man cowering in a corner, bleeding on his carpet and begging Daniel to call off his animals. Instead Daniel called over some friends, and together they gave the fellow a sound beating, then threw him into the bay. The would-be burglar, in turn, sued Daniel for false imprisonment, mental anguish and a couple of other crap charges. But unfortunately for him before the man could collect damages he was blown away by a shotgun blast—a scared woman alone with her husband's .12-gauge pump— trying to burgle another house a few doors down from Daniel's. (The man was obviously fond of the neighborhood.) Somehow I always felt that in this case justice had prevailed.

I walked up to the front gate and pressed the buzzer. The dogs went wild, throwing themselves against the fence, trying to get at me. After a few minutes a female voice came through the speaker box: "Yes?"

"Is Daniel there?" I asked, bending down, shouting into the box, shouting over the commotion created by the dogs.

"Who wants to know?" responded the voice.

"His cousin, Thomas Clay."

Through the speaker box I could hear broken fragments of a shouted conversation, then through the speaker box again there came a loud high-pitched whistle, and the dogs fell silent. The gate buzzed and I pushed my way into Daniel's yard. Once in, the gate automatically swung back and clicked shut. The dogs came over, sniffed my extended hand and then skulked away into the bushes, evidently disappointed that I was not to be their dinner.

Daniel's yard spread away before me in two well-maintained, professionally landscaped corridors of color. Off to one side a pick-up truck, jacked up and suspended above large wheels, was parked. Beside it was a new Jaguar XJ6 with heavily tinted windows. Both of these vehicles were painted the same dark forest green. Directly in front of me was Daniel's house—modern, stark, imposing, expensive.

The front door opened. A small blond girl wrapped in a large beach towel stepped out onto the front porch and waved me forward.

I advanced and entered the house.

"He's in the Jacuzzi," the girl announced. She turned and headed down the hall. "Shut the door," she said over her shoulder. "Lock it."

I did as directed, then followed after her.

The interior of the house was open and unobstructed, with rooms flowing into one another. What few inner walls there were loudly proclaimed their existence in bright Caribbean pastels. Along these walls and on the tables in the rooms through which we passed, were primitive clay sculptures and grim-faced ceremonial masks of long lost Central and South American civilizations, stolen or bought on the black market somewhere. Why Daniel was so attracted to these monstrosities I could never understand. Some of these figures may have been high art, priceless national treasures, but to me—admittedly no connoisseur of lost cultures—they looked like the forgotten results of a kindergarten craft class. But then, what did I know?

Without conversation my guide and I made our way toward the back of the house. Suddenly the girl turned to her right and descended a narrow, dimly lit stairway. Halfway down the stairs she let the towel slide from her body. Naked, nicely curved, with hips swinging, she proceeded on. I continued after her, scooping up the towel as I went.

At the bottom of the stairs was a small sun-drenched room. In the center of this room was a bubbling hot tub surrounded by redwood decking; in the hot tub itself was Daniel. All about orchids bloomed and strange green plants sprang up. Behind Daniel, running from floor to ceiling, large windows opened onto a view of Sarasota Bay. Tied up to his dock I could see two boats—a 32-foot sailboat and a long low-slung speedboat, both again painted the same dark green as his car and truck.

Daniel looked up and smiled at me. His handsome face and long curly blond hair had changed little over the years.

"You know, you ought to feed those damn dogs of yours sometimes," I said, lowering myself onto a large fluffy pillow laid out on the decking opposite him. "They seem a bit hungry to me."

"I keep all my bitches hungry," said Daniel. He reached up for the girl's hand. "Don't I, sweetheart?"

The girl—a natural blond—took his hand, smiled and stepped lightly into the swirling waters. She was young, fifteen or sixteen, a runaway probably. Her eyes were green, her breasts full; her mouth, I noticed, had a tendency to hang open. Around her neck was a thin gold chain with the words, in gold—SPOIL ME—spelled out at the end of the chain. Whether she knew it or not, cared or not, she was being set up, recruited. As a sideline, a hobby really, Daniel ran a string of cocaine whores—young girls who, in return for a steady supply of powder, would perform any sexual service on demand—and soon this girl, I could tell, would be added to his stable.

I had seen it before; it didn't bother me. People, for the most part, tend to dig their own graves, create their own private hells. And if what this girl wanted, needed, or thought she wanted or needed, at this particular time in her life, was cocaine and the cold comfort of Daniel's company, so be it. I was not outraged in the least. It all seemed quite natural to me, quite Darwinian.

The girl reached behind her into an elaborately carved wooden box. Carefully she lifted out a small mirror and brought it around in front of her. She offered the mirror first to Daniel. Daniel picked up a slender silver tube lying on the mirror and snorted a rail of cocaine. "Want some?" he asked, as the girl extended the mirror toward me.

"No thanks," I said.

Daniel tilted his head back and let his sinuses drain. "Someone told me you'd quit."

"It's just not that big a deal for me anymore," I explained.

Daniel nodded his head.

The girl snorted a quick rail herself and then returned the mirror to the box.

"Hop in," suggested Daniel. "You haven't given up everything, have you?" He slipped an arm around the young girl's shoulder and pulled her close. His hand found a loose breast bobbing on the surface and he began fondling it.

The girl smiled up at me. Her tongue flicked out along her lips—the gesture was involuntary, of no erotic significance; a simple chemically induced reflex.

"Maybe later," I said. I was beginning to feel a bit like an intruder.

"Hey," said Daniel, brightening up, "you remember that girl back in high school we used to do together? She was a riot. 'Meet you in the middle.' Remember? Barbara something. Both Ends Barbara, you used to call her."

"Yeah, I remember," I said, remembering.

"Man, was she hot or was she hot? I wonder whatever happened to her."

"She got married," I said. "I saw her brother down at Coley's a couple of months ago, and he said she married a doctor and moved to Beverly Hills. A proctologist."

"Jesus, her own private asshole for a doctor," observed Daniel, slipping deeper into the coke, deeper into the hot tub.

"No," I said. "You've got it backward. It's her own private doctor for her asshole."

"Whatever," said Daniel, glancing quickly at his watch, then sliding beneath the churning water.

The girl looked up at me again. Her eyes were empty, her smile fixed.

A long minute of silence passed. Daniel stayed underwater. Another minute ticked by—the water bubbling; Daniel below.

"Is he all right?" I asked finally.

"He's okay," the girl said.

"No, I mean, is he okay? Is he all right?"

"Yeah, I told you," said the girl, a little annoyed. "He's okay. Not great, but okay. At least he don't beat me. I used to live with this guy—"

Suddenly Daniel burst to the surface, his face red, his watch before his bulging eyes. "Two minutes and fifty seconds," he gasped triumphantly. "Whew! Pretty damn good. I've been practicing."

"Wonderful," I said, settling back down on my pillow. I had almost jumped in to save him.

"How about you?" he asked, still panting. "How long can you hold your breath?"

"Well, I don't really know."

"I bet not for two minutes and fifty seconds."

"No," I conceded. "Probably not."

"Damn right," agreed Daniel heartily.

Games, I thought, somewhat disgusted. Goddamn games.

"Hey, sweetheart, get me a daiquiri," commanded Daniel, his head now resting against the decking. "Want one?" he asked, looking over at me.

"Sure," I said.

"Two tall ones," said Daniel.

Without uttering a word the young girl stood up, stepped out of the hot tub and walked around in front of me. I lifted the towel that I had picked up off the stairs, her towel, and offered it to her. She looked at the towel, then at me, then she laughed. Naked, quite proud of her nakedness, she walked on up the stairs, still laughing.

"Well, tell me, cousin," I said, once we were alone, "what do you think about Grandfather getting whacked?"

"Good riddance. The old fucker's been charging me a bundle for using his farm to do a little night work."

"Yeah, Fulton mentioned something to me about you landing planes out there."

"He did?" asked Daniel, sitting up straight, genuinely surprised.

"He did," I confirmed.

"Motherfucker. The old fart. Well, now it makes sense to me. I couldn't figure it out before. But now it makes sense. Fulton must've found out and told Grandfather what I was using the airstrip for. That's why he doubled my fee for landing rights. He even made me put in lights for the runway. I'm surprised he didn't make me build a goddamn control tower too. Ten thousand a week, the old fucker was charging me. Goddamn."

"The cost of doing business, I guess," I said.

But Daniel didn't hear me. He was still thinking about Grandfather and the ten grand a week.

From above I could hear the soft padding of bare feet

descending stairs. The young girl materialized and handed me a cold glass of frozen green.

"Thanks," I said.

The girl just looked at me.

"You seen Brooks yet?" I asked, turning my attention back to Daniel.

"Yeah, what a fucking dork he turned out to be." Daniel extended his hand and received a glass. "He and some turnip-head detective came around here yesterday asking a bunch of questions. Asking a lot of questions about you and James. How's your alibi?"

"Married. How's yours?"

"Ironclad," said Daniel, stroking the young girl's thigh as she slipped back into the hot tub. "Right, sweetheart?"

"All night," the girl parroted. "We were here together all night."

Daniel smiled and kissed her on the cheek.

The girl reached around behind her again, extracted the mirror from the box and rewarded herself with another rail for remembering.

After that I drank up quickly and left.

FIFTEEN

My visit with Daniel had been as unproductive as I had imagined it would be, and somewhat more depressing. I headed downtown in search of better results. It was there, in a little white clapboard house, that I hoped to find Laura. Laura—the younger sister of James and Michele Clay.

Long before it became parentally acceptable, commonplace, the three of them—James, Michele and Laura—had been latchkey kids. To me, at the time (the late '50s, the early '60s), it seemed that they lived wondrous lives of freedom—each with a key to their front door, hamburgers and pancakes whenever they wanted them and no one to tell them what they could or could not do. Undoubtedly there was also a downside, which at age nine didn't occur to me.

Their father, Philip Clay, the one-term congressman turned lobbyist, was so busy with his wheeling and dealing that he was seldom home, seldom even in the state. Their mother, an attractive woman with an abundance of auburn hair, was left to fill her time as she might. Perhaps a latchkey wife herself, bored, she turned to her friends for solace and was steered into the field of good works; parties, pageants, parades, all in the name of charity. Eventually she became so absorbed with helping others that, it can be argued, she neglected her own. After my cousins were grown, she, the mother, the wife, divorced Philip Clay and moved to Arizona, where she effectively disappeared from the scene and from the lives of her children.

Of the three of them (my cousins) it was Laura who first showed signs of rebellion and rejection. Always in trouble, in school and out. Running fast, running wild. I remember her as a child: dirty; her face smeared; her clothes in rags; barefoot, her shoes kicked off, lost; her knees and elbows scraped and bleeding. Then would come those rare occasions—family gatherings, Christmas, whatever—and she would be forced into formal attire (and force, indeed, often being required); but once dressed, clean, presentable, she was transformed almost magically into something else, something demure, delicate and ladylike; but still, just beneath the surface, beneath the clean face and the frill, sparkling in those bright eyes, you could tell that she was still looking for some chaos to cause. Little Laura, the tomboy. A year older than David, Daniel and me, but treated by all of us—cousins, family extended—as though she were a younger sister to be watched, guarded, protected. Because one never knew with Laura; she could go off in so many different directions.

It had been quite some time since I had last been to Laura's house. Occasionally I would see her out at the beach or in a bar somewhere and we would talk. But basically, for the most part, we lived separate and unconnected lives. I now sat in my car, in front of her house, admiring the picture of disorder and neglect which presented itself: paint peeling; tall grass and weeds to the windowsills; newspapers, still rolled up, baked brown by the sun, littering the drive; an empty wine bottle on the front door step.

If she had wished Laura could have lived in a much grander style, in a more elegant setting. She was not, by any means, stupid, or even poor—she could have tapped her father for funds had she wanted. It was simply that earthly comforts and considerations were of little importance to her. She seemed to live in a state beyond, or maybe above, all that. There was an almost calculated sense of carelessness about her, about her attitudes toward life, and toward death. Currently, as far as I knew, she lived alone, had few friends and certainly no job. (This—a job, work, the active pursuit of wealth or even subsistence—ran counter to the guiding principles of her life.) Somehow—"with a little help from my friends," she would say and smile—she was able to muddle through. And a muddle, to me, it appeared precisely to be.

I got out of my car, walked around in front of it, kicked a

rusty beer can out from under one of my tires and moved on up to the house. Taped to the front door was a note. BACK IN A MINUTE. WAIT. The door had been left slightly ajar. I pushed it open and looked inside. The house seemed empty. I called out Laura's name. No answer. I entered the front room, found a rather unstable chair near an open window and lowered myself into it.

A fan rotated in one corner, blowing occasional gusts of hot air in my direction. In another corner a scratchy record on an inexpensive stereo thumped out a '60s beat. It looked as if someone had left the house in a hurry—then again, knowing Laura, I knew that might not necessarily be the case.

Laura, not surprisingly, had devoted little time and less effort to the problem of interior decorating: an old sofa with metal springs popping through the sides and back; a table of stacked slabs of slate in front of the sofa; dust balls on the floor; spider webs on the ceiling; an ash tray on the slate table full to overflowing with cigarette butts and half-smoked joints; beer cans and more wine bottles; lipstick-smudged glasses; posters announcing rock concert dates long past, slapped against fingerprinted walls; a sandwich with one bite taken out; cockroaches scurrying from crack to crevice; yellowish houseplants curling to brown; a worn rug; forlorn articles of clothing strewn about; coffee cups still half-filled with coffee; a plate of something on which a mold colony had permanently established itself.

I sat in the chair with my hands folded and tried not to touch anything, living or dead.

Those posters, I imagined—the dates, the bands, the places—must have had a special meaning to Laura. For almost ten years and countless thousands of miles (quite an investment), she had been a groupie, a token member of that inner circle of fame, fantasy and fatalism, her location in the descending hierarchy somewhere between the man with the night's receipts and the roadies. Go anywhere, do anything, absolutely anything. Always ready. "Let's party!" Laura began her career, her education, in Tampa. She was sixteen, standing up front at some concert, clapping and shouting and screaming. Someone in a band spotted her—young, ready for the picking—and commanded that she be brought backstage, and from there on it was one long non-stop carnival-odyssey to nowhere. Sex, drugs and rock 'n' roll. Airports to limousines to plush hotel rooms—"Charge it!"—to concert halls, then back to hotel rooms—"More! Charge it!"—and then in the morning to the airport again and on to the next town. The USA and Europe. The people and places becoming a blur. The blur itself trampled beneath the repetition and the pace. Then with five years in, going for her master's now, she began to slip. Hell, she was already twenty-one. The bands not quite so famous, the airplanes replaced by buses. Down, down, down, from band to band, from hand to hand, she was passed—damaged goods, holding on by sheer cunning and strength. She couldn't believe, wouldn't believe, what was happening to her, that it was over. Hadn't she partied with Mick and the boys? Hadn't she once been the steady girlfriend, almost the fiancee, of some near-famous drummer? Hadn't she been in charge of drug injections—"Oh, nurse"—for one entire band? Hadn't she been a house guest at Hef's, cruised the Caribbean on a private yacht? Wasn't she important? Yes, she had, and no, she wasn't. Then finally, feeling for the bottom, the end now undeniably in sight, the coup de grace: kicked out of some minor nobody's convertible on Sunset Strip, tossed a dime and a hundred dollar bill and told to call home. And that was it. No audience. No applause. No encore. Spent, used up both physically and mentally, twenty-five looking thirty-five, sitting there on her ass on the hot pavement in L.A., the money in one hand, the other hand raised in a gesture of defiance, screaming at the car as it drove away. The graduate groupie, with a Ph.D. in hard living. Eventually the call was made and more money was sent and she flew home (coach), and after six months or so of intense therapy she was almost coherent again. At least she wasn't making those long-distance midnight calls to people who hung up on her anymore.

Then another half year on, and you could begin to see the difference. That entire next summer, sunrise to sunset, she stationed herself at the beach, letting the sun draw out the poison, heal the wounds. Her body firmed up, her skin tightened and turned a golden brown. She remembered how to smile again. She became a vegetarian, adopted an off-beat Eastern religion and bought a battered army surplus Jeep. Then she went big-time, turned pro. As she explained it to me late one night in a bar: "If I'm gonna get treated like a whore I might as well get paid like one too." And so she set herself up as an escort. She had gone from free love to pay sex, and it didn't make a bit of difference to her. She teamed up with another girl, and together they made themselves available for parties. Her friend, an attractive little redhead whom I only met once, had a speciality—or so I was told, having never actually witnessed the event—called, rather crudely, a cum cocktail. At some point her friend evidently decided that she'd had one cocktail too many. She went to the beach and put a bullet through her heart. She left a message scrawled in the sand saying: FUCK IT. JUST BURY ME. After that Laura gave up the business—apparently she didn't enjoy performing solo—and allowed herself to be kept in modest style by a succession of men who demanded from her a minimal degree of effort or exertion.

And this, I believed, as I sat there in the chair, listening to a Jeep loudly rounding a corner two blocks away, was currently how she made ends meet.

The Jeep roared up to Laura's house, jumped a curb and jerked to a stop in the middle of her yard. Out bailed Laura. Through the open door I could see her swinging toward me: her hair, long, thick, blond and braided; her eyes, bright and impish; her body, trim; her movements, easy, ready.

She bounced up the stairs and into the room. She was wearing cut-off jeans and a white sleeveless T-shirt. Before I could rise she was on me, bent across me, kissing me on the cheek.

"How long, Thomas? How long has it been?" she demanded, looking down at me with mock seriousness; her hands on her hips. "Does it take a death in the family to get you to come and see me?"

"Murder always brings out the best in me," I said.

She flopped down happily on the floor in front of me. She brought her long tan legs up to her chest, her chin resting on her knees.

"Well, did you do it?" she asked eagerly.

"What the fuck kind of question—"

"Come on. You can tell me. I can keep a secret."

"Laura,—"

"Okay. Just kidding."

She turned, reached into the ashtray on the slate table and dug out half of a joint. She lit it and looked at me. "Get one if you want," she said, gesturing toward the ashtray. "I've got plenty."

"No thanks," I said. The marijuana currently circulating the city was so strong that it made me uncomfortably incoherent.

"God, you're such a prude," she said, taking a puff, smiling.

"Right," I agreed, not caring to debate the matter.

Laura picked a beer can up off the floor, took a tentative sip, testing for texture and temperature, then finding its vintage acceptable to her palate, she turned the can up and emptied it.

"You don't seem too upset," I observed.

"Tears for the dead?" she asked. "Rain in the ocean. Piss in a pond."

"If you say so," I said.

Laura had always been able to confuse me. She was my favorite cousin, but I could never read her, never tell whether or not she was being serious. One moment she might be laughing and then the next ready to break down over nothing. I just sat there and watched her perform. Because that's what it was—a performance. But why she felt it necessary to perform for me, I couldn't understand.

"Who's that note for?" I asked, pointing to the door.

"You," she said. "Anybody who comes by."

I shook my head. She shrugged her shoulders and took another hit off the joint. I knew that she was lying, and she knew that I knew. But it didn't matter to her. Something was wrong, something was making her afraid.

"Have you talked to Brooks yet?" I asked.

"Who's Brooks?"

"Mason Brooks. From school. You remember him, don't you? A little nerdy kid with a big head. He's some kind of cop now. He's in charge of investigating Grandfather's murder."

"Mason Brooks," she said to herself, letting the name filter back through time until it linked up with a face. "Mason Brooks. The little boy you almost killed."

"I didn't almost kill him," I protested. "I just flushed his head down a toilet."

"Yeah, I remember him now."

"Well, like I said, he's in charge of this investigation, and—"

"What investigation?"

"Grandfather's murder."

"Oh," she said. "Well, I guess that's rather unfortunate for you, isn't it?"

"It's neither fortunate nor unfortunate, because I didn't have anything to do with it."

Laura smiled at me through a cloud of marijuana smoke and nodded her head.

"Listen, the point is that sooner or later he's gonna come by here and ask you what you were doing, where you were the night before last."

Laura thought for a moment. "I was here," she said. "Alone. By myself."

"That's not a very good answer."

"That's okay. I'm innocent. Like you." She stubbed out the tail-end of the joint. "At least until proven guilty, right?"

"Yeah, well, that's the theory."

"And a wonderful theory it is too," she said, searching through the ashtray for another half-joint.

SIXTEEN

I stepped out onto Laura's front porch and stopped.

"Come back when you're ready to confess," called out Laura from inside.

"I will," I called back. "You've got a couple of visitors here to see you. Of the police variety."

"Great," she said. Then after a moment she shut her door and locked it.

In the street, sitting on the hood of my car, waiting, smiling at me, was Brooks. Inside the car itself I could see the top of Dectective Dawson's flat head bobbing up and down, looking under my seats, going through my glove compartment.

I walked down the steps and on toward my car.

"Trying to get your stories straight?" asked Brooks as I got closer.

"I've got something right here you can get straight," I said.

"Wouldn't be interested," said Brooks.

Dectective Dawson lifted his head up, looked at me, then at Brooks.

Brooks slid off the car and stood up. "Let's go, Detective," he said, stretching. "We've violated enough civil rights for one day."

Detective Dawson squeezed out of my car and held the door open for me. Somewhat suspiciously I slipped into the driver's seat. Detective Dawson slammed the door hard, just missing my foot. He smiled at me, then followed after Brooks, who was already knocking on Laura's front door.

I started my car and pulled away from the curb. At the end of the block, before turning, I glanced in my rear view mirror and saw Brooks and Detective Dawson talking with Laura. She had them seated on the front porch steps, in the bright hot sunlight. Laura knew how to handle cops. She had dealt with them before.

I turned onto the Trail and headed south, away from downtown. As I drove the rumbling in my stomach reminded me that I had not eaten all day. Along the street half a dozen fast food options advertised themselves. The choice was less than a choice. They were all basically the same.

I pulled into the first parking lot I came to and entered the building. Bright, cheerful, clean. As pre-packaged as the food served. I ordered a hamburger, received it immediately and sat down at one of the little plastic tables.

Judging by the crowd—mostly teenagers—I estimated the time to be somewhere between three and four o'clock. David, I knew, would be working until at least five or five-thirty, but Michele might be at home. Sometimes she knocked off early. I decided to swing by her condo after I'd disposed of my burger and hope for the best.

In the corner opposite me I happened to notice two young girls sitting together, drinking Cokes. The girl facing me had long black hair tinted blue and green and gold. She was wearing an extremely short skirt. As she sucked on her straw—full lips, white teeth—she was constantly crossing and recrossing her legs. She seemed to be looking in my direction. I tried to focus on something else, but my eyes kept drifting back. Suddenly she whipped her ankles around the back of her chair and threw her legs open wide—pink underwear with little white flowers on it. She held her legs open and smiled.

It didn't seem fair. Some pimple-faced kid—with a Mohawk haircut, no doubt—was probably poling this young thing, and legally I couldn't touch her. Ordinarily I would not have allowed such legal niceties as the mere fact that she was obviously underage stand in the way of a good time, but with cops now popping up all over the place I knew that I had to be more careful.

I made a mental note to remember that face and those legs if I ever saw them again, finished my sandwich and left.

Back on the Trail, heading south again: new buildings

going up, old ones coming down; the churning of dollars so loud you could almost hear it.

And some of that churning, some of that building was being done at Michele's behest. After graduating from college, she came back to Sarasota and went to work for Grandfather. She was given, per Grandfather's instructions, a revolving set of difficult and unpleasant tasks, at which she acquitted herself admirably. Her promotions came quickly. When Father surrendered the controls of Grandfather's companies and pushed the eject button, it was Michele who was tapped to take his place. She had been in charge for less than three years now, but according to most reports she was working wonders—unless, of course, you happened to be seated across the bargaining table from her. She seemed to have a lot of the old boy's blood in her and a lot of his vindictiveness too.

Then off the Trail, over the bridge and back onto Siesta Key. I drove on through the village—really nothing more than a stylish cluster of banks, bars, restaurants and boutiques—past my house, past the public beach and turned in at the flower-lined entrance road leading to Michele's condominium. Her car—a red Porsche 911—was parked next to a small bubbling fountain.

In front of the main outer door, I noticed a group of elderly men standing around, discussing the events of the day. I parked my car in the visitor's section and hurried to join this gossiping group. Worse than old women, they were—hushed tones, fugitive eyes, a forefinger laid knowingly against a bulbous nose. Finally one of the old gentlemen remembered why they were all standing there with their keys in their hands, and with a laugh, as a group, we entered the building together.

While the gentlemen, still whispering, trooped away to the mailroom to collect their dividend checks, postcards and magazines, I made straight for the elevators. I was glad that I had been able to get into the building without having to call up to Michele and ask her to buzz me in. Michele was not above telling someone—me—to go screw. This way at least I could get to her door, and from there maybe I could talk my way in.

I stepped into the first open elevator I came to, pushed the button marked P and rose soundlessly to the seventeenth floor.

There were four large penthouse apartments. Michele occupied the one on the northwest corner.

I knocked on her door. I waited. No one came. I knocked again; this time more insistently. In fact, I was still knocking when the door opened—a double chained crack. Standing there, filling the crack with a silk peach-colored bathrobe, was Michele, her face hard as stone.

"Why the hell do I pay two hundred damn dollars a month for security if they're gonna let every common criminal and derelict in town in the building?" she asked, looking at me.

"Fine," I said. "And how are you?"

"What'd you want, Thomas?" she demanded.

"To talk," I said.

"Go ahead. Only make it quick."

"Here?" I asked, glancing down the hallway. "A bit public, don't you think?"

"Okay. Wait." She shut the door. I pressed my ear against it. Inside I could hear muffled voices. A minute later the door swung open. "All right," she said, moving away from the door. "Come on in."

Michele's apartment was clean, cold and elegant—very much like the owner herself. Angular steel sculptures, abstract paintings, cube tables, leather sofas and chairs. Throughout the apartment the floors were marble, the interior walls white plaster, the outer walls glass and, in places, the ceilings mirrored. The lighting was predominantly neon and seemed to come from nowhere, rising up mysteriously or else descending from hidden nooks. Cut flowers in elaborate elongated vases softened the feeling to a degree, but on the whole the place always reminded me of some sort of surrealistic waiting room through which people passed rapidly, with eyes averted.

Michele slipped into a large padded leather chair and tucked her feet up underneath her. I sat down across from her on a sofa. Next to her, on the floor, in a pile, I noticed two dresses and two pairs of shoes.

"Couldn't you decide what to wear today?" I asked.

Michele looked down at the dresses, then back at me. "You said you wanted to talk, so talk."

"Well, I was just wondering if you'd seen Brooks yet? You know who Brooks is, don't you? Mason Brooks from—"

"Yes, I know who Mason Brooks is, and no, I haven't seen him yet. He made an appointment to come by here at five o'clock." She glanced over at the clock on the wall. I looked at it too. It was four-fifteen.

"He made an appointment?" I asked, somewhat surprised.

"Naturally," she said. She reached out and picked up a small silver box off the table between us. "Anybody who wants to see me makes an appointment. And you might remember that yourself next time." She opened the box, extracted a cigarette and lit it.

"Sure," I said.

From where I was sitting, from the angle, from the height, all that I could see outside was the sky meeting the watery horizon—blue on blue, calm and forgiving.

"I saw your picture in the paper yesterday," I offered.

"Oh," said Michele, lifting her chin up slightly.

"Did you enjoy the play? *Hamlet* wasn't it? 'To be or not to be.' "

"*Macbeth*," she said. " 'Double, double toil and trouble; fire burn and caldron bubble.' "

"Impressive," I said. "And I thought you only knew numbers."

Michele just looked at me and said nothing.

"Pretty weird about Grandfather, huh?"

"Yes. Very strange. Did you have anything to do with it?"

"Me?" I asked.

"Why not? You hated him, didn't you? Everybody else did."

"I didn't hate him. I just didn't like him very much."

Michele took a long pull off her cigarette and blew a cloud of smoke up at the ceiling.

In the back rooms of the apartment I could hear someone moving about. Eventually a door opened and Vanessa, barefoot, bare shoulders, wrapped in a quilted green bedcover, stepped into the room.

"Auntie Vee!" I exclaimed. (This was a name given to Vanessa by Laura, and she hated it intensely.) "What a pleasant surprise!"

Vanessa looked at me, raked her fingers through her hair and moved over to the bar area—more marble and mirrors. She dropped an ice cube into a lead crystal glass and poured in a couple of ounces of Scotch. Leaning against the bar, she surveyed her surroundings and drank.

"What time's that cop supposed to get here?" she asked.

"Five," said Michele.

"Then I guess I should clear out before he gets here."

"It would probably be better," Michele agreed.

Vanessa finished up her drink with one swallow, walked around next to Michele and picked up one of the dresses and a pair of shoes from the pile on the floor. She stopped and looked down at Michele for a moment, then turned and walked back to the rear of the apartment. Out of sight, a door slammed.

"Listen, I know that it's none of my business," I began, "but—"

"You're right," snapped Michele. "It's not. So leave it alone."

"Right," I said.

After several minutes of silence Vanessa reappeared fully dressed. She walked up beside Michele's chair again, bent down and kissed her full in the mouth. She licked her tongue along the length of Michele's lips, then straightened up. She put an arm around Michele's shoulder and pulled her head over against her hip. Both of them looked at me with eyes hard, defiant and blue.

"Why don't you take it with you?" suggested Michele, still looking at me.

"Why don't we just drop it off the balcony?" countered Vanessa.

"It certainly would make a nice splat," Michele observed.

"Girls! Cousin! Auntie!" I objected with mock horror.

They both shook their heads.

"Call me," said Vanessa.

"I will," Michele assured her.

Vanessa stepped over to the door and opened it. "Come on," she said. "And if you say one word to me, I swear to God I'll knee you in the nuts."

"However the lady likes it," I said, standing. "I'm only here to please."

SEVENTEEN

In silence, as requested, Vanessa and I rode the elevator down to the lobby. Still without talking, we walked over to the main outer door. I opened it and bowed slightly. Vanessa stepped through it, then spun around. "Leave her alone," she hissed, her eyes flashing. "Stay the fuck away from her. Understand? And don't come near me either."

"Secrets?" I asked. "Something to hide, maybe?"

"I'm warning you. Back off." Then she turned and walked away quickly.

I stood there and watched her as she disappeared around the corner of the building. I wondered what the big deal was. Everybody in the family knew that she and Michele were lovers, and had been for a number of years. No one cared. Not even Vanessa's husband, Doctor Jack. He had other playthings.

Strange, I thought, very strange.

I turned and headed back to my car. Two steps and I stopped. Again, seated on the hood of my car, still smiling and waiting, was Brooks. And now, sitting next to him, was Detective Dawson too—all two hundred and fifty plus pounds of him. I could almost see the dents in the hood from where I was standing.

This whole operation was getting to me. Simultaneously it was making me angry and afraid. I was becoming overly conscious of the people and things around me; every passing pair of eyes seemed to be watching me.

I walked on toward the car.

Again Brooks hailed me, his entire face one large smirking smile. "Like a chicken with its head cut off, a dog with its tail on fire. Note, Detective, the circles getting progressively smaller and smaller. Why don't you just tell me you did it and I'll take you in and we'll call it match point? You lose."

"Why don't you just go fuck yourself?" I said, circling around to the right and climbing into my car. "And take your big monkey with you."

"Watch out, citizen," warned Brooks. "If Detective Dawson didn't know that you were kidding he might take offense."

"Well, I sure as hell wouldn't want that," I said, starting the engine.

Then I flipped, really flipped—the sun, the heat, the pressure, the pursuit, I don't know. I started pounding on the horn and screaming through the windshield at Brooks and Detective Dawson to get the hell off my goddamn car. They didn't move; they didn't even turn around. They just laughed. I jammed the car into reverse. The machine lunged backward, nearly hitting a palm tree. They both slipped easily off the hood and landed on their feet. "Don't go away mad," I think I heard one of them say. I threw the car into first and stomped on the gas. The thing jumped away from me—wide-eyed pedestrians, speed bumps and a blur of greenery whizzing by. I was already in second gear, about to go to third, when I checked the rear view mirror: behind me, receding rapidly, I could see Brooks and Detective Dawson waving and laughing and trading one-handed palm slaps.

This wasn't the way my life was supposed to be. This was Grandfather's revenge, a curse from beyond the grave. And it had me totally shattered.

Once I got back on the main beach road I realized that I was driving much too fast and breathing hard. I slowed down and turned on the radio. In my heart I knew there was no logical reason that I should have allowed Brooks to get under my skin the way that he had. After all I was innocent or, at least, not guilty. But still, still . . .

I crossed onto the mainland again and drove east, out into the country and on toward David's house. David now lived with his wife and two children in an exclusive development built around a golf course. David loved golf and played the game religiously. A fact that to me was always terribly funny.

Somehow—wrongly, I admit—I tended to associate golf with old men in checkered pants, whacking little white balls into the weeds and talking business and taxes. And this was the very antithesis of the David I had known, admired. Or it should have been.

The worst of the bad. The best of the lot. David then—young, wild, carefree: pissing on a potted plant at a teenage party at someone's parents' house; totaling his father's new Cadillac; skipping school, getting suspended, dropping out; fighting—everybody, anybody, for reason or none; getting girls pregnant, a whole string of them, including one who took the long swim to Mexico (he didn't even go to her funeral); stealing a motorcycle, riding it to California, dumping it in the Pacific Ocean; coming back home, standing outside the high school late one night, throwing rocks through the windows—one hundred and fifteen—saying to the cops, "Okay, but I've just got a few more to go"; rejected by the Army for being too nuts; selling drugs, shooting drugs, living on cheap wine, heroin and speed. David, the instigator. David, the antagonist. This was the David of old. This was the David who inspired awe and commanded respect.

And then he got married.

And now: husband, father, stockbroker, golfer, cutter of grass. Pale by comparison, a tragedy of conformity. But then, it was his life, and he had to live it.

I pulled into David's drive and stopped my car. A cocker spaniel bounded out of the bushes to greet me. Sprinklers shot arcs of water across a flawless lawn. A healthy looking child rode a bicycle down the pleasant and properous street. Farther along I could hear the combat of a half a dozen lawn mowers. It was early Friday evening; an hour of sunlight left.

In front of me, at the peak of the curved drive, were two cars, a blue Mercedes 380SL and a brown BMW 325e. Both David and his wife seemed to be home. I walked up to the front of the house—white, rough-finished concrete exterior topped with a red barrel-tile roof—and rang the doorbell.

The door swung open before the last bell in the chime sequence had sounded. And there stood Anita, David's wife; her eyes fierce, protective, like those of a mother jungle cat.

David had been one of Anita's first cases. She had been a

young lawyer, right out of law school. He had just been busted on a possession and sales rap. Through some fancy legal maneuvering she had been able to get him off on a technicality. She then proceeded to take David under her wing and into her life. She straightened him out both physically and mentally, got him a good job as a stockbroker with a nationally known firm (he was a natural at sales—be it drugs or mutual funds) and then married him.

Now, some four years later, Anita was a junior partner with a prestigious local firm, and David was a rising star in the brokerage community. And as she saw it, it was her duty, her obligation to her family and herself, to shield and protect David against all intruders from the past, from the good old days of sin and corruption, because one never knew when the contagion might again manifest itself.

"He's not here," she said, blocking the doorway with her small trim body.

I glanced quickly back at the Mercedes. I said nothing.

"I tell you he's not here. He's gone." Her hair was black, shoulder-length and beginning to go to an early gray. I had always liked her, liked the way she looked, even though on more than one occasion she had made it plain that she couldn't stomach me.

"Five minutes," I said. "That's all. I promise you it's important."

She didn't move.

"To me and to David," I added.

Her eyes slipped from mine. Her gaze wandered into the street. The sprinklers were twirling; next door, children were laughing. Finally she sighed and stepped aside. "Five minutes," she said. "Out by the pool." She turned and walked away toward the kitchen.

I entered the house and shut the door behind me. The front room was long and rather narrow—white walls, a white ceiling, white rugs, white sofas, tables and chairs. A connected series of more colorful rooms ran off to the right and left and then swept toward the back in parallel wings. Attached to the outside of the front room, and extending along the side for perhaps a hundred feet, was a lanai crowded with green plants. From where I was standing, through a sliding glass door, I could see the back of David's blond head. I crossed the white room and slid open the glass door.

"Any expert advice for the financially naive?" I asked, stepping out onto the lanai.

"Buy low and sell high," said David, turning, looking up at me.

Since I had last seen him he had grown a beard—neat, cut close, slightly darker than the rest of his hair. As a rule I tended to be suspicious of anyone who wore a beard in the tropics, subtropics, whatever. It seemed unnatural and certainly looked uncomfortable.

"Something new, eh?" I remarked, reaching up, stroking my own face, surprising myself with the coarseness of the accumulated stubble of two and a half days that I found there.

"Yeah," said David, smiling. "It drives Anita wild."

"I'll bet," I said, sitting down next to him.

David took the last sip from a Heineken bottle. "You look like hell, cousin,"

"Thanks," I said.

He laughed and stood up. "Wanta beer?"

"Sure," I said.

He laughed again, patted my shoulder and entered the house.

A large sparkling swimming pool was stretched across the backyard. In the pool, at the shallow end, two young boys were playing—throwing a bright yellow tennis ball back and forth, shrieking. Beyond the pool a manicured lawn curved down a slight hill. At the bottom of the hill, at some indefinable point, the green of the lawn merged with the green of a golf course, which then spread itself out in all directions.

David stepped back out onto the lanai. He had a plateful of hamburger patties in one hand and two cold beers in the other. He passed one of the beers to me.

"Are both those kids yours?" I asked.

"No. Only the little blond-headed guy there," he said proudly. "The other one's a neighbor's kid from across the street. You know, you ought to have some kids. They're great."

"I'll just stick with beer for now," I said, raising my bottle.

"Your loss," said David. He moved over to a gas-fired grill situated at the edge of the lanai, lifted the lid and began dealing out hamburger patties. "Oh, by the way, I saw an old friend of yours today."

"Let me guess. Mason Brooks, detective extraordinaire."

"The same."

"Did he make an appointment?" I asked.

"Appointment, shit," said David, replacing the lid and sitting down again. "He and some other character just barged right in on me. And I had a client too. Ate up my last thirty minutes at the close. Son-of-a-bitch cost me some dollars. I told the fucker I wouldn't speak to him again unless he came by after hours. I don't need that kind of shit. I told him Anita was with Bradford, Turner and Wilson, and if he ever tried pulling that cheap shit on me again I'd file a civil suit against him for harassment so fast it'd make his fucking head spin. You've got to stand up to these pushy bastards."

"Right," I said. "What did he have to say?"

"Questions mostly. Like did I know any reason why anybody would want to whack Grandfather? And where was I last Wednesday night?"

"Where were you?" I asked, looking out at the golf course.

"At home with Anita and the kids, naturally. He also had a lot of questions about you and James and Laura. I'd watch out for that son-of-a-bitch if I were you. You can tell he's smart, and he's tricky. And he's going to nail somebody."

"It's not going to be me," I vowed.

"Just make sure it's not, 'cause I'd hate to have to drive all the way up to Starke just to visit you," said David, taking a sip of his beer.

Running along the length of the lanai, spaced at appropriate intervals, were half a dozen or more bird cages hanging from the ceiling—some elaborate, some plain, all occupied. Suddenly, simultaneously it seemed, the birds in the cages came to life, chirping and singing, making one hell of a racket. The sun was dropping fast now.

"Birds in cages, huh?" I observed. "You know the Chinese or the Japanese or somebody buy caged birds and release them whenever fate has been especially kind. But you keep them locked up, singing for your own pleasure. That's rather sad and selfish, don't you think?"

"Not all," said David, standing. "Just watch."

David walked over to the nearest cage and opened the door. The bird inside immediately stopped singing, hopped up to the open door and looked out. He poked his little head around the corner, twisted it up and down. Then he hopped back up onto his perch pole, turned his back to the door and began singing to the bars again.

"Some animals enjoy cages," explained David, shutting the bird cage door and returning to his seat. "It makes them feel secure."

"Yeah, and some people enjoy captivity too," I said.

"It's all relative," said David, taking another sip of his beer.

I was amazed at how far David had fallen. Burgers on the grill, kids in the pool, birds in cages. Thirty-six holes a weekend if it didn't rain, two weeks a year vacation regardless. Bide your time, protect your ass and hope the man in front of you croaks before they find out how incompetent you really are. It was depressing. And what was even more depressing was that David—the rebel, the terror of the establishment—seemed happy, satisfied.

I knew that I had to go out and get drunk tonight.

EIGHTEEN

My plan was a gem of uncomplicated thought: I would start drinking my way westward, stopping for a quick one at each bar that I came to, until I wound up painlessly back on Siesta Key. The program was valid, its intent noble, its execution, however, flawed. I had not calculated correctly how many grog-shops now lay between David's house and the beach. The outlying areas of the city had been growing rapidly; every half mile along my route seemed to possess at least one tavern.

Four hours and eight bars later I pulled up somewhat irregularly in front of Lizard's Long Neck Lounge. I was nearing home. In fact, this was my last stop before the bridge.

Lizard's Long Neck Lounge (known to all as simply Lizard's)—a place where the homicidal and the suicidal came together to meet and greet, where the short fuses sizzled and the time bombs ticked, where all manners of illicit pleasures could be purchased and then, depending on the vice, performed or consumed in the back parking lot, where people sat alone and drank and stared at blank walls or else shouted, danced and screamed. In short, it was my kind of place. Plus on the weekends they had a band; no cover charge.

I rolled up to the front door feeling the full effect of an excess of alcohol and a lack of substantive nutrition. I pushed open the door and was immediately assaulted by the loud shrill of electric guitars and untrained voices. To my left a spotlight filtered through a cloud of cigarette smoke to focus on four members of a band, all of whom I hoped had day jobs. To the right a cluster of tables was positioned directly in front of the speakers—some people just couldn't seem to get enough aggravation out of life. Ahead was a small dance floor filled with bobbing bodies. In the back was the bar.

I made my way through a swaying sea of baseball caps and cowboy hats up to the bar. In one corner several motorcycle boys wearing their colors were trying to intimidate a group of adventurous yuppies. In the opposite corner two undercover cops who everyone knew were staked out, watching with their ears.

I asked for a Beefeater with a splash and sat down on a vacant stool. Throughout the crowd there was a liberal sprinkling of refugees from the '60s, showing the physical results of lives ill-spent—gray beards and balding men with long loose strings of hair drooping from dissolving crowns, holding onto some hip myth not reflected in mirrors; the women slack-muscled, drugged out, generally sleazy. Behind me the bathrooms reeked of urine, and if one had been so desperately in need of relief as to enter one of these rooms they would have found phone numbers and sayings of wit and racism scrawled on the walls and plumbing that functioned only sporadically.

I took a sip of my drink and looked around the room. I saw no one I knew; it was just as well. I didn't care to engage in light pleasantries or philosophical debates. What I wanted, needed was a good deal less cerebral. A nice round young mouth and no conversation. There were several likely candidates on the dance floor. I decided to wait until the band took a break, which I hoped would be mercifully soon, and then see what I could negotiate.

One young girl in particular looked extremely promising—bud-breasted, gypsy-dark, dancing with an abandon that bordered on exhibitionism. She pumped and hunched and swung and shook it loose. Yet as I watched I couldn't tell with whom she was dancing. There was a wooden partition about four feet high between her and me. I imagined that her partner—for she kept looking down and laughing—must have been on his knees doing something either highly erotic or comic or both.

Finally—proving that there is a God—the music shrieked to a halt, and the young girl filed off the dance floor trailed by—and here proving that there are also dark forces in the universe as well—three midgets.

Midgets, I thought, almost uttered audibly. And I thought I was debauched.

The foursome settled cheerfully at a nearby table. I promptly ordered myself another drink. "Make it a double," I said. This, I knew, would, at the very least, be worth watching. Though for me watching has on occasion developed into something of a contact sport. For after several drinks my watching inevitable slips into unapologetic staring. It's a habit I've never been able to break. People just interest me.

The little guys kept jumping up, running around and sitting in each other's laps. The young girl kept laughing and drinking. I wondered if they might in some way be connected with the circus. Sarasota had once been the winter home of the Ringling Brothers, Barnum and Bailey Circus, and although they later folded their tents and moved down the coast to Venice, there was still a small collection of performers and other assorted personnel left in town.

At some point one of the laughing fellows noticed that I was watching them, probably staring by now, and they all calmed down. The little men began whispering among themselves. The young girl looked over and smiled in my direction. I raised my glass in a salute and smiled back.

One of the small men from the table suddenly stood, hiked up his pants and strutted over to where I sat. His face was red and angry; his head too large for his body. "What're you looking at?" he demanded.

"Not much," I said. I meant this not as an insult, not as a disparaging reference to the man's diminutive stature. It was simply the way the words came out.

"Oh, yeah," he said. "A funny guy, huh? Just wait." And with that he moved quickly and crookedly back to the table.

I turned and took a sip of my drink. And at that instant, I felt something solid whiz by my head. It ricocheted off a wall and spun around several times on the floor. Finally the object, intact, came to rest—a jar of Grey Poupon mustard. My first thought was somewhat illogical: I didn't even know they served food in this joint; then equally illogical: Imported mustard? Then from behind I felt a sharp piercing pain, and I turned to see the same angry little man below me, his face distorted, a penknife now in his hand. He was dancing back and forth, cursing and threatening me. I bent and reached out for him. And as I laid my hands upon him something shattered against the back of my skull, and my world faded to black.

When I finally came to, I found myself suspended between two strangers, heading for the door. The crowd in the bar was standing, laughing and applauding. Feebly, I raised a hand to acknowledge the applause, and then I was outside, seated on the curb.

'Hey, man, you oughta get that thing looked at," one of the men said. "I knew this guy that got shot in the ass while fucking somebody else's wife, and a week later the fucker died of some kinda lead poisoning or gangrene or something."

"I think I knew that guy," the other man said.

"Huh?" I asked.

"Your ass," the first man explained. "Better get it looked at."

Then both men re-entered the bar.

I lifted one cheek up off the sidewalk, touched a tender spot and brought away a hand smeared with blood. "I've been stabbed in the butt!" I shouted. "By a goddamn midget!"

Across the street and farther on, I could see Sarasota Memorial Hospital rising above the trees. Taking the man's advice, I limped to my car and drove myself around to the emergency room entrance.

The lights were bright; the staff was busy. A pretty blond dressed in white passed by.

"Excuse me, nurse," I called out.

The woman in the white jacket spun around and heaved her large pointed breasts into my face. Pulling a name tag pinned to her lapel close to my eyes, she snapped, "Doctor. Doctor Walker."

"Oh, of course," I said. "Excuse me."

"Well?" demanded the doctor.

I turned and pulled my hand away from my wound.

The doctor looked quickly, glanced at her clipboard and asked, "Do you have any medical insurance?"

"Yes, in fact I do," I said. "It's with—"

"All right. Room six." She pointed down the hallway. "Fill

these out." She handed me a stack of papers. "I'll be there shortly."

"Thank you," I said, and I walked on down the corridor. Crying, bleeding, broken bodies. The things we do to each other and ourselves.

As I was finishing up the admission forms the doctor entered the little cubicle. "What did you do?" she asked. "Sit on a nail?"

"No, I was stabbed—"

"Don't tell me," she said, holding up a hand. "I don't need the extra paperwork."

"Right," I said, handing her the forms.

She looked over the papers quickly, checked for my signature, then set them down on a table. "Okay," she said. "Drop 'em." She cleaned the wound, added a Band-Aid and threw in a tetanus shot.

"Can I get something for the pain?" I asked.

"It looks like that's what got you here in the first place," she observed.

She gave me two aspirin. I put them in my shirt pocket.

"Well, there you go, sweet cheeks," she said, patting my rump. "You won't be able to enter any hot buns contests for awhile, but you'll live."

"Tell me the truth, doc, how would you rate them?"

"Well," said the doctor, studying my posterior. "I've seen worse." She smiled and turned and walked to the door. "In a morgue."

NINETEEN

The next day I woke up feeling bent and broken. My head pounded; my body ached. There was no one in the bed beside me. Without looking out the window above my head, I could tell that it was going to be a miserable day (weather-wise). Eleven o'clock, the curtains drawn back and the room still semi-dark.

If I could have gone back to sleep, I certainly would have. But I couldn't, so I swung my feet onto the floor. I reached for a bottle of aspirin that I kept under my bed for just such emergencies. Naturally the bottle was empty. Had I been clever I might have remembered the two aspirin the doctor had given me the night before. But, needless to say, I was not clever.

I stumbled up onto my feet, gained a degree of equilibrium and turned to the window to confirm my suspicions: gray clouds merging with a gray sea; whitecaps kicking up midway out to the horizon; sand swirling; palms dancing in the wind; rain falling on the deserted beach.

I moved away from that cheerful scene and entered the bathroom. The reflection which greeted me in the mirror was only vaguely recognizable. Behind those baggy bloodshot eyes, beneath that scraggly beard, was the outline of a face that had smiled at me in more prosperous times. Today no smile was expected, and none received.

I was about to step into the shower in the vain hope that I could wash it all away and begin again from scratch, when I heard a knock at the front door. I walked back into the bedroom, gingerly slipped on a pair of jeans and stiff-legged-it downstairs to see who was compounding this disaster of a day.

I opened the door; I lifted my head. Briefly a figure passed through my blurred field of vision. A fist flew into my face. Pain—distinctly red in color—bounced from one end of my body to the other. I staggered backward, tripped over my tangled feet and landed on my already injured ass. Brooks stormed into the room. Dissimilar points of pain simultaneously called out for aid and attention. I rolled over onto my stomach. A foot flipped me over onto my back again.

"Payback's a motherfucker, isn't it, asshole?" demanded Brooks, standing over me, glaring down.

"Jesus Christ," I cried. "What's that for?"

"Everything," said Brooks, still standing over me, still glaring down.

Detective Dawson entered the room and shut the door behind him.

"Besides," continued Brooks, "I didn't want you to slip away before we could settle our account."

"I'm not going anywhere," I protested.

"You never know," Brooks said. He moved over to the sofa and sat down.

Detective Dawson plopped down next to him.

I worked myself up onto an elbow and wiggled my nose. It was bleeding slightly but didn't seem to be broken.

"I hear you've been out wrestling midgets," said Brooks, smiling.

"It wasn't much of a match."

"So I heard." Brooks looked around the room. "Where's your girlfriend?"

"Lauderdale. She went to visit her mother."

"Convenient," said Brooks. "After you left Lizard's last night, where'd you go?"

"You tell me."

"To the hospital."

"You've got more spies than the Russians."

"And then?"

"Home."

"Maybe," said Brooks, leaning back, lighting a cigarette. "And maybe not. Maybe you went hunting."

"For what?" I asked.

"Whores."

"No doubt, this is all leading up to something, so why don't you just tell me what it is that you think I've done and quit fucking around."

"We're talking murder. Again."

"Brooks," I said, sitting up, "your head's getting soft, your brain's getting weak. Why don't you go back to Tallahassee and do whatever it is that you do up there, because you're not even close this time."

"As I said, maybe and maybe not."

Brooks was wearing another one of his expensive three-piece suits—this one a light tan color. His face was enveloped in a wreath of cigarette smoke. His eyes were intense. His smile had evaporated.

"Early this morning, around three o'clock," he began, "the semi-nude body of a young white female, sixteen to twenty years of age, was discovered in the parking lot of the Van Wezel Auditorium. She had a bullet in her brain and her hands in her underpants. She hadn't been dead for more than a couple of hours. The bullet came from a small caliber weapon. Perhaps a .22. Perhaps from a .22 caliber, ten-shot, semi-automatic, blue-steel Ruger. Perhaps from the same weapon that killed your grandfather. Judging by the girl's clothes—they were in a neat little pile next to the body—and the circumstances surrounding her death, we believe that she was a prostitute working 41. We're running a computer search on her fingerprints and checking the motels along the Trail, but I believe her occupation is a pretty safe bet.

"Now you say you went home last night like a good boy after you left the hospital. Well, maybe. Or maybe you went out looking for something strange. And maybe you found it."

"And maybe you're full of shit," I said, sitting up somewhat straighter. "All I'm hearing from you is a lot of supposition, a lot of perhaps and maybe."

"You're becoming defensive."

"Defensive?" I laughed. "I can't imagine why."

"Well, we'll know more when we get the coroner's report. But for right now what we need is a hair sample."

"A hair sample?" I asked.

"If you didn't do it, then you have nothing to hide, right?"

I thought for a minute. "All right, asshole, but I'll tell you one damn thing, this is all going to make you look mighty fucking stupid."

"Detective," said Brooks.

Detective Dawson pulled himself up out of the sofa and removed a small pair of scissors and a plastic baggie from his inner coat pocket.

"Just a little off the top," I said, running my fingers through my hair.

Detective Dawson stopped and looked back at Brooks.

"Not exactly," said Brooks, smiling again. "You see we found a hair, a blond pubic hair, in the dead girl's mouth. So that leads us to believe that she was performing an act of oral copulation on someone at the time of her death. A full coroner's report will tell us whether or not she succeeded in accommodating her client before she was killed."

"So you think someone came and she went."

"Precisely."

"And you think that that someone is me."

"It's a thought."

"Okay, but tell me, what were her hands doing in her underwear?"

"Maybe the client, maybe you, asked her to play along."

"You're corrupt. And you're wrong. I don't blow away whores and I don't get blow jobs in parking lots."

"Prove it to me," said Brooks.

"You know I don't have to," I said. "This is an invasion of privacy or an illegal search and seizure or something."

"I know."

"But just 'cause you're such a shithead, Brooks, I'm going to do it."

"Detective," said Brooks.

I stood up and unbuttoned my jeans. If I hadn't been so angry, I might have felt marginally embarrassed. But I didn't. I just wanted to show Brooks what a fool he was and to get him off my case. I had had more than enough of his unfunny crap to last a lifetime.

Detective Dawson moved around from behind the campaign chest and knelt down on one knee. He flapped open his baggie and placed it on the floor. Carefully, he selected several strands of hair and separated them from the rest. With his scissors he took aim.

"I'll bet you enjoy your work," I observed.

Detective Dawson looked up and smiled. Slowly he lowered the scissors. He twirled the strands once around his thick forefinger. "Sometimes," he said. Then he gave the hairs a good hard yank.

TWENTY

After Brooks and Detective Dawson had gone, taking with them their most rudely extracted sample, I moved into the kitchen and made myself a cup of coffee. With the coffee in hand, I stepped out onto the lanai—I was still hurting—and called my cats. The animals were hiding somewhere, probably just under the house, and there they'd remain until the rain had ceased. I walked back inside and eased myself down into the recliner.

I could feel the noose tightening. I could see my options fading away. The hovering darkness of the day and the general emptiness of the house itself further depressed me. I had to escape. If I simply sat and waited I felt as though I would surely sink into a state of complete apathy. I decided to go back out to Devon Woods and have another little chat with Fulton. Maybe he could offer a new perspective on life and events. He was a wise old man.

I went back upstairs, showered, again passed on a shave—it just seemed like too much of an effort—threw on some clothes and was gone.

It was probably close to one o'clock by the time I reached the farm. The rain was still coming down. The fields were deserted—not a man or beast in sight. The farm buildings looked extra drab.

I drove around to the back and pulled up in front of Fulton's quarters. Immediately he appeared in the open doorway: a freshly pressed blue work shirt, a drink in his hand. He smiled and motioned for me to enter. I slipped out of my car and ran for the door.

"Raining," observed Fulton, waving his glass toward the outside world.

"It sure is," I agreed, shaking myself off.

"We needed it," he explained.

"I guess."

"What're you drinking?" he asked. (This was a rather odd question. Fulton only drank Heaven Hill whiskey, and everyone knew that he stocked nothing else.)

"Whatever you're having," I said.

"Wise decision," said Fulton. He walked around to a rickety little table, picked up a glass, looked through it, then poured in a couple of inches of whiskey. "You eaten yet?" he asked.

"No," I replied.

"Good," he said. He crossed over to a small refrigerator in his cooking corner—a stove, pots and pans and dishes laying about—and retrieved an egg. He cracked the egg, added it to the glass, then handed the glass to me. "If it doesn't kill you, it'll cure you."

"Thanks," I said. I looked down at the egg yolk floating bright yellow on the golden brown surface. It didn't appear to be especially dangerous, but it didn't look overly appetizing either.

I raised my glass; Fulton raised his. I shut my eyes and threw it back. The egg and the whiskey merged, then slipped quickly down my throat.

Fulton laughed, snatched the glass from my hand and farted. "Whoa, boy!" he exclaimed. "We're having some fun now. Sit down, son."

There were two large easy chairs in the room. I landed in one.

Fulton refilled my glass with five ounces of whiskey, added a tablespoon of sugar and splashed in a little sulfur-tainted well water from a pitcher on the table. He handed the glass back to me and sat down in the other easy chair. "So?" he asked.

"Well," I said—and then I explained what had transpired in the forty-eight or so hours since I had last seen him.

"A heap of shit," he conceded after I had ticked off my list of complaints.

"And so I've come to you," I said, "for advice and counseling."

"If you're guilty, get a lawyer. If you're innocent, don't worry about it."

"That's all?" I asked, amazed, angry, disappointed.

"That's it. It doesn't do any good to get yourself all worked up over things you can't control. I talked to that detective fellow—"

"Brooks."

"Yes, Brooks," said Fulton, taking a sip of his drink. "Now as I understand it he might not be just too favorably disposed toward you because you tried to drown him when you boys were only kids, but—"

"I didn't—"

"Don't interrupt me, son. But I don't believe that the past will unduly influence him. He seems like a fair enough minded man to me. He knows literature. He admired one of my poems when he was out here the other day. Any man who appreciates good poetry can't be all bad in my book."

"Jesus," I sighed.

"Don't start praying now, son," Fulton advised. "It's entirely overrated and, in your case, it's entirely too late. Man by nature isn't a beggar, he's a demander. If you have to reach out in someway I recommend cursing. I've always found it to be extremely cathartic."

I could tell that Fulton had been drinking for a good while and was in an expansive mood, so I just sat back and let him expand.

"You know, I'll be sorry to be leaving this place," he said.

"Where're you going?" I asked.

"The way of all flesh. Dust to dust, ashes to ashes."

"Oh," I said.

"Yeah, with your grandfather going off and getting himself so properly recycled like he did, it set my mind to thinking, to wondering, to worrying. You see, I'm the only one left who knows the story, the whole story. And if I don't tell it to someone it'll all die with me."

"What story?" I asked.

"Your story. The story of your heritage."

[157]

"I might not be exactly the best one to tell," I said. "I don't know how long I'm going to be around here either."

"Well, that doesn't matter. You're here now and I'm ready to tell. Want another drink?"

"Might as well," I said, handing over my half-empty glass.

Fulton stood up, freshened our drinks and returned. He handed one of the glasses to me and sat down again.

"Now, son, you know precious little about your family, about those who came before you."

"Well, it's never been exactly a prime topic of conversation," I said.

"Yes, I know. Strange. Strange family."

"You're not telling me anything I don't already know."

"Well, I will," he said. He leaned forward and cut loose with a foul one. He picked up an old photograph in a small silver antique frame and passed it over to me. "You know who that is?"

"No," I said, looking at the faded grainy photograph—a tall handsome man with one arm, standing in front of a wood frame house; white steps leading up to a porch and then a door; the door open yet within only darkness.

"That, son, is your great-grandfather, Adam Clay."

"What?" I exclaimed. "But we were always told there were no photographs of him. No paintings, pictures, drawings."

"Only one," said Fulton.

I looked at the photograph, the man, again: the loose jacket sleeve—the clothing dark and heavy—folded in half and pinned at the shoulder; the good arm resting on the banister; one foot—a square-toed boot—on the bottom step; the body half-turned as if inviting one inside; on his head a broad-brimmed hat; the man's hair white, flowing out from under the hat; the nose slender, birdlike; the face wrapped in an untidy mass of white beard; the eyes fierce, unapologetic, looking out over the years, decades, a century gone now; the eyes threatening, daring; the eyes laughing at the seriousness of the threat.

"But where, how—"

"In a box, left to me, left to me to keep and hold, by your grandmother. And how, where she got it—probably stole it from wherever it was hidden one night—I don't know."

"Jesus, I can't—"

"I told you the time for prayers has passed. That man never prayed."

"All right," I said. "You've got my attention. I'm listening."

"Where and when precisely he was born, I don't know. He may not have known himself. Suffice it to say that the place was somewhere in the northern hills of Alabama, and the time some few years before the Civil War. At least enough time for him to hear the drums and the bugles and see the flags and the uniforms and watch the soldiers marching young and proud and the girls and the mothers waving and crying. And again him being old enough or at least tall enough to find the captain's desk and sign his name or make his mark and have his right hand shaken—maybe the first and last time he ever had his right hand shaken by a gentleman. And then off to war. But not in defense of slavery or states' rights or any other rights or unrights, but just for the drums and the flags and the waving crying women, most of whom wouldn't have looked at him twice on the street. And probably, in truth, for him anyway, anything was better than going back to that farm and plowing those few desperate acres from sunrise to sunset. Because now, you see, at least he had a uniform—or part of one.

"So away they marched, the women and the drums and the flags nowhere to be seen now—well, all right, they had one (a flag) because they had to remember who they were, which side they were on—marching in the rain and the cold and the heat and the sun, looking for that other flag and that other group of young boys ready to die for what neither group understood, thinking, wondering what they had all gotten themselves into. Then somebody yelled 'Charge!' and someone else whooped out a rebel yell and they were off. Musket balls and bayonets and sabers, young boys dropping right and left, flames and cannon flashes, and always the screaming, of pain, of fear, of dying. And whether or not he ever got to fire his rifle, I don't know. Because one of those loose-flying-unaimed-lucky-shot musket balls tore into his right arm and he dropped or fainted. And later, when the smoke had cleared, when the armies like two mindless beasts had separated to lick their wounds and regroup and get ready for another turn at each other, he was found and taken to the doctor's tent. And the doctor, knee-deep in death and dying and mud and blood and guts and body parts, must have said, 'Oh hell, another one. Give me the saw.'

"Then it was over, the peace, the surrender, the whatever signed, and the officers saluted—'Good game.' And then they went home, some walking, some being carried, some—like your great-grandfather; he was in as good a shape as he was ever going to get by this time—riding a horse if they had one or could steal one, because the other general had agreed to allow them to keep their animals for the next season's plowing. Hell, he had already re-won half a damn country back, so what did he need with a few starving horses?

"And so he lost an arm and gained a horse—a better swap than a lot of them made—and rode back home. But, you see, there was no home left, no house, no physical structure, only a few bricks and pieces of burned lumber, and the people, his people, family gone too, leaving no word, note or communication. So standing there looking at what was no longer there, his horse beside him tearing at the ground, reminding him of his own hunger, with no drums now, no flags, no smiling ladies, only the rain and the red clay mud, he looked down and thought: Clay. And thus was he reborn or at least re-christened, because, you see, the old name had done him absolutely no good and he needed to begin again. So the new name was Clay, and where the Adam part came from, came to him—maybe standing in front of another desk with another gentleman behind it, ready to sign his name again, but this time not for song and glory but just for wages, food—I don't know. Maybe out of some distant bible reading: Adam, the first man, a new man. At least he didn't call himself Jesus or Judas."

"So it was all made up then," I said. "The name I mean."

"A man can call himself anything he wants. What matters is whether or not he can stand and face the door when the name is called."

Fulton pulled himself up out of his chair, walked over to his desk, picked up his pipe and leather tobacco pouch and returned. He lowered himself again into the chair, eased off a silent one and packed his pipe. He then lit the pipe.

"At some point, after some years," he began again, "your

great-grandfather found himself in New Orleans, which even today is the way many visitors arrive in that wondrous city. They wake up one morning, reach for their wallet and discover that they're in New Orleans. Your great-grandfather, however, was somewhat luckier than many in that he at least knew where his wallet was. And so it was here in New Orleans, in that fair southern city of charm and beauty and evil that he killed his first man. At least it was a Yankee, which must have been of some minor comfort to him. It had something to do with a woman. Naturally. A woman, two men and a pistol. Well, the pistol went off, the woman screamed and your great-grandfather decided that a change of address would suit him just fine.

"He boarded a southbound sailing ship—he had acquired by this time a certain skill at the one-handed dealing of cards, and the winning which is so necessary if one is to pursue that career—and watched with pleasure and satisfaction as the blue of the Gulf of Mexico replaced the brown of the Mississippi River and its estuaries. By nature a restless man, he must have walked the deck of that ship for almost an entire afternoon before he could scout up a game. And fortunately for him the captain of this particular vessel fancied himself to be something of a wizard at games of chance. And it was here that your great-grandfather made one of those decisions that people sometimes make, which, in retrospect, irreversibly change their lives. After he—your great-grandfather—had relieved the captain of what gold he personally had on hand, as well as the future earnings of the man's next three voyages to the Caribbean and back to New Orleans again, he offered to return to the captain all monies that had been won—minus the customary ten-percent fool's tax—cancel all debts owed and teach the captain how to play the game so that he would not again have his pride and pocket so deeply wounded, in exchange for which the captain would educate him in the rudiments of sailing and navigation. It was a fair trade all around. By the time the ship docked at Port-au-Prince, your great-grandfather had picked up a backup skill and the captain stood a better than even chance of not getting cleaned out again in the immediate future.

"In Port-au-Prince your great-grandfather acquired, won, bought a small sailing schooner and began the life of an island trader. He had a few local boys to hoist the sails and swab the deck and load and unload cargo while he stood behind the wheel and shouted orders and negotiated the contracts. And so it was the life of easy adventure now—the sea and the wind, the exotic ports-of-call and the even more exotic women, the rum and still the turning of the cards. Then after more than twenty-five years your great-grandfather, probably pushing out on the other side of fifty now, decided that it was time to slow it down, to retire. He chose Tampa. And why Tampa? I don't know. Maybe he had visited it once in his trading days and liked what he saw, the wild Caribbean atmosphere for his soul and the moderately stable political climate for his money. At least he was home again—more or less.

"But retirement for a man like your great-grandfather was not more possible than keeping an unchained lunatic home-bound on a full moon night. Despite the money—he had more than enough now—and the games and yes, still the women, he rapidly became restless. So he bought—again, won or bought— a shallow draught steamer (he was through with sailing now) and set himself up as a commercial shipping concern. His route was between Tampa and Sarasota. His cargo was primarily fish and people. His rate was a penny a pound for both.

"And one mildly amusing little anecdote here: once while loading a group of pilgrims at the Tampa docks for a run down to Sarasota, a preacher with the group objected to your great-grandfather's practice of pricing people with savable souls and salted fish at the same rate. So your great-grandfather, conceding the apparent injustice of his rate schedule, offered to accommodate the gentleman by doubling the price for human cargo. At which point the preacher promptly shut up and stepped onto the scales.

"And so Tampa to Sarasota, Sarasota to Tampa, back and forth. But still something was lacking, was missing from his life. And that something was an heir, a male heir, to carry on his name—even if he had made it up himself while standing in the mud. He still needed, wanted something to show that he had been here, had breathed the air, had lived.

"And when he saw her—your great-grandmother, a young giggling girl then, sitting at the docks in Sarasota, maybe waiting for a package or a letter—it didn't take long. A few tall tales, a kiss in the moonlight (even a one-armed man can kiss and lie), a ring, the words, the bed and bam, the first one, the only one, out of the chute—your grandfather. January 12th, 1900. Yes, I know the date.

"So, seeing the result, your great-grandfather—he didn't want to go to all the trouble of packing and moving until he was sure—relocated himself down in Sarasota and let the rest of his hand play itself out. It was only a matter of time now."

"And what about you?" I asked.

"What about me?" countered Fulton.

"You said grandfather—January 12th, 1900. What about you?"

"Oh, me. Yes, the next year—1901. My mother the daughter of a fisherman, my father a crewman on your great-grandfather's steamer. I was born, my mother died, my father vanished, went drunk, went crazy. My mother's people wouldn't have anything to do with me, considered me a Jonah or something. So your great-grandfather took me in, called me son and treated me like one."

"And then it was just waiting?"

"That's right. Waiting. Your great-grandmother died in the hurricane of 1911. You've seen pictures of her, haven't you?"

"Yes," I said.

"I thought so. And your great-grandfather lived on a few more years, then died the violent man's, the gambler's, the bandit's perfect death—drank his shot of good night brandy, laid his head down on his pillow and never woke up."

What light was now left in the day was a gray unpleasant color. Fulton stood up, turned off the overhead fan and lit a kerosene lamp. (He had electricity—thus the fan—but sometimes, for effect, he liked to go primitive.) "Another one?" he asked.

"Sure," I said, extending my empty glass. "I'm going to use your facilities." I stood; my head spun; I staggered.

"Through that door," he said.

When I returned there was another full glass on the table next to my chair and Fulton was seated, ready to begin again.

"All right," I said, taking my seat.

"Yes. All right. So after the lawyers and the bankers got

through with your great-grandfather's estate there was nothing left."

"Nothing?" I asked. "But what about the boat? And there must have been a house. You said he had plenty of money."

"Debts. You can never have too much money."

"All right," I said, taking a sip of my drink and settling back into my chair.

"So your grandfather and I were left to fend for ourselves. He was fourteen, I a year younger. Your grandfather became a carpenter's apprentice. A friend of your great-grandfather, a lawyer who was slowly going blind, hired me as his clerk, his bartender, his eyes. My chief duties were making these"— Fulton held up his glass—"and reading to him. And reading not the law, but Homer, Shakespeare, Shelley, Keats. You see how things work out. It's all fated.

"And then after a couple of years the lawyer too slipped his chains, leaving me his books and his bottles, and I was again on the street. Your grandfather by this time had gone independent, and he hired me on as a helper. It wasn't as much fun as drinking and reading, but then again the chances of my having landed another job as a reading bartender were limited. You have to take what you can get.

"Then a few years more and it was war again. But now the war to end all wars, and I went off to die a noble and heroic death, only to discover that all the poets had lied to me, and that there was little that was either noble or heroic in death— only death itself, dirty and silent and cold. And whoever started that rumor about dying for your country, about dying well, about the great sacrifice, should have had his body drawn and quartered and his head stuck on a pole at the entranceway to all wars so that the participants would know to hope for nothing.

"But not your grandfather. Whereas I volunteered—in fact, I had to lie about my age, not that anyone really cared—he waited. And it was not that he was a coward, afraid to fight. No. It was simply that as he saw it, it was a waste of valuable time. There was no money to be made sloshing around in the mud in France. Hell, there wasn't even anything to loot or steal. It was here, in this country, that there were opportunities for a bright boy. And that was far more important to him—the opportunities, the money—than what a bunch of politicians and generals thought or believed. Because, you see, that's just the way his priorities were arranged.

"But then came the draft, and it looked like they might have him. But no one had counted on how resourceful, even at that early age—eighteen—he could be. He found himself a doctor, you see, and made a deal. Your grandfather knew the man was no gentleman. The doctor was probably not even shocked by the proposition. Your grandfather was always a good judge of character—or lack of it. The deal was that your grandfather would add to the doctor's house three new rooms free of charge—he had his own crew now, his own company—and in return the doctor would certify him medically unfit for military service. So the hands shook and your grandfather remained free on his own recognizance.

"Then came November 11, 1918, and the Armistice. And now your grandfather had no further need of the doctor's services, so the work on the house came to a stop. It had always been a go-slow project, because, you see, your grandfather didn't know how long it would take, how many young men needed to die before the quotas were filled and the opposing nations could honorably declare that they'd had enough. And then the whispers and the funny looks started. So your grandfather went back to the source, found the weakness and exploited it. He married the doctor's only daughter—your grandmother. And fast enough the whispers stopped. And in time the rooms were finished. And after that neither man ever spoke to the other again."

"But did they love each other?" I asked.

"Who?"

"Grandfather and Grandmother."

"Maybe. At first. Or maybe she just wanted to get out of the house. Maybe she was impressed by this young man with his shirt off, shouting at the other older men, telling them what to do. I don't know and it doesn't matter. So they were married—and no one bothered to ask anyone's permission either, as I'm sure you can imagine. Maybe she did it, agreed to it, out of spite, as a way of lashing out against her first captor. I don't know. I was still in France then, being shuffled from one hospital to another—shot twice, gassed once.

"Well, finally I made it home, and how things had changed. Then I realized that things were in fact the same, exactly the same, and that it was me who had changed. But still there was a difference, no doubt. That's why your cousin James and I get along, why he trusts me. We understand. Because we see something of ourselves in each other. Because it's all the same—all wars, all fighting, all dying."

"And James?" I asked.

"I expect we'll be hearing from him soon enough," said Fulton, repacking his pipe and putting a match to it. "He's out there. I know it."

Out there, it was totally dark now. The wind was still blowing, the rain still falling. A small green lizard scampered across the floor, crawled up one wall and leaped onto Fulton's desk.

"But now back again," said Fulton. "Call it 1920, and I came home to a different me. And by now your grandfather was already moving up the path to prosperity and beyond. He was branching out. Oh yes, he was still in the construction business—with three crews on the job instead of just that one—but now he was getting into property ownership and sales, rent collection, management and finance. And that last one, finance, bordered more on loan sharking—interest as high as 30%—than on any legitimate banking activity. And he was more than willing, perhaps even eager, to confiscate any collateral put up against a loan that fell delinquent.

"So I got back and your grandfather asked me to come in with him. As a partner, he said. But I knew the truth would be something less. And I was tired of taking orders. Then I saw your grandmother—a beautiful woman, she was, refined and charming; wearing, that first time I saw her, a single blue sapphire around her neck, the color matching her eyes; her long blond hair pulled up—and it looked like your grandfather already had everything in the world anyway. And I had nothing, least of all a woman like your grandmother. So I went up to Tampa and shipped out on a tramp steamer for Europe again. And there for more than ten years I lived the life of a vagabond poet. And it wasn't a bad life either—the living was cheap, the women cheaper, the people interesting and always new things to see. So I wandered. Europe, the Middle East, India, the Far

East, Africa. Working when I had to, but mostly just traveling, moving from one place to another, trying to forget her."

"Trying to forget who?" I asked.

"Her," said Fulton, pointing at the painting on his wall, the nude painting of the young woman that I had seen so many times before. "Your grandmother. The one woman I'd met just one time and couldn't forget."

"What?" I cried.

"Yes," said Fulton. "I loved her from the first moment I saw her, coming down the stairs at your grandfather's house by the bay, at a dinner party that he gave in my honor when I returned home."

I was stunned; I couldn't speak. I could only gaze up at the painting and think: Grandmother? Grandmother?

"And later, when I came back from my ten years of exile, she told me how she felt, how she felt about me, how she had been waiting for my return, how she had always known that someday I'd be back. And so we became lovers."

"Wait! Wait!" I cried again.

"Oh, you needn't worry, son. I'm not your secret bastard grandfather. Your father and his brothers had already—"

"No, no." I shouted. "It's just—"

But Fulton wasn't listening; he was remembering, reliving.

"And we had our own little place in town, she and I. Your house now, the beach house. She had it all planned out and was just waiting for me to come back, and I didn't even know it, didn't even dare to consider that the possibility existed. Wandering the back roads of the world, following strange women up back stairways, drinking until I passed out.

"To your grandmother," said Fulton, standing, his glass in his hand. "Up!" he commanded.

I stumbled to my feet.

We turned, faced the painting and raised our glasses.

"To Margaret O'Shaughnessy Clay," declared Fulton. "The most beautiful woman I've ever known. May she forgive me for the years I made us miss because I just didn't know."

We drank.

Fulton swept the empty glass out of my hand. "Another drink? It looks like you could use one."

"I could," I said, and I collapsed back into my seat.

Fulton tottered over to the table—he was getting fairly well lit by now—mixed up a new batch of high octane and returned. He handed me my drink, slipped into his chair and began again.

"And so when I came back that second time, after the ten years, I found that your grandfather had bought this place, and he asked me to come out here and manage it for him. And it was then, one bright afternoon shortly after I'd arrived and set myself up in this very room, that she came to me and told me how she felt. And I didn't know whether to laugh for joy or cry for the time that I'd squandered.

"And sometimes when he was away overnight or longer on business she'd dismiss the servants and send the boys into town to stay with their friends and invite me in. And we would pretend that this was the way we really lived—both of us smoking his cigars, drinking his cognac and making love on the floor.

"Then one day, suddenly and without warning, in the early '50s it was, she broke it off, called a halt to it. And she never told me why. She was like that. But at least I'd had twenty years on and off with her—on a secondhand, behind-the-back basis admittedly. But still, in the end, that was one whole hell of a lot better than nothing at all.

"And as for your grandfather, he continued to prosper, to buy and sell and buy some more. And he didn't need a degree in business administration or in anything else. It was all just common sense and a large streak of sheer meanness. Through the '30s, the '40s, the '50s, and then you yourself saw it, began to notice it, the pattern, the method to his madness—watching the business cycles, waiting for an opportunity, scheming. Boom to bust and back again. Wait until they panic, then buy 'em out, sometimes force 'em out, over the edge, engineer their downfall. Nothing was above or below him. And it didn't matter too much to him what it was that he was buying as long as it looked like somewhere down the line it could be of some value. In fact, often times it was more important to him who owned it rather than what it was—land, buildings, homes, hotels, livestock, orange groves, shares in a company, whole businesses, any business. He was impartial. He'd ruin anybody. See it, spot it, wait for the cycle to turn, for the debt to get too heavy, for the panic to set in, then buy it—pennies on the dollar—hold it awhile, build it up, make it better, wait a bit longer, make 'em hungry, make 'em beg, then sell it at a premium—anything and everything, nothing was sacred. Some of the things he bought he didn't even see them; he just knew who owned them. Yes, your grandfather was a man . . ."

And at some point Fulton must have stopped talking, must have stopped trying to explain—although I don't remember when that might have been—and pushed me out the door. Because the next morning, fully dressed, shoes on, I woke up in my own bed with the telephone ringing in my ears and my liquor-soaked brain pounding in my head.

TWENTY-ONE

Through a grayish deep-sleep fog, faint at first, then louder, I heard it. I reached out blindly, knocked a lamp off the bedside table and picked up the telephone.

"Hello," I moaned, lowering my head back onto the pillow.

"Good morning, Mr. Clay," sang out a cheerful voice. "My name is Jennifer and I'm calling for the American Cremation Society. We're offering, for this week only, special rates in your area on a wide variety of services. First, we're offering—"

"Wait," I pleaded, pressing my hand to my forehead, trying to equalize the pressure. "Cremation?"

"Yes, Mr. Clay," the voice happily continued. "My name is Jennifer and I'm calling for the American Cremation Society, and we're offering, for this week only, special rates—"

"All right, " I said. "Where's Brooks?"

"Brooks?" asked a puzzled Jennifer. "I'm sorry. I don't understand."

"Brooks!" I shouted, sitting up much too fast. "Goddamn Mason Brooks! Did he put you up to this? How much is he paying you?"

"Mr. Clay, I'm sorry. There is no Mr. Brooks here. But if you'd like, I could let you speak with—"

"Wait," I said, lowering myself slowly back into a position of throbbing recline. "Hold on. Let me get this straight. You're calling me at"—I glanced over at the clock on the table—"ten-thirty on a Sunday morning to see if I want to get my bones toasted once I croak, right? At a discount, correct?"

"Well, sir, in the profession we prefer the term—"

"Listen, lady,—"

"Jennifer."

"Oh, right. Listen, Jennifer, screw you and screw the profession. And why don't you go out and get yourself a real goddamn job and quit bothering people on Sunday morning!"

I slammed the telephone down.

Jesus, I thought, a goddamn phone solicitor. For a fucking crematorium. What a creepy ass job.

Grandfather's funeral was slated for noon, out at Devon Woods. (Special permission had been granted, regulations waived, so that he could be buried out there, next to Grandmother. Apparently one couldn't be planted just anywhere.) If I went back to sleep I knew that I wouldn't wake up again until after dark, and if I didn't put in an appearance my absence might be misinterpreted as a sign of lack of love and respect.

I forced myself out of bed, stripped off my clothes from the night before and stumbled into the bathroom.

"Christ," I said, looking at myself in the mirror. I picked up my hairbrush, squeezed out a white line of toothpaste along its length and began brushing my hair. "What the fuck?" I asked, looking at myself again in the mirror. I dropped the brush into the sink and stepped into the shower.

It had been an inauspicious beginning.

After my shower I cleaned my brush, brushed my teeth (twice) and decided that the time for a shave had arrived. The electric razor screamed in my ear and my beard seemed more than a little resistant, but in time, with only one cut, I discovered a hidden face, worn and somewhat pale. "Morning," I said to the unfaltering reflection.

I went back into my bedroom, found a clean pair of jeans and a clean shirt and slipped them on. On light feet, with a light head, I groped my way downstairs.

In the kitchen I opened the refrigerator and found a cup of cherry yogurt and two Miller Lites. Taking the yogurt and one of the beers, I moved into the living room and sat down in the recliner. I turned on the television: cartoons, preachers, politicians—one and the same. I turned off the television and ate and drank my breakfast in silence.

Soon the digital timer on the VCR read eleven-thirty. I removed the second beer from the refrigerator for the ride and drove on out to Devon Woods.

The sun was shining; there was a light breeze from out of the west. It was a lovely day for a funeral. I pulled in behind Daniel's dark green Jaguar and got out. There were eight or ten other cars parked in front of the house. Not surprisingly one of these was a black Corvette.

I walked around to the back of the house, to a little clearing off to one side of Grandmother's rose garden. A small group was gathered together, talking quietly. I walked on and joined this group. Before I could enter the conversation, a clerical person of some unknown and unannounced persuasion cleared his throat and requested our attention. We all turned toward the hole and the casket suspended above it. The minister began his act.

Daniel, David, David's wife (no children), Laura, Michele, Vanessa, Fulton, Simon, the rest of the household staff, a few of the workmen—hats in hand—and me. No sons (as Father had predicted), no friends, no business associates. Hell, he was dead. There was no longer any need to pretend.

The minister was brief and to the point—"we are gathered . . . sinner . . . forgive . . . comfort . . . amen." Fulton then stepped forward and began reading a poem that he had crafted for the occasion. As he read the workmen removed the wooden slats supporting the coffin and lowered the box into the ground. Not much; fifteen minutes tops. The scent of roses in the air.

Once Grandfather was safely and securely deposited in the earth, those in attendance broke momentarily into groups of twos and threes, spoke quickly, then hurried toward their automobiles. I stood alone and watched the dirt going into the hole.

After awhile I could feel someone standing behind me. I knew who it was. Nevertheless I turned.

"Ah, Mutt and Jeff," I said.

"Making sure he won't come back to haunt you?" asked Brooks.

"Amusing," I said.

Brooks stepped up next to me. We looked at each other for a second, then focused on the hole. It was filling rapidly.

"I just thought that I'd drop by to see who showed up," offered Brooks after a moment.

"Any surprises?" I asked.

"Not really. Both of your uncles have been out of town for more than a week. Dr. Jack Clay has been in Chicago with one of his nurses attending an AMA meeting, and Mr. Philip Clay has been in Washington lobbying for some type of citrus import quota bill. And as we both know your father is in Spain. But still one might have thought, perhaps even hoped—"

"All right. Cut the shit. So what are you telling me? That in your opinion my uncles and my father should've been here for the funeral, or that they all have adequate alibis?"

"Well, their reasons for not being here are naturally their own, but as to their alibis, they're a hell of a lot better than yours."

"Give it a rest, Brooks. Just give it a fucking rest."

"I'd love to," said Brooks, kicking a few dirt clods into the hole. "But things just seem to keep coming back to you."

"In what way?" I asked.

"Well, like this deal with the whore who get whacked Saturday morning."

"What about it?" I demanded. "I know damn well the hair sample couldn't have matched. So what've you got?"

"Yes, sadly you're right," said Brooks. "The hair sample didn't match. And Detective Dawson was so hopeful. Weren't you, Dectective?"

"Hopeful," said the detective, directly behind me now.

"But, you see, we also conducted a search of the area around the Van Wezel and of the bay itself, and guess what one of the divers came up with?"

"Spanish treasure?"

"Even better. A gun. A pistol. A .22 caliber, ten-shot, semi-automatic, blue-steel Ruger. Your pistol. The numbers checked out."

"My pistol?" I asked, dumbfounded.

"Without a doubt," said Brooks. "Unfortunately the pistol was wiped clean so we couldn't get any prints. But a ballistics report confirms that the bullets taken from the whore—we still don't know her name yet—and from your grandfather all came from the same pistol. Again: your pistol."

"Wait!" I shouted. "Wait just a goddamn minute!"

Brooks was smiling; Detective Dawson was breathing down my neck—foul gusts of onion-breath.

"Now I told you that goddamn thing was stolen from me! More than six fucking months ago!"

"You told me," conceded Brooks. "But that doesn't necessarily make it true. You've told me a lot of shit so far. Maybe it was stolen or may be you just reported it stolen. Perhaps you've been planning this thing for a long while."

"I didn't plan anything!" I protested. "I didn't do anything!"

Brooks just looked at me and smiled.

The pressure was on; the roads were blocked. I was desperate.

"All right, listen," I said. "I've got this duplex. Downtown. Nobody knows about it. 1857 Oak Street. I was there Wednesday night. With Susie Allen. John Allen's wife. You go there. I'll give you the key. Take your fingerprint people. Dust the place. Get a set of her fingerprints. Then go see her. Confront her. Alone. Show her the prints. Tell her where you got them. She can't lie. She'll have to admit that she was there. With me. Wednesday night."

'I've already talked to her once," said Brooks calmly. "Naturally she lied. Everybody connected with this damn case lies. Besides even if we did find a set of her prints it would only tell us that she had been there, not when."

"Christ," I said, shaking my head, looking out across the grave.

Somewhere in the garden a bird was singing. White billowy clouds whirred by overhead. In a nearby pasture two colts ran and pranced about.

"All right," said Brooks finally. He held out his hand. "Give me the fucking key. 1857 Oak. We'll check it."

With unsteady fingers I slipped the key off my key ring and dropped it into Brook's hand.

He passed the key to Detective Dawson, turned, took two steps, then turned back. "Don't even dream about leaving town," he said.

Detective Dawson patted me on the shoulder, smiled, then joined Brooks. Together they disappeared into Grandmother's garden.

The workmen were finishing up the grave now. A few more pats of the shovel, smoothing it over, rounding it off. The grass sod and the granite headstone—identical to Grandmother's, both bought at the time of her death, his held in storage, just waiting for the final date to be chiseled in—would come later.

I walked back to my car feeling numb. All of the other cars had already gone. I was about to open the door when I noticed a small piece of white notebook paper tucked under the windshield wiper. I plucked the paper out. I looked around. No one was in sight.

There was writing on the paper (printing in ink): MEET ME AT THE HANGAR TONIGHT AT TEN. NEED TO TALK. The paper was signed James.

TWENTY-TWO

On the way home I stopped at a 7-Eleven and picked up a six-pack of Miller Lite (might as well stick with the same poison, I reasoned) and a ready-made chicken salad sandwich. Back at the house, sandwich and beer in hand, I settled down out on the lanai and began my vigil. Almost eight hours to kill. I was hoping Kim would be home soon.

After a time my cats showed up, hungry, howling in protest. I poured out a bowl of dried cat food and watched them eat: their heads butting together in a state of dreamy animal innocence.

On the beach there were quite a few people walking about and a surprising number in the water itself. It looked so pleasant out there that I almost went upstairs and put on a pair of swimming trunks. Instead I opened another beer. The beer ran out after a couple of hours and I was forced to switch to gin.

And so I passed the day—drinking, watching, waiting. Waiting to hear what James had to say, needed to talk to me about. In my mind I tried to picture what he would look like (it had been more than five years now), but I couldn't come up with anything concrete. It all seemed so vague, so remote.

The sun set and the night drifted in, and still I sat and drank and waited.

It was around nine o'clock when I finally rousted myself out of my chair and went upstairs. I washed my face, brushed my teeth and hair and changed shirts. Downstairs again, I made myself one last drink and slipped on my shoes. Then I heard the low putt-putt of Kim's ancient Volkswagon pulling up out front. I was relieved that she had made it home before it was time for me to go; I would've worried. So many things can happen on the road.

I walked out to greet her. We kissed before words were spoken.

"I missed you," she said softly, her head laying against my chest, her small body—I had nearly forgotten how small—resting in my arms.

"Long drive?" I asked, reaching into the back seat for her overnight bag.

"Alligator Alley," she said. "A killer."

I patted her firm little rump. She was tired I could tell. Anywhere was a long drive in her car. One felt every bump, every pine cone in the road. She probably hadn't slept much either, what with all the feasting and drinking and family fun.

I guided her up the stairs and inside.

She looked around the room once (I hadn't noticed—coffee cups, beer bottles, newspapers, plates) and shook her head. "You need a maid," she said. "Or a mother."

"Or a mistress," I countered.

Her eyes narrowed. "Dream about it."

I sat down on the sofa.

She slipped into my lap—small, so small. Again her head went to my chest, then in a moment it shot up. She looked at my drink on the table, then down at my shoes. "Where you going?" she asked.

"I have to meet someone," I said, glancing over at the timer on the VCR. "In half an hour. James. My cousin."

"The one no one's ever seen?"

"We've seen him," I said. "Just not in awhile."

"Can I go?" she asked, brightening up at the prospect of adventure.

"Next time," I promised. "This is special. He asked me to come alone."

"This still about your grandfather?"

"I'll explain the whole thing when I get back. Okay?" I kissed her and slid her off my lap.

"Okay," she said. She lay down on the sofa, unbuttoned the top two buttons of her shirt and pulled the fabric over to one side to reveal the upper half of a healthy breast. "I wait for you."

"I'll wake you if you don't," I said.

"Okay," she said, and she closed her eyes.

Devon Woods at night was an altogether different place—like some strange and dangerous animal sleeping. It was best if one walked carefully, made little noise and watched for surprises.

I parked my car in front of the main house. The house was totally dark. There were no other cars about. No lights came from the bunkhouse and only one from Fulton's quarters. I got out of my car, closed the door gently and headed toward the fields. I opened the back pasture gate, left it ajar and walked on.

The sky was patchy with clouds. Between the clouds, stars and a half moon shown through at shifting intervals, offering ample light. Soon I came upon a double-rutted dirt path that led toward the hangar. I followed this path as it twisted along, my senses extra aware, my mouth dry, my palms wet.

Up ahead I could see a single light shining through the tree. I walked on slowly. Eventually I was able to discern the outline of a building and a van parked next to it. Then I heard someone call my name. I stopped. "Here," I called back.

"Come to the light," instructed the voice.

I did as directed.

Then I saw him—James, standing there at the edge of the shadows. I would have known him anywhere. The eyes—the giveaway—still wild, still intense; the hair long, streaked with gray now; the nose, the chin the same as I remembered; the body as lean and tight-muscled as ever.

He smiled, stepped forward and embraced me. He pushed me away, held me at arm's length, shook me, looked at me, then hugged me again.

"I wasn't sure you'd come," he said, turning, letting an arm linger on my shoulder.

"Yes, you were," I said.

"You're right," he agreed, smiling.

"What're you doing out here?" I asked.

"Waiting," he said.

Then from out of the dark, from behind, I heard footsteps in the grass. And there was Daniel. He patted me on the back. "You come to help?" he asked, escorting James and me out of the light, over to the side of the hangar.

"I doubt it," I said.

"He's here 'cause I asked him to come," said James, his voice taking on a different tone, assertive.

"Sure, sure," said Daniel. "Just save it till after business. Okay?"

"Okay," said James.

Daniel patted me on the back again. "Good seeing you, cousin," he said, then he walked over to the van.

Next to the van were two other men—neither of whom I knew. In the light earlier, I had noticed that Daniel had a pistol tucked in his belt and a walkie-talkie in his hand. I could now see that both of the men standing by the van were armed—one with a black rifle, maybe an M-16; the other with a shorter weapon, perhaps an Uzi. James, I could tell (I knew), was unarmed.

"Over here," said James, leading the way a short distance into the dark.

We stopped and squatted in the grass.

"Waiting for a delivery?" I asked.

"Any time now," he said.

"What's your connection with this operation?" I asked, looking around.

"Helper, the lights, whatever."

"Like your job?"

"It beats working."

I then realized that everyone except me was dressed in dark clothing. Cleverly I had changed into a clean white shirt before coming out.

"So what'd you want to talk about?" I asked.

"About Grandfather," said James, staring into the night. "I saw it. The whole thing. Kraft and I were there. He got excited, started barking."

"Yeah," I said. "Sorry about him. A fine dog, had a lot of heart."

"True," agreed James. "Anyway, according to Fulton—I talked to him last night after you left. Jesus, you were drunk."

"Thanks," I said.

"According to him, you're ass-deep in this shit."

"That's putting it mildly," I said. "Every damn time I turn—"

"Wait!" commanded James, holding up a hand. "Here it comes." James moved away from me a couple of feet. On the ground in front of him was a small black box with a row of switches on it.

Then I heard it too: an airplane cutting through the night, running without lights. Louder, closer, it came.

"Hit it!" shouted Daniel.

And James began flipping switches, and the lights along the runway came to life. Christmas in September.

The airplane—a small two-engine job—eased down nicely. It turned around at the far end of the runway and began coming back this way.

Daniel and the other two men hopped in the van—a dark green color, Daniel's colors—and drove out onto the runway. The airplane came to a stop with its propellers still whirling. The van backed up to the side of the plane. Daniel and his men jumped out and began tossing duffel bags from the plane into the van.

James and I squatted in the high grass and watched.

Then suddenly, from out of nowhere, a spotlight flashed on the plane. A blowhorn informed everyone that we were under arrest. A helicopter swooped in low over the trees and began circling. Then one of Daniel's men reached into the van and came out with a rifle; he opened fire on the spotlight. And now there was shooting—automatic weapon fire—coming from everywhere and more spotlights and screaming and shouting and cursing.

A light swept across James and me. I stood and threw my hands into the air. James reached up as if to pull me down; then they were shooting at us, bullets impacting around us. And James grabbed his stomach and collapsed at my feet. "Christ!" he cried. He was bleeding. "Stay down, asshole." he groaned. I ripped my shirt off and thrust it into his hands. He pressed it against the wound; rapidly it turned red.

And now I could see Daniel driving away in the van, driving fast, driving and firing his pistol out the window, racing toward the dirt path that I had come down earlier—the only way in or out by car or truck. Suddenly more lights flashed on him, on the van. And the path, I could see now, was blocked—two squad cars. But Daniel kept going, accelerating, firing out the window, firing at the spotlights, at the cars in front of him. I could see his face twisted into a demented smile of pure joy and excitement. Then from out of the weeds, like a firing squad springing to life, they stood and opened up on the van—a mixed pattern of bullet holes appearing in its side. The van swerved violently to the right, tilted up on two wheels and slammed head-on into a tree. Then from above the shooting and the chaos, like a wounded and dying beast crying out in pain, I could hear the sound of a horn blowing steadily.

The airplane was halfway down the runway now, the engines revved to an ear-splitting whine, a spotlight tracking its progress. Then it was airborne (but just barely), struggling, veering away at a desperate angle—the wings almost perpendicular to the ground. An engine sputtered; a wing tip scraped the runway. And the plane, as if it were a child's toy, cartwheeled loosely end over end—parts and pieces flying off—then burst brightly into an orange fireball, heating the night air and setting the scrub brush aflame.

And there, by the light from the fire, I could see Daniel in the van, head down, slumped over, draped across the steering wheel. And the horn was still blowing. Then two deputies, both wearing some type of black SWAT team getup, approached the van. One man took up a position next to the door on the driver's side, an M-16 at the ready; the other, armed with a pistol, threw open the door. Nothing happened. Both men looked at each other. Then the man with the pistol poked Daniel, and slowly, ever so slowly, Daniel rolled out of the driver's seat and hit the ground. And the horn fell silent.

On the runway a man, one of Daniel's men, lay in a pool of blood. Next to him another man stood with his hands on his head.

The shooting had stopped now; it was strangely quiet.

Then Brooks was beside me, kneeling down next to James, a walkie-talkie in his hand. "I said I want that chopper down here immediately!" shouted Brooks into the walkie-talkie.

"I've got a wounded man here that I want out now! Repeat: now! Copy?"

"Roger," came the reply.

And Brooks grabbed one of James' hands and said, "Hang in there, buddy. You're going home." Then he turned to one of the deputies—there were several standing around—pointed at me and said, "Cuff that son-of-a-bitch and throw his ass in a squad car. I'll deal with him later."

Downtown in the Sheriff's Department building, I sat alone—still handcuffed—in a room without windows. After several hours Brooks and Detective Dawson showed up and began asking me questions. I refused to talk until they removed the handcuffs. I also threatened to sue them, the county of Sarasota and the state of Florida for something or other, but, in truth, this didn't appear to have much effect of them. Finally, after more than forty-five minutes, still not having answered a single question—I was rather proud of myself—a key was magically produced and the cuffs were removed. Then the questions began—questions to which they already had answers. And as they questioned, they also explained.

It seemed as though the DEA and the locals had been working on the bust for quite some time. It was already set up. Brooks was invited along because their quarry—the late Daniel Alfred Clay—was still a prime suspect in a capital murder case. They had not expected to get James—he was still in surgery. And I'd blundered into the trap by simple blind fool's luck. Apparently they had already established that I had nothing to do with the drugs.

After a couple of hours and more than a dozen rude threats of endless incarceration, I was released and told to get out of there—my presence was offensive.

Downstairs in front of the entrance to the building, I found my car parked, waiting for me. If I had thought about it I might have considered this to be more than passing strange in light of the fact that I had left the car out at Devon Woods and still had the keys in my pocket. I didn't, however, think about it. I simply got in and drove home.

The sun was just coming up.

TWENTY-THREE

Again, someone pounding on the front door. Again, another bright and sunny Florida day. Again, waking up in my bed alone. The patterns of my life were becoming painfully familiar.

The pounding at the door continued unabated. I pulled myself out of bed and worked my way into the jeans that I'd worn last night. On my bedside table, propped up against the lamp, I noticed a piece of paper with writing on it; the handwriting slow and methodical, each letter formed with delicate deliberateness—BE HOME AROUND 5. TELL ME EVERYTHING THEN. LOVE K. I folded the piece of paper in half, slipped it into my back pocket and went downstairs.

This time I opened the door more carefully, more cautiously, remembering the fist in the face from the other moring. And there was Detective Dawson—huge, red, sweating in the sunlight. I wondered what time it might be.

"Mr. Brooks sent me to get you," stated Dectective Dawson flatly.

"What for?" I asked. "You got an arrest warrant? Where is he, your Mr. Brooks?"

Detective Dawson looked at me with tired and sleepy—or maybe just dull—eyes.

"If he wants me, let him come and get me himself," I said. "He knows where I live. I'm getting sick and fucking tired of getting yanked around like some goddamn dog on a short chain." I tried to shut the door.

Detective Dawson shouldered his way into the room. "Come on," he said. "Get dressed. Put a shirt on. Don't give me any trouble or I'll slap the cuffs on you and take you down there like that."

"All right," I said. "I'll go." I turned and headed back up the stairs. "But I think my civil rights are being violated."

"You're white," said Detective Dawson, settling himself wearily on the sofa. "You don't have any civil rights."

I looked back to see if this was an attempt on the detective's part at humor. I couldn't tell.

In an unmarked car Detective Dawson drove north on 41. After we had passed all of the logical places to turn if we were going downtown, I asked him where he was taking me. "You'll see," he replied.

We pulled into the parking lot of a rather shabby motel and came to a stop. It was a mom-and-pop operation—a two-story L-shaped affair, thirty rooms maybe; neon flickering irregularly; the marquee splattered with misspelled words advertising rooms by the day, week, month or season—to say nothing of by the hour; yellowish grass and derelict bushes; cars whizzing by; whores strutting their stuff on the sidewalk in broad daylight; air-conditioners groaning; Christmas music (weirdly) piping out of the p.a. system; in one corner machines offering ice, soft drinks, snacks and condoms. A heavy air of impermanence hung about the place: just one more stop on a long rough road.

"Ordinarily I don't do this sort of thing," I said.

Detective Dawson just looked at me and said, "Get out."

In the parking lot there were several other sheriffs' cars—marked and unmarked. Off to one side was a small brown-water swimming pool. Half a dozen unprosperous-looking persons sat around the pool, watching all of the activity with uneasy interest.

Detective Dawson led the way up an outside set of stairs and along a cement walk. In front of us, some thirty feet away, a door opened and two men stepped out of a room. One man was carrying a large cardboard box; the other had a suitcase.

"You gentlemen finished?" asked a voice—Brooks—from inside the room.

"Done," said the man with the suitcase.

"She's all yours," added the second.

The men nodded to Detective Dawson and walked past us. The detective stopped before the open door, allowed me to catch up with him, then pushed me into the room.

"Ah, wonderful!" declared Brooks upon seeing me. "So glad you could come."

"What choice did I have?" I asked.

"None," smiled Brooks.

The room smelled stale; the air within locked up too long. A thin grimy green carpet covered the floor wall to wall. A couple of cheap lamps provided the lighting. What few pieces of furniture there were in the room were old and scarred. The bed was unmade; the sheets tangled in a knot. Clothing and dirty towels were tossed about randomly. A television set, padlocked with an iron brace over the top, looked down from a metal rack midway up the wall. In the back was a small dressing table littered with cosmetics and creams. The waste-paper basket overflowed with empty sacks, cups and containers from fast food outlets. A half-empty bottle of tequila waited by the bed. The ashtrays were filled with lipstick-smudged cigarette butts. A crumpled newspaper—Friday's—was crammed into a corner. And on the bureau, as if guarding all this, there stood four faceless styrofoam heads, each topped with a woman's wig.

"Nice place," I said, turning to Brooks. "Yours?"

"A funny guy," said Brooks. He looked over at Detective Dawson. "Don't you just love funny guys?"

"The man's hilarious," offered the detective.

Brooks and Detective Dawson and I were the only people in the room. Through the open door I could see a couple of deputies loitering around downstairs.

"How's James?" I asked.

"Out of surgery," reported Brooks. "But still unconscious. Still in intensive care."

"Well, I guess that's something anyway," I said.

"Yes," agreed Brooks. "That's something. Oh, by the way, here's your key back." Brooks flipped the key to my duplex into the air.

I caught it. "Did you get any fingerprints you could use?" I asked.

"We didn't try," said Brooks. "Like I explained to you that

[187]

really wouldn't have told us much. We did, however, pay another visit to Mrs. Susie Allen."

"And?" I asked.

"Maybe she's getting tired of lying too. Almost everyone gets tired of lying eventually. She admitted that last Wednesday night she was at the duplex with you from 8:35 until almost 9:30."

"All right!" I exclaimed. "That's what I've been telling you clowns all along."

"But she said that she had to wait for you," continued Brooks, "and that you didn't arrive until 8:35. You were supposed to meet her at 8:15, right? She had a watch. She noticed the time."

"So?"

"So since the time of death is still pegged at somewhere between 8:00 and 9:00, and since it only takes about fifteen minutes to drive from your grandfather's farm to your duplex, not even driving especially fast, that would've allowed you plenty of time to do the old boy and still get back for a quick roll in the hay with your friend's wife."

"Wrong, wrong, wrong," I said, sinking down onto the bed. "You've got it wrong."

"Perhaps," said Brooks. "But if you had hoped that Susie Allen's statement was going to put you in the clear then you're the one who's got it wrong."

I sat on the edge of the bed in a state of ever increasing depression. Things really seemed to be breaking against me. Even my hoped-for alibi had turned liquid. I was almost past the point of caring.

"But now on to the business at hand," announced Brooks cheerfully.

I looked up. I hated it when he was cheerful; I knew that could only mean more shit coming my way.

"These lovely accommodations," began Brooks, swinging his arms open wide, "belonged to one Elizabeth Jane Andrews, a runaway from Steubenville, Ohio, a prostitute, seventeen years old as of September 15, dead as of Septmeber 23. The girl in the parking lot, remember?"

"No!" I protested. "I don't remember. And I'm getting mighty goddamn tired—"

"Right," said Brooks. "You'll notice she was fond of chang-ing her hairstyle."

On the bureau, in front of me, the four faceless heads stared back blankly—one red-haired wig, one brunette, two blond (one long, the other considerably shorter in length).

"Looks like she had all the bases covered," I said, standing. "What color was her real hair? Black?"

"If you've never seen her how could you've known that?" asked Brooks sharply.

"Come on, Brooks, give me a little credit at least." I walked over to the bureau. "It's the only more or less natural hair color missing, if you rule out gray and white, which wouldn't, under ordinary circumstances, do a seventeen-year-old whore much good."

"Not bad," said Brooks.

"I just wonder why two of them are blond?" I touched the hair of the short blond wig; it felt uncomfortably alive.

"Maybe blonds really do have more fun," suggested Detec-tive Dawson.

Brooks and I both turned and looked at the detective. He lit a cigarette and stepped outside.

But there was something familiar here, something about that short blond wig—the hair used in its manufacture was of a fine texture, the ends curled inward at about where the shoulders would be.

"You notice a difference in that one?" asked Brooks.

"I don't know," I said. "There's something about it."

"It's newer," said Brooks, "and, according to one of the technicians who was just here and who supposedly knows about these sort of things, a good deal more expensive than the others. We found a sales slip for it in the trash. It was purchased less than two weeks ago in Tampa."

"Maybe she bought it as a birthday present for herself," I said.

"And maybe not."

And I knew Brooks was right. Vaguely I was beginning to get a picture.

"How tall was she?" I asked.

"5'10". Barefoot."

"How much did she weigh?"

"110."

Brooks looked at me; there was a strange smile on his face. I wondered if he was thinking what I was thinking.

"And then we have these," said Brooks, pulling a pair of earrings out of his inner coat pocket and dropping them into my hand.

"Are they real?" I asked.

"Real as $20,000. Diamonds and sapphires."

I held the earrings up by the two tiny gold posts extending from the backs of the top diamond sets. A combined total of three inches of sparkle and glitter dangling there in front of my eyes. They were beautiful—like fire, like stars at night. And now I knew.

"A seventeen-year-old whore, living on cheeseburgers, living like this, with $20,000 worth of stones lying in a drawer," observed Brooks. "Strange, don't you think?"

"Yes," I said. "Strange, indeed. You certainly have an interesting case."

"That's it?" asked Brooks.

"What more can I say?" I handed the earrings back.

And Brooks just smiled his strange smile again.

TWENTY-FOUR

Detective Dawson drove me home without uttering a word. It was just as well; I didn't feel much like talking. I got out of the car, slammed the door—no words of parting—and hurried inside. (I knew, but still I needed to be absolutely certain.)

Kim had cleaned up the house, maybe last night, maybe that morning, and yes, I noticed now—there was definitely a difference. I went outside again, around to the side of the house and dove into the garbage can. I pulled out an accumulated pile of newspapers and took the bundle back inside. On the dining room table I spread the papers out. Quickly I found the one that I was looking for—Thursday's, the last day of summer, the farmer in the feed cap standing in six inches of North Dakota snow—then located the section, page and picture. And there they were. The same. Exactly the same. There could be no doubt, no mistake.

I moved into the living room and checked the timer on the VCR—4:10. Where had the day gone? What did it matter?

I stepped out onto the lanai. My cats were waiting on the sundeck, howling to get in. I went into the kitchen, filled a large pot with cold water and threw it on them. The animals dispersed rapidly. They didn't seem totally surprised.

I made myself a gin and tonic—a double, or maybe a triple—and returned to the lanai. The wind, the sun, the sand, the pounding of the surf.

4:30. I knocked back the rest of the gin and tonic, locked up the house and went out the front door. Across the street a palm tree that I must have seen ten thousand times before for no reason caught my eye. I stood for a moment admiring it as though I had never seen one—the trunk curving gracefully upward, the palm fronds twirling in the wind. Then I got in my car and drove over to Michele's condominium. I was hoping that I would get there before her.

I didn't. The red Porsche was already there. I wondered if perhaps she had not gone to work today.

In front of the outer door to Michele's building, I saw a small elderly woman struggling with two bags of groceries and a purse. She was apparently trying to get the door key out of her purse without dropping the groceries. I hurried up to the lady and offered my assistance. The lady smiled, slipped both bags into my arms, dipped into her purse and extracted the key. She opened the door and we both stepped inside. I handed the bags back to the lady—she looked very much surprised to get her groceries back so soon; perhaps she had imagined that I'd offer to carry them to her apartment for her—and moved on to the elevators.

I entered an elevator just emptying a chattering load of blue-hairs, pressed the button marked P and rose swiftly to the seventeenth floor. No one was in the corridor. I walked up to Michele's door and knocked.

After several moments the door opened a crack.

"You should call before you come up," said Michele, her voice none too friendly.

"I didn't want to bother you," I explained.

"Well, that's precisely what you're doing." Her eyes were as cold as her voice.

"All right," I said. "But since I'm already here why don't you invite me in?"

She looked at me for a second, then shut the door. From the other side now I could hear chains clearing their slots. Eventually the door opened and I was allowed in.

Michele's apartment seemed little changed since my last visit. There was, however, one noticeable addition—a stylish gray suitcase parked next to the mirrored bar.

I sat down on one of the leather sofas; Michele lowered herself into a chair opposite me.

"Make it quick," she said. "I'm in a hurry."

"I can see," I said. I nodded to the suitcase. "Skipping town?"

"A business trip," she countered.

"Right," I said.

Michele looked tired—deep dark half-circles under her eyes. She didn't seem to be able to control her hands; they twitched and picked and pulled at nonexistent threads not dangling from her clothing.

"Did you hear about Daniel and James?" I asked.

"Yes," said Michele. "It was in the paper. Shocking."

"I haven't read the paper yet," I said. "But I was out there when it all went down."

"Oh really. How interesting," said Michele, not displaying the least bit of interest, concentrating on her clothes.

"Yes," I agreed. "And almost educational too."

"What do you mean?" she asked. She looked up uneasily.

"I mean that James asked me to meet him out there last night because he had something to tell me. He said he saw who shot Grandfather."

"That *is* interesting," said Michele. "Who did it?"

"Unfortunately James himself was shot before he could tell me," I explained. "And now he's in intensive care, still unconscious."

"Most unfortunate," said Michele, sitting back in the chair, letting her hands finally flutter to a stop on the armrests. "Perhaps I should send him some flowers."

"If he ever wakes up, I'm sure he'd appreciate it," I said.

Michele smiled slightly. "Yes," she said. "I'll have to do that." She stood up and ran her hands down the front of her dress. "Well, thanks for coming. It was very considerate. But now I have a plane to catch."

"That's not the reason I came," I said. "Maybe you'd better sit down."

"I can stand quite well, thank you," she assured me. "Now what is it?"

"I came to warn you that he knows, he knows about you."

"What are you talking about?" she demanded. "Who knows what about me?"

"Brooks, Mason Brooks, he knows about you, about Grandfather, about the whore. And what he doesn't already know, he'll probably be able to figure out sooner or later. I just got back from the Sun 'n' Fun Motel. The cops took me over there to show me the girl's room. What was her name? Elizabeth something or other. I saw the wig and the earrings. If I could put it together, certainly Brooks can too. It's his job."

"So you think you know the story, do you?" she asked calmly. She walked over to a small desk, opened a drawer and pulled out a shiny chrome-plated pistol. "You think you're pretty smart, don't you, Thomas?"

"Okay," I said. I stood up. "Maybe I'm wrong. Maybe—"

"Sit!" she commanded. She pointed the pistol at me. "And shut the fuck up!"

I sat.

She came around in front of me again and slipped into her chair. The pistol was still pointed at me. She was smiling.

"So you saw the wig, nice match"—she touched her own hair—"and the earrings, and now you think you know everything. You don't know anything. Nothing. But I'm going to tell you, loving cousin, because you're such a very bright boy."

"That's really not necessary," I said. "I just thought—"

"Shut up!" she commanded again. "Or I'll shut you up. Permanently."

"All right," I said. "I'm all ears."

"You're all shit, but that's beside the point." She picked a cigarette out of the silver box on the table in front of her, lit it and blew a cloud of smoke into the air. "You see, I'd been thinking about it for a long time, about different ways of doing it, then I saw her, Elizabeth Jane, walking down 41, and it all came together in an instant, like a bolt of lightning. I saw it all with perfect absolute clarity, from beginning to end. It was brilliant, my plan. A true thing of beauty. Simple yet complicated. She was made for the part. Elizabeth Jane. Just the right height, the right weight, and with the wig in the dark no one could've told us apart. It was the perfect crime. I could be in two places at once.

"So I saw her and I pulled up beside her and asked her to get in the car. And do you know what she did? She propositioned me, right there on the street, said she'd do anything with anybody for money. I told her that I wanted to buy her dinner. She made a rather crude comment about liking fish, then she saw that I was serious, that I really wanted to buy her dinner. And I think that shocked her. So she got in the car and

I took her to dinner. We went to the Summerhouse. We drank three bottles of good champagne, then went back to her motel room. What a filthy place! I suggested the Hilton instead, and she thought that would be wonderful. The next morning was Saturday. She said something about her birthday. She was the type of girl who had twenty birthdays a year. I told her that I wanted to buy her something special. We drove up to Tampa and I bought her the wig and also a long black-haired one for myself. Then I bought her some clothes. She looked great. I asked her if she would like to make $500 for one hour's work. And again she said she'd do anything, anything for money. So we spent the night in Tampa. I tried to show her how to dress, how to walk, how to act. Though her part was simple—just to sit still for one hour—you can't be too careful. She was a quick study. We dressed up that night, she in the wig and the new clothes, and went out on the town. We looked like sisters. One poor fool in a bar somewhere even asked if we were. That's when I knew it would work. We came back to town late Sunday. I gave her some money and asked her to stay off the streets until after it was over. It was only three nights away. Somewhat reluctantly she agreed.

"But you see how beautifully things were working out. I found her on Friday, had her set to go by Sunday and the play was scheduled for Wednesday. The pieces just fell into place."

Michele stabbed out her cigarette and immediately reached for another. As she told her story she appeared to grow more confident, more relaxed. The pistol, however, remained pointed at me. She lit the new cigarette and continued with the tale.

"Wednesday afternoon I called Elizabeth Jane at her motel and set up a meeting to go over the plan, to make sure she understood her part—as I've said, it was simple yet essential. We met down the street from her motel. She ran through her role perfectly, times and all, then I gave her some more money. And it was then that she first asked what it was all about. The money was making her curious. I told her it was a joke on a friend.

"Vanessa and I arrived at the Van Wezel at 7:30. She was in on it from the beginning. She hated the old bastard as much as I did. We mingled with the crowd in the lobby for awhile, talking to as many people as we could and even managing to get our picture taken. At 7:55 we went in and sat down. We had two aisle seats together toward the back. The play began promptly at 8:00. Ten minutes into the first act I got up and went to the bathroom. Elizabeth Jane was already there waiting. We stepped into adjoining toilet stalls and began undressing and passing clothes back and forth under the partition. It was almost funny. Like a girls' school game. I slipped into Elizabeth Jane's clothes as she got into mine. We were the same size, you see. We had already tried on each other's clothes. The fit was perfect. As a precaution against being recognized by any possible late-comers, I put on the black-haired wig that I'd bought in Tampa and a pair of sunglasses. Then another ten minutes and the change was complete, and Elizabeth Jane, wearing the blond wig, my clothes and earrings, was in my seat watching *Macbeth*, and I was on my way out to Devon Woods.

"I had timed the drive ten times or more. Twenty minutes tops. I arrived at 8:40 and rang the doorbell. Grandfather came to the door himself. He looked surprised to see me, especially wearing a black wig. Nevertheless he invited me in. We stepped into the library and he sat down. I asked him if he was alone. He said he was. I didn't have time to waste making any big speeches or dramatic scenes. I simply pointed the pistol at him—your pistol, Thomas—and told him to get up. At first he seemed stunned, then he started to move. On the way out the door he grabbed his checkbook off a table and asked me how much I wanted. I laughed at him and told him to keep walking. He was barefooted. I should've let him put his shoes on. He cursed and complained all the way out to the back pasture. When I finally got him there, when I told him to get down on his knees, that's when he really started begging and trying to bribe me. I walked around behind him and told him to lie down on the ground. He threw his arms out and continued to cry and beg. It was a pitiful sight. I gave him a little push with my foot. He nodded his head and said, all right. Then he just relaxed and fell forward. He landed face-down in a pile of cow shit. I didn't even know it was there. He may not have either. I looked at him for a moment, all spread out on the ground, his feet cut and bleeding from the rocks and sticks and thorns and things, his arms out from his side like a man on a cross, his face in a pile of cow shit. Then I shot him. Two quick ones to the back of the head.

"Then nearby I heard a dog bark. And I looked in that direction, over in some bushes, and I thought I saw something move. I fired four shots, then ran back to my car and drove away. Only later, when your friend, Mason Brooks, came around and mentioned that James' dog had been killed, did I realize who it was. But who the hell would have thought my own spook-ass brother would've been lurking around in the weeds, watching?"

Michele leaned forward and crushed out her cigarette. This time she didn't light another one.

"By 9:10," she continued, "I was back at the Van Wezel, feeling pretty good about it. I immediately went to the bathroom, and again Elizabeth Jane was there, looking just like me. I kissed her and told her to get into the stall again. You see, Vanessa and I had synchronized our watches earlier, and she was the timekeeper inside. By 9:20 the change was again complete, and Elizabeth Jane was headed back to he motel room with more money in her pocket for one hour's work than she'd ever made in her life, and I was sitting in my seat, feeling wonderfully alive. At 9:30, right on schedule, the curtain came down for intermission. As the house lights went up Vanessa turned and smiled at me and said she loved me. Then I saw her smile collapse and she asked me where my earrings were."

"But wait," I said. "I don't understand how you could've known that the intermission was going to be at exactly 9:30?"

"Simple," said Michele, savoring the opportunity to exhibit her brilliance. "As a patron of the arts, a member of the arts council, information like a play's running time and when intermission is going to be is easy to find out. You see, the company that put on *Macbeth* travels around the country doing it, the same play, three-hundred and some days a year. They've got it down to a fine art. All I did was ask."

"Oh," I said. "Okay."

"But it's the earrings, Thomas," she moaned. "The earrings, don't you understand? I trusted her and the little bitch stole my earrings, Grandmother's earrings. Can't you understand how that made me feel?"

"Bad?" I guessed.

"Worse," she said, standing up now. "It made me feel like . . . like . . . well, like murdering the bitch. Then Vanessa said not to worry about it. She'd buy me some new ones. And I thought what the hell, I'll write it off. But I was still mad about it."

Mad, I thought, was hardly the word.

Michele walked over to the bar—the pistol still pointed at me, her eyes ever alert—poured herself a couple of inches of Johnnie Walker Black and brought the glass back to her seat.

"Then Friday afternoon Elizabeth Jane called me at work," began Michele again. "And now that really freaked me because I'd given her a phony name and a bogus life story. And there she was on the phone, saying how we needed to talk. Can you imagine it? Trying to blackmail me on an open phone line. I told her to hang up and I'd call her back. At first I couldn't figure out how the little whore had tracked me down. Then I remembered the photograph in Thursday's paper and the story about Grandfather in Friday's. Also I later realized that there was a possibility that she could've gone through my purse sometime during the weekend before—perhaps when I was in the shower—and found my driver's license or a credit card. I don't know. But you understand that I had to kill her too, don't you, Thomas?"

"Absolutely," I agreed. The conversation was getting almost too strange. But I had no real options except to listen and hope for an opening, an opportunity to do something.

"Besides," said Michele, sipping her Johnnie Walker, "she *had* stolen Grandmother's earrings."

"She deserved it," I said.

Michele nodded her head and smiled. "So I went to a pay phone and called the little cunt back and asked her what she wanted. Money, she said, more money. She thought she'd hit the gravy train. The greedy little tart. So I said, fine. I told her to get the earrings and meet me in the parking lot of the Van Wezel at midnight and I'd pay her off, big. She was so goddamn dumb she laughed. She didn't even know a threat when she heard one.

"Well, the little piece of garbage didn't show up until after one o'clock. And when she finally did, she was drunk or stoned or something. And she didn't even have my earrings. I was pissed, Thomas, let me tell you."

"Rightly so," I said.

Michele took another sip of her drink. "So anyway, I told her to get in the car. We sat there for a moment, then I said that I had her money and asked her where the earrings were. She smiled this goofy smile and said she'd decided to keep them. I almost shot her right there. Instead I leaned over and kissed her and asked her to come with me for a walk over by the bay to look at the lights on the water. We walked over to a little grassy spot close by and I pulled the pistol—still your pistol, Thomas—and told her to strip. She had a nice firm young body. Then I told her to get down on her knees and do what she did best. I pulled up my dress and let her go to work. It was her job, right? She didn't really seem all that afraid. Maybe she was just tired of living. I don't know. Well, anyway, it was kind of beautiful—the stars, a light breeze coming in off the bay, the quiet, and little Elizabeth Jane on her knees, her hands deep in her underpants, licking for life, enjoying it, getting into it. So I shot her. Then I wiped the pistol clean, tossed it into the bay and drove home."

"But how'd you ever get my pistol to begin with?" I asked.

"Thomas, Thomas, poor innocent Thomas," sighed Michele with a faint smile. "Can't you guess? I knew that you had a pistol because you told me that you bought one when that fellow was breaking into everyone's house on the beach. You even advised me to get one too. So I did." She waved the chrome-plated pistol at me. "Thanks. But to get yours was no problem. You're such a creature of habit, Thomas. What do you and your little Chinese girl do every Saturday night?"

"Well, sometimes we go out and have a few drinks."

"Sometimes? Ha! There could be a hurricane on the horizon and if it's Saturday night you're gone. So I just waited until late one Saturday and called you. Naturally you weren't home. So I walked down the beach, slit open the screen to your lanai with a kitchen knife and just stepped right in. Thoughtfully you'd forgotten to lock your sliding glass door. Then I walked upstairs and found the pistol in the drawer of your bedside table, right where you told me you kept it."

"Oh," I said.

Michele smiled again and finished off her drink.

"All right," I said. "Call me stupid, but—"

"Stupid," said Michele happily.

"All right, great," I continued. "But I still don't see why you wanted to kill Grandfather in the first place. He wasn't going to live forever."

"He was trying," countered Michele. "And I wasn't getting any younger either. I wanted it while I could still enjoy it. And he was standing in my way. You see, Grandfather's operations were a mess—spread out, unorganized, with a bunch of old birds in important positions doing nothing. What I wanted to do, what needed to be done, was to combine all of the companies together under one holding company, weed out the unprofitable business lines and sell them off, then take the rest public. I could've made a fortune, not only for myself, but for everyone in the family. But the old fart wouldn't buy it. He wouldn't even listen. When I approached him about the plan, his exact words were, 'over my dead body.' So I simply obliged him."

"Then the whole thing was just about money?" I asked.

"*Just?*" laughed Michele. "Why money's the best reason in the world for murder."

Michele stood up and backed over to the bar. "Now get up," she commanded. "Story time's over. My suitcase, please. We're going to the airport, and you're going to drive."

"And what's going to happen once we get there?" I asked, standing.

"I haven't decided yet," said Michele. "Maybe I'll just lock you in your trunk or maybe I'll shoot you too. It'll be interesting to find out, won't it? Now come over here and pick up my goddamn suitcase or you'll never even make it to the airport."

I stepped over to the bar and picked up the suitcase. It was rather heavier than I had imagined. "Planning on being away long?" I asked.

"Long enough." Michele slipped the pistol into her shoulder bag. Her hand remained inside the bag. "The door, please, Thomas. Destiny awaits."

I was tempted to say something, but decided not to. I opened the door; Michele followed me out and closed it behind her. I pushed the button for the elevator. Michele jabbed me in the back with the pistol in her bag. "Just remember," she said. The elevator came almost immediately and we rode without company to the lobby.

Downstairs I was hoping for a crowd so I could maybe cause some confusion. There was no way that I was going to get in my car or any other car with Michele. Unfortunately the lobby was deserted. I had no definite plan of attack or escape. Vaguely I visualized myself swinging the suitcase at her or going for the shoulder bag. But nothing seemed really very practical. So I just kept walking—through the lobby, past a maintenance man ("Good evening, Ms. Clay." "Good evening, Howard."), through the outer door and into the parking lot.

Twilight: shadows dissolving, lights coming on, stars appearing low in the sky.

"Where's your car, cousin?" asked Michele, half a step behind me.

"Over here," I said, leading the way. I knew that I had to do something now. Later would surely be too late.

We walked on. The pounding of my heart drowned out all feeble thoughts trying to reach my brain. My feet and arms operated independent of command.

And then we were there, beside my car; my hand involuntarily reaching for the key.

Then from two cars away: "Going somewhere?"—Brooks. A pistol pointed. Detective Dawson next to him. Another pistol. Both crouched, only the heads, shoulders and weapons visible.

Michele spun, grabbed me around the neck and pointed the pistol at my head. "Back off!" she shouted. "Back the fuck off or I'll kill him!"

I bent slightly. I heard the pistol click—maybe the safety. I placed the suitcase on the ground—it was getting heavy—and straightened up again.

"Don't let me stop you," said Brooks calmly. "Might as well go for three as two. But if you do waste my old buddy there, then Detective Dawson and I'll be forced to blow you away too. Your best bet would be to put the pistol down and get yourself a good lawyer. I can recommend several. Or if you're really intent on doing it the hard way, I'd advise that you try to take out either Detective Dawson or me with your first shot and hope like hell you get a second."

And now, behind me, I could feel Michele beginning to shake. Her entire body jerked and banged against mine. I was worried that the pistol might go off accidentally. She was sucking down short excited half-breaths and mumbling, whining, crying about something I couldn't understand.

Then suddenly I felt her move to the right. Her arm came off my neck. She let out a scream of what sounded like physical pain. The pistol swung away from my head, and she fired once in the direction of Brooks and Detective Dawson.

The sound of the pistol going off was so loud—the pistol itself so close, no more than six inches away—that at first I thought I had been shot. I leaned away from the pistol, took a tentative step and stumbled over the suitcase. I fell to the ground.

Immediately I looked up and heard four quick shots. Then, rag-doll loose, I saw Michele fly backward through the air and slam up against my car. She slid down the side of the car, leaving several smudge trails of blood, then toppled over against me. Her head finally came to rest in my lap.

With pistols still drawn, Brooks and Detective Dawson circled cautiously around the cars and stopped in front of Michele and me. Slowly Brooks reached out and took the pistol from Michele's hand.

Michele looked up at Brooks and, through a bloody mouth, said, "All right. You can stop now. You've killed me enough."

Brooks said nothing.

"You'll be okay," I said, stroking her fine soft baby-blond hair. "An ambulance is on the way."

And Michele turned her head—her eyes filled now with total contempt—and said, "Fuck you." Then her head dipped an inch, and my cousin was dead.

Brooks looked at me. He slipped his pistol under his jacket. He turned to Detective Dawson. "Call it in," he said.

TWENTY-FIVE

The next day I slept late. I called into the office around noon and was assured—a little too positively, I thought—that my smiling presence would not be missed in the least. "Take the rest of the year off," our receptionist, Julie, advised handsomely. "You've had a rough week." (The entire sordid tale was in the newspaper, recapped and put into chronology; they had most of the facts right.) I thanked her for her concern and promised not to overexert myself. Then I went downstairs and fixed a cup of coffee.

With the coffee I stepped out onto the lanai. Another beautiful Florida day—not a cloud in the sky, the blue above, the bright white sands all around, the almost mirrored calm of the Gulf. It was a grand day to be alive, to reflect on the unattractive alternative. An alternative which I had come frightfully close to achieving.

As I sat there I thought about my life, about how much of it I had taken for granted, about how unworthy, in truth, I really was. And soon I came to the inescapable conclusion that a change was needed, was demanded. A change of life, of place and position; a change, new challenges. Even the best of life-styles can become tainted with repetition. One can only absorb so much easy living without falling into a stupor of benign complacency. And my sponge was soaked.

Later that evening, after dinner—lobster tails, wild rice, stir-fried vegetables and a bottle of Chardonnay—Kim begged me to take her to the hospital to see James. She had heard about him, read about him, and now she wanted to see the mystery man for herself. He was out of intensive care and according to all reports on the road to a rapid recovery. I was curious to see him again myself, our last encounter having ended rather abruptly.

James had a private room on the seventh floor; the place was flooded with flowers. He was still hooked up to various monitoring machines, with wires and tubes running from his body, but for someone who had just been shot and operated on I thought that he looked remarkably well. A confederate in crime had smuggled in a six-pack of beer for him. He was on the fourth can and seemed quite content. I introduced him to Kim, and immediately he responded with a flurry of Vietnamese. I was surprised that he could remember so much (it sounded like a lot to me anyway) after so long. Kim seemed surprised—pleasantly so—herself. She pulled up a chair next to his bed (a somewhat forward gesture for someone as outwardly reserved as Kim), and soon they were going at it, ninety miles an hour—Vietnamese to English and back again—as if they had known each other for a lifetime, as if I weren't in the room. I stood by the window, reading James' get-well cards and watching them out of the corner of my eye. What I saw made me simultaneously happy and a bit sad. The circle was turning.

After a time the door opened and Laura, smiling brightly, entered the room with a small suitcase. "More beer," she announced cheerfully, setting the suitcase down on the floor beside James' bed. "And a little smoke." She flipped a plastic baggie, obviously containing marijuana, onto James' chest. "Just don't get caught with any of this crap or the doctors'll raise unholy hell."

"Yes sir, little sister," said James, reaching out for Laura's hand.

Laura leaned over and kissed him.

James and Kim promptly resumed their rapid-fire conversation. James opened a beer and passed it to Kim. They raised their beers and Kim proposed a toast in Vietnamese. Then they drank.

Laura turned to me. "What're you doing here, cousin? You look out of place. Like the third one that makes the crowd."

"I feel like it," I said. "You staying?"

"No. I just came by to drop off the supplies. I've got to run."

"I'll walk you down to your Jeep then," I offered. I wanted to give Kim and James a chance to be alone together; although admittedly, in retrospect, that hardly seemed necessary.

"Thanks," said Laura, hooking her arm around mine. "You're a dear."

"I'll be right back," I said. "I'm going downstairs with Laura."

Not a head turned; no one heard me.

Laura and I walked out of the room.

"They seem to be getting along quite nicely," observed Laura as we moved on toward the elevators. "That's your girlfriend, isn't it?"

"For the moment," I said.

Laura smiled and led me into an empty elevator.

I was glad to get outside again, out into the night, into the warm fresh air. Hospitals have always creeped me out—the cleanness, the sickness, the white clothes and the sanitized smell.

"Life's strange," I said as we walked through the parking lot.

"Only if you take it seriously," countered Laura.

"You mean that you didn't think it was strange to find out that your sister killed Grandfather?"

"No," said Laura calmly. "I already knew. I was there."

"What?" I asked, stopping.

Laura turned and faced me. "Yes, I was there. Upstairs. I was there when you came and left. And when Michele came later. You just missed each other."

"What?" I asked again. "Then you've known—"

"Yes. I heard everything, saw everything from the window in Grandmother's sitting room."

"Wait," I said. "Wait."

"It's quite simple," she assured me. "I used to go out to Devon Woods every evening. I'd park in the back so no one would know that I was there—nobody but everybody. And then I'd stay with Grandfather until he fell asleep. I'd wear one of Grandmother's old nightgowns and hold him, lay in bed with him. We'd talk. Mostly I'd listen. He was afraid of being alone, of dying alone, but in the end everyone really dies alone anyway, even people who die together still die apart—small individual deaths. But that's what he wanted, so what the hell."

"But wait," I said. "Wait."

"Vanessa used to stay with him before me. She was his mistress for a number of years. But then he got too old to do it—you know, the down and dirty. And after that the very sight of her made him mad, made him remember what he couldn't do anymore. So he kicked her out of his royal bed, banned her from Devon Woods and asked me to come out instead."

"Vanessa?" I asked, dumbfounded.

"It was kind of sweet, in a way: listening to him talk, talking about the old days or what he had done that day, talking about the family or people I didn't know, holding him, his frail little body struggling to be strong. I think I would've been a good nurse."

"A nurse?"

"Yes. A nurse," she said, walking again.

I followed and caught up with her. "But if you knew everything and saw everything, then why didn't you do something, why didn't you tell somebody, like the cops maybe, or Brooks?"

"Why did you go to Michele's apartment?" she asked. "What would've been the point? In the end, things worked themselves out."

"Yes, but you couldn't have known that. I could've been killed too. Hell, I almost was."

"But you weren't," she said. She stopped beside her Jeep, kissed me on the cheek and climbed in.

"But wait. Hold on," I demanded. "I still don't—"

"Sssh," she said, placing a finger against my lips. "It's over. Don't worry about it. Nothing can be changed now, and probably never could have been."

Then she started the engine, smiled and winked at me.

I stood there for a moment watching as the Jeep made its way through the parking lot, turned onto the Trail and then disappeared in a sea of red tail-lights. Behind me I heard a car door slam. I knew; I waited. And then there he was—Brooks—standing beside me again.

"Where's your partner?" I asked, looking around. "The intrepid Detective Dawson."

"He's out night sailing," explained Brooks. "He's quite a yachtsman, I'm told. You might not think it by looking at him."

"I guess that just goes to show how wrong you can be about some people, right?"

Brooks didn't say anything; he just looked at me.

"Right?" I asked again. "Like the way you were wrong about me."

"I never really thought you did it," said Brooks, taking a cigarette out of a pack, putting it in his mouth and lighting it. "It takes a certain amount of balls, knowing the consequences if you're caught, to pull the trigger on somebody in cold-blood, unless of course you're insane."

"I'm not sure if I've been vindicated or insulted."

"But I did think that if I put enough pressure on one end of the balloon something would pop out the other end."

"And so I was the pressure point, huh?"

"I can think of worse ways of passing a week."

I looked at him; he was smiling.

"Anyway," continued Brooks, "I'm going back to Tallahassee tomorrow and I just wanted to drop by and say that it's been a pleasure working with you."

"You mean *on* me."

"Whatever. No hard feelings, I hope." He extended his hand.

I hesitated; I thought.

"All right," I said finally. "No hard feelings." And I extended mine.

And Brooks laughed and jerked his hand back. He turned and walked over to his car. He got in and drove away.

I looked down at my hand, still hanging in space. I stuffed it into my pocket. "Asshole," I said aloud, referring to whom I wasn't sure.

The air was filled with the scent of flowers—jasmine, oleander. The stars were out in full force. The traffic pushed noisily along 41—people going places, doing things, night things. And I felt as if I were knee-deep in cement, waiting to be dropped over the side.

Finally I kicked myself free, went into the hospital again and back up to the seventh floor. With my hand on the doorknob, I stopped outside of James' room. Inside, I could hear someone laughing—Kim laughing, light and carefree. I wondered when was the last time that I had heard her laugh. I couldn't remember. It had been that long ago.

TWENTY-SIX

The following morning—a Wednesday, it was—I went into the office but accomplished little. I was simply going through the motions, and not even doing that very well. I couldn't concentrate; there was a total lack of enthusiasm on my part. After a couple of fruitless hours of shuffling papers, requesting information, then canceling the requests, I decided to break for an early lunch—a nice long liquid lunch.

In a bar downtown I ran into an old acquaintance whom I had not seen in several years. The man claimed that he was now importing mahogany (and probably a good deal more, though he didn't say) from Honduras. We drank and he told me of the wonders of Central America. It all sounded pretty good to me, especially the part about the fourteen-year-old girls.

A little after three o'clock I rolled out of the bar and into the burning glare of another bright day. Returning to work was totally out of the question. Not only would it have been in extremely bad taste to have shown up drunk, but it could also have been financially foolhardy—once, when more than slightly inebriated, I almost committed John Allen and myself to the purchase of some five hundred plus acres of canker-infected orange trees.

Instead, I went home and took a swim. The light rolling of the waves, the uncompromising sun overhead, the Beefeater in my brain. It was lovely—floating. So relaxing. So quiet.

Unfortunately, at some undefined point, I over relaxed, fell asleep and almost drowned.

After my near brush with a soggy death, I trudged home—

the current having carried me a couple of miles down the beach—and got back just as Kim was returning from school.

"Well," she said, "look what the tide washed up."

"Almost washed out," I said.

She kissed me. I put an arm around her and together we climbed the outer stairs and went inside.

"How about a little French food tonight?" I suggested.

"You taking me out?" she asked happily.

"Sure," I said. "Put on your red dress and we'll go scarf down some snails."

"You scarf snails," she said, heading upstairs. "Not me."

(Slugs, no matter how cleverly disguised, were one culinary delight that Kim had decided early on she could easily forego.)

We arrived at the restaurant at around six-thirty and were informed that all of the tables had been taken. We were asked if we'd like to wait at the bar. The crowd was primarily elderly, twosomes and foursomes—discount diners, "early birds" as they were referred to, somewhat condescendingly, in the local vernacular, who, as the name would imply, arrived early to take advantage of the lower priced meals (and slightly reduced portions) that many restaurants in the area offered to those who could get their act together and get to the trough before the usual dinner crowd. The cutoff time seemed to be six o'clock, but people tended to linger. And why not? They had paid for it, earned it. There was, however, one notable paradox in this arrangement: many of the "early birds" (and not a few of them looked a little birdlike too—nibbling away, heads bobbing and twitching, fluttering from one table to another, chattering up a storm) were quite rich, and as a group they were probably far wealthier than the succeeding "y-crowd"— the parking lot packed with Mercedes and Cadillacs (the vehicle of choice), mink coats in the summertime, diamond bracelets and gold Rolexes dripping from wrists like loose skin. Maybe by five o'clock they were bushed and just wanted to eat early, or perhaps after years of enforced frugality and sacrifice, old habits were simply hard to break. A bargain was still a bargain, no matter how much money your accountant told you you had.

Around seven o'clock the crowd began to rotate—out with the old ("new menus; evening, suckers"), in with the new. A table was found and we were seated. I was already well on the way to my second glorious drunk of the day. I was totally content. We ordered; the food came. It was excellent. The service was no more rude than one would hope to encounter in a restaurant advertised as being "a little corner of France in Sarasota." And the price was not too outlandish. I charged it and forgot about it.

Standing outside again in the fading orange twilight, I looked up and casually noticed the lights of the hospital. Yes, I knew precisely where I was; yes, it was all part of my master plan. I glanced over and saw that Kim was looking at the lights too. She was truly beautiful—bright, alert, young; standing there, looking up at those lights as if she could reach out and touch them. And if I had had any doubts before, they now vanished utterly. For I knew that my plan, scheme, whatever, was a good one—very possibly even noble.

"Hey, let's go visit James," I suggested off-handedly. "I think I can see his room from here."

Her face lit up. She turned to me. (Perhaps she already knew; I don't know.) "All right," she said. "Let's."

It was all so simple.

Back to James' room. A little small talk. An excuse. Then out—leaving them alone again.

I went downstairs and outside. Next to the emergency room entrance, I saw a vacant bench and sat down.

And soon, in a steady stream, by car and ambulance, they came: the broken and bleeding cargo. A crying, dirty, little blond-haired girl being carried in with an injured foot, crying more from the terror than the pain. A large black woman with a rag to her face; she had come by taxi. A small boy bravely cradling an arm, walking under his own power; a man guiding; another small boy following, stopping—"My brother broke his arm. He fell out of a tree." "He'll be all right," I assure the boy. "Yeah, I know," says the boy, obviously disappointed. An ambulance whirring up, lights and sirens, stretchers and bodies, shouts and commands. A second ambulance, much slower, no lights, no sirens; two grim-looking attendants wheel out a body covered with a sheet. A police car, two policemen and a prisoner; the prisoner, handcuffed, covered with blood, looks at me; "Today's my birthday," he informs me. "I'm twenty-one. Legal." One of the policemen slaps the man on the back of the head—"Happy birthday, motherfucker." A small red car speeding up to the entrance; the brakes lock, the car slides; a youngish man with a pale face in a panic; a very pregnant woman already in a sweat, about to drop her load on the sidewalk. "Watch my car!" the man shouts—a BMW. I watch the car and think about a time, perhaps a year ago; Kim asking me if I want her to stop taking "the pill"; I say no; she says okay, and never raises the subject again. Now I'm watching the car and wishing that I could have said yes, but I couldn't—the old corrupt blood, the old selfish self unable to give. And on and on. Another ambulance, again no lights or sirens; an old man on a stretcher breathing through an oxygen mask; the same look of terror that I had seen on the little girl's face earlier. A security guard approaching, standing next to me, pointing at the BMW—"Hey, buddy, you can't leave that car there." "I should hope not," I say. "Then move it," orders the security guard. He has a pistol. "Not mine," I say. "Not yours? Then whose is it?" he asks. "Couldn't say," I say. The security guard walks inside. A short time later a tow truck arrives and the offending vehicle is hauled away.

After the car was removed, I stood up, walked over to the glass doors at the emergency room entrance and looked down the corridor. The time was eight-fifty.

I went back upstairs. Outside of James' room I stopped. There was no laughter now. No voices. It was quiet. Slowly I pushed open the door. The room was dark—only a dim light, moonlight, coming from the window. On the bed I could see two figures. I approached the bed. They were both asleep—Kim with her clothes on, outside the sheets, her head resting on James' shoulder. I touched her lightly. "Time to go," I whispered.

She turned and looked up. She blinked. "Yes," she agreed. "Time to go."

It was over; it had begun.

We rode the elevator down in silence.

Once outside Kim said, "I don't know if I should go home or not. He gets out in two days."

"Where would you stay till then?" I asked.

"Well, I could stay at your duplex," she suggested.

"My what?" I asked; I was stunned.

"Your duplex. On Oak Street," explained Kim happily. "I could stay there."

"But, but, how—"

Kim laughed. She grabbed my arm and pulled me toward the car.

"Poor boy," she said mockingly. "Thinks he so smart. Tomorrow I go stay with my friend."

"And tonight?" I asked.

"And tonight is tonight," she said. And then she kissed me hard.

TWENTY-SEVEN

Some three weeks later I was invited out to Devon Woods for dinner. Kim and James were living there in the main house.

Things were moving fast now. Grandfather's will had been read, his wishes carried out. No legal challenges had been mounted. Property, shares, monies had been distributed to the surviving family members and friends. James and Fulton became equal partners in, and owners of, Devon Woods. James, as I've said, moved into the main house with Kim, and Fulton bought himself a bottle of good bourbon. David was selected to run Grandfather's companies. He later put a plan of corporate reorganization into effect and was widely hailed as a financial genius. I've always suspected that he may have found a blueprint of Michele's vision among her private papers, for he did precisely what she had said needed to be done. About that matter, David was to remain uncharacteristically quiet, and soon became rather reclusive. I never learned nor could guess what Laura did with her windfall. She continued to live in the same rundown house and to drive the same old accident-waiting-to-happen of a Jeep. For my part, I benefited far more handsomely than I had any right to deserve. All parents, uncles and aunts (except Vanessa) profited to a greater degree than their children. Vanessa was, indeed, cut out of the will. Later, however, she was to make up for it by divorcing or being divorced by Doctor Jack; to avoid further scandal a favorable settlement was reached. It looked somewhat unseemly for the good doctor to remain married to a woman who was publicly known to have been the lover of his father's murderer. Vanessa was also later indicted for conspiracy or manslaughter or something, but was never brought to trial. She had a team of high-priced Tampa lawyers and eventually plea-bargained her way into six months of house arrest. Her sentencing was celebrated with a running series of parties at her home. She never missed a beat; like a true cat, she landed on her feet. Simon, for his years of faithful service, received a check for one million dollars. He continued to work out at Devon Woods, but now he arrived in a chauffer-driven limousine. Daniel's house, cars, boats and bank accounts were seized by the government. Michele's estate dissolved under the weight of back taxes and loans secured against inadequate, and in some cases, invisible, assets. To everyone's surprise it was revealed that Grandfather was something of a secret philanthropist. Large sums of money passed to assorted charities and grants were established for the continued benefit of mankind. And in the end, to a greater or lesser extent, everyone seemed satisfied. At least no one complained openly.

And thus things stood—or were actively in the process of evolving—on the night that I drove out to Devon Woods to have dinner with Kim and James.

I arrived at the appointed hour and was greeted at the door by James. I handed him the bottle of wine that I had brought with me and stepped inside. Outwardly, the house seemed much as before—the same furnishings, the same fixtures. James stepped into the dining room, placed the wine bottle on the table, then returned and escorted me into the library.

"What're you drinking?" he asked, moving over to a small table on which several cut-glass decanters and an ice bucket were positioned. "We still have a few minutes till dinner."

"Gin and tonic," I said.

James mixed two drinks, gave one to me, then lowered himself into a leather wingback chair. I sat down next to him in an identical chair.

"I see you've become acclimatized to living indoors again," I said, glancing around the room.

"For the time being," said James. He took a sip of his drink.

"How does Kim like it out here?" I asked.

"Well, it's farther for her to drive to go to school and she has to get up earlier, but except for that, she says it's okay."

"Just okay," I remarked. "Typically understated."

"Typically," agreed James.

From under James' chair a small black puppy emerged and began chewing on James' foot.

"A new dog," I observed.

"Kim brought him home a few days ago," said James, flipping the animal over on his back. "I think he has real promise."

"How'd you like two cats to go with him?" I asked.

"Cats?" asked James. "Oh yeah, Kim told me you had a couple of 'em. You giving them up?"

"Have to," I said. "I'm thinking about doing some traveling and I need to find a good home for them."

"Sure," said James. "Bring 'em out. One thing we've got is plenty of space. Where're you going?"

"South," I said.

"South?" asked James. "Hell, there's not much south of here except Miami and Key West."

"South, as in south of the border," I explained. "Mexico. Central America. In that general direction. How far I'll get, I don't know."

"Well, good luck to you," said James, raising his glass.

"Thanks," I said. And I raised my glass and drank.

Behind us I could hear footsteps—bare feet on a wooden floor—coming from the game room. And then there she was, standing in front of me: Kim—small, vibrant, alive; a hint of mischief in her eyes; a little of that bad that makes some girls so good. (I had not seen her since that night we went home together from the hospital; in the morning, when I woke up, she, her clothes, every trace of her, was gone.) And now here she was again, standing in front of me with a painting—the back of the canvas turned toward me—in her hands.

"You look wonderful," I said, rising from my chair. "I see he's feeding you well enough."

She came forward and kissed me. "I get my daily ration," she said, smiling over at James.

I sat back down and looked at her, and I knew that for once in my life I had done the right thing.

"What's that?" I asked, pointing at the canvas.

"A present," she said. "For you."

"For me? Are you sure I rate a present?" I asked.

"Yes," she said. "I sure." Then she spun the canvas around and held it out in front of her.

The style was perhaps the first thing that I noticed. The style was the same, exactly the same, as the painting that I had in my bedroom, the painting of the young naked girl bearing a small bejeweled box, passing through a thin gauze curtain, approaching a man seated before her wearing black patent leather boots, a man whose face and body are out of view. And then I saw it, realized it. It was the same moment, the same situation, except now, in Kim's painting, it is the view as seen through the girl's eyes. And what she sees is an old man: fine white hair combed carefully over to one side, a shrunken frame in a large high-back wicker chair, weathered and tanned face and hands. And at first I thought that it was Grandfather—there, looking back at me—then I examined the face more closely and realized that it was not Grandfather at all, but me! Me fifty years hence! And behind me, the old me, the me to be, is a window looking out, not on a desert scene as in the original, but now looking out on a beach—palm trees, a winding stretch of unpeopled white sand, the water clear and blue, running out to a bright orange sundown horizon. And for a moment I couldn't speak. I could only sit and stare at the future.

"You like it?" asked Kim finally.

"It's, it's—I don't know," I said. "It's me."

"You," said Kim, handing the painting to me. "Yours."

I held the painting at arm's length and continued to look: the face not altogether unhandsome, a degree of dignity, somewhat refined; a curious knowing smile—perhaps a little world-weary but not, as long as the money holds out, bored.

"Me," I said. "If I live that long."

"Oh, you will," Kim assured me, sitting on the armrest of James' chair now.

"Christ," I said. "Weird."

"Weird," agreed James.

I pulled the painting closer. In the lower right-hand corner, in small letters merging with the background: LOVE K.

"Dinner ready?" asked James, standing, pulling Kim up alongside him.

"Ready," said Kim.

"What're we having?" asked James. Arm in arm they stood, each supporting the other just a bit.

"Your favorite," said Kim. "Cold rice and fish heads."

"Hot damn," laughed James. "Let's eat."

TWENTY-EIGHT

It was my last night in town. I was ready to go. I had sold my half of Allen-Clay Realty to John, put my house and duplex on the market (listed now with Allen Realty; it only seemed proper), sold or given away all furniture and accessories, loaned my two paintings to a local gallery (they caused quite a stir and prompted several commissions for Kim) until such times as I would send for them and purchased an airplane ticket, first-class, to Cancun. My plan was to work my way south along the Caribbean coast, and when I found a place that appealed to me—as I knew I would; I'm basically easy to please—I would stop and call it home.

One last bit of business, however, remained: my car. John had bought the T-bird as a present for Susie. I was to drop off an extra set of keys and the title at their home before I left. The agreement was that I would leave the car in the airport parking lot the following morning and they could then pick it up at their convenience.

It was probably after ten o'clock when I pulled up in front of John and Susie's house—a long low red-brick affair perched on a slight wooded rise.

I rang the doorbell. A dog—a big dog—barked. A male voice told the dog to "shut the fuck up." The animal complied, the door opened, and John welcomed me in with a slap across the back that propelled me into the living room. On the couch, cool-eyed and confident, sat Susie, smiling slightly.

"Well, partner, so you're really on your way," declared John.

"Too late to turn back now," I said, trying to work my vertebrae into alignment again.

"Sit down," said John. "You missed the champagne, but we've still got lots of beer left." On the coffee table there was indeed an empty champagne bottle and two glasses.

"Drinking to my departure?" I asked, lowering myself onto the couch next to Susie. "Good riddance, eh?" I slipped the extra car keys and the title onto the table next to the empty bottle.

"Not departure," countered John happily. "Arrival."

I noticed now that John was not merely in an excellent mood; he was positively ecstatic. Such exuberance in such a physically big man was an unsettling sight. One could only hope that he would not literally explode with enthusiasm.

"You tell him, honey," sang out John joyously. He circled the coffee table and came up next to Susie.

Susie turned to me, looked me dead in the eyes and, in a tone that sounded more like a threat than a statement of fact, declared, "*We're* going to have a baby."

"*We?*" I squawked.

"We," explained John, draping an arm around Susie's stiff shoulder and squeezing her tightly.

"Motherfucker," I said, looking at Susie. And now I knew, now I understood.

"You should see your face," laughed John, pointing at me. "You'd think you were going to be the father."

"Well, congratulations," I managed to say. "Yes, congratulations," I repeated.

"Feel this," said John, reaching out and picking up my right hand. He pressed my palm against Susie's flat stomach—she wasn't showing yet. "That's my son in there," he boasted.

"Yes," I said, jerking my hand back like fingers from fire. And there was life in there, a new life, a new life that I was half responsible for, or at least an unwitting accomplice in its creation. It was all too strange. I wanted to bolt for the door.

Susie turned and looked up at John. "Why don't you get Thomas a beer, sweetheart?" she said sweetly.

"Sure," said John, already up and three steps toward the kitchen before I could say no thanks.

Once John was out of the room Susie leaned forward and

grabbed my hand. "I'll be a good mother," she whispered, her eyes somehow calmer, quieter now.

"I know you will," I said. And then I did something that for me was totally out of character: I kissed her hand.

She eased back and smiled.

John re-entered the room and handed me a beer.

I turned the beer up and began gulping it down.

"If it's a boy—and it will be," said John confidently, "we're going to name him Jonathan Thomas Allen."

I choked; I gagged. Beer shot out my nose. I thought for a moment I might black out and drown on dry land.

"Not for you, asshole," laughed John, almost beside himself with good cheer. "For Susie's father. He's named Thomas too."

"Oh sure," I said, wiping the beer from my face and the front of my shirt. "Naturally."

I finished the rest of my beer in a hurry and stood up. I offered my congratulations again, shook hands all around and promised to write. And then I was gone.

Gone—leaving everything, leaving it all behind, leaving it to others to sort out, to comment on and consider, to do with life (their lives) what they would or would not, to make, break, build, burn or destroy.

I was gone. *Pasado.*

If you have enjoyed this book and would like to receive details of other Walker Adventure titles, please write to:

Adventure Editor
Walker and Company
720 Fifth Avenue
New York, NY 10019